Books By
JOHN GARDNER
on the Ballantine Books List:

THE
RESURRECTION

John Gardner

BALLANTINE BOOKS • NEW YORK

BALLANTINE BOOKS
A Division of Random House, Inc.
201 East 50th Street, New York, N.Y. 10022

To My Wife

Eagle of Pengwern, it called far tonight,
    it kept watch on men's blood;
Trenn shall be called a luckless town.

Eagle of Pengwern, it calls far tonight,
    it feasts on men's blood;
Trenn shall be called a shining town.

—*Anonymous, Wales, ninth century*

THE
RESURRECTION

PROLOGUE

A country cemetery in upstate New York. Spring. The sky very blue, clouds very white. Trees, higher up the slope; this side of the trees an iron fence surrounding a cemetery; below the lower cemetery fence a broad valley, the Tonawanda Creek winding slowly and placidly like yellow mercury among willows. The pastureland on each side of the creek seems as smooth as a park from this distance. Two red barns, over by the highway, like barns in a painting.

Nothing ever changes within the bounds of the iron fence: The grass grows green, explodes into field flowers, turns brown in September, bends under snow in the wintertime, grows green again; the sharp edges of chiseled names grow less sharp, mysteriously, year by year; birds build in the grass and trees, more each year, all the hawks and foxes dead; but nothing changes. Like sound waves on an empty planet, Nature's confusion spends itself unnoticed, or almost unnoticed. One of the markers is newer than the rest and has a green metal flowerbox in front of it, and in the flowerbox, blue flowers. The name on the marker, James Chandler, means no more than the names on the other markers except that there are still a few who are not fully reconciled.

One of them is an old woman who comes out from Batavia in an old black Chevy, driving slowly and clumsily down the middle of the road, turns at the cemetery gate and rattles up the two-rut lane to the fence, parks in high weeds, and looks out her window with what seem blind eyes. Sometimes she doesn't get out of the car. Sometimes she does get out, stiffly, works her way to the marker and the flowerbox, and looks at the name awhile, then waters the flowers and goes back to her car, moving more slowly than before, what she came here to do now done. She is old and will stop coming soon, or will soon come one last time and never leave.

And now every three or four years a middle-aged, well-dressed woman comes, or will come in the future (here there are no distinctions), sometimes with a man who holds her arm politely as she walks, then stands back when she looks at the marker, and the woman bows her head as if praying or waiting for something to be over; when she looks up she says brightly, in a voice alien in the world of the dead, "It's beautiful up here, don't you think?" The man looks at the valley and smiles and after a moment takes her arm and they return to the car. Sometimes the man and woman have three children with them, two of them beautiful, the third, the youngest, owl-faced, impish, no relation, you would say, to the rest of the family. And now the three come alone, separately sometimes, sometimes together. Only the oldest comes often. And now this:

Dusk. The car careening up the lane has its lights on. The girl, the oldest daughter—a woman now—is driving. She has sun-bleached hair and, despite the darkness, dark glasses. She gets out lightly and quickly, shuts the door of the convertible behind her, reaches over into the back seat for a potted plant. (There has been no plant by the marker for some time.) She comes to the fence and stops. There is someone before her. She says cheerfully, but as if prepared to be alarmed, "Hello."

The woman standing by the grave looks old, but when she speaks her voice is not. She says, "Hello."

The girl crosses to her slowly. The trees higher up are black against the sky; their branches move in the late-summer breeze. The girl says brightly, "That's my father's grave. Did you know him?"

The woman says nothing, smiles vaguely, as though perhaps she hasn't heard. The girl says: "You startled me.

I didn't notice your car and—" She hesitates, realizing perhaps that there is no car, has been no car in sight all the way from Batavia. The woman before her is obviously no country walker: She is dressed in black, with a white flower on the lapel of her suit, the white luminous in the failing light. The girl stands motionless.

"I'm sorry," the woman says suddenly, vaguely. "I came to say—"

They look at one another, standing perhaps six feet apart, and then, slowly, the older woman rises her white-gloved fists to her chin, her elbows close to her body, like one troubled by the cold. The younger woman bends down, her eyes not leaving the older woman's face, and puts the plant on the ground, then rises again. She whispers, "Viola." The other one does not seem to understand.

A tiresome business, from the point of view of the dead. Say it were not what we know it is, some trifling domestic tragedy, but something more grand—the fall of civilization, the end of the world, the death of all consciousness, or, to speak recklessly, the Second Coming! Not a dead eyebrow would rise. The dead might, perhaps, rise; but they would not be impressed. Burdocks have grown up along the fence, hiding in their musty darkness the neatly lettered but no longer legible sign, *Perpetual Care.*

PART ONE

1

AT forty-one James Chandler felt secure, on top of things. He had reached the rank of Associate Professor; his articles and his book were beginning to be noticed; he was happily married and had three small daughters whom he loved very much, though he could not say he knew them. He had just finished a long monograph entitled "Am I Now Dreaming?"—perhaps his best work yet, at least in the sense that here, at last, he had achieved what seemed to him perfect control, a marriage of substance and form. He had undertaken it partly because the epistemological problem teased him, involved as it was with the old realist-idealist dilemma and threatened as it was at every turn by solipsism. But mainly he had chosen his subject because of the whimsicality of the thing. The monograph was an intellectual exercise, a *tour de force* which had taken him two full years to complete and which, he knew, was at bottom no more—or less— than an immensely elaborate joke on the idea of philosophy itself, a complement to his more serious *Philosophy as Pure Technique*.

There was of course not much question in Chandler's mind about which of his thoughts and perceptions were real and which illusory dreamwork—for the most part, at least—but that was irrelevant; the problem was to find, if one could, satisfactory checks. It was R. G. Collingwood who had hit upon the secret, not only the general but also the specific approach: Who but the historian had developed techniques for dealing scientifically with that which was not only relative but also, in terms of present space-time, lost? But denying the ultimate value of logical abstraction and ignoring the element of abstract science in his own philosophy—the clue to *das absolute Wissen* itself in his *Essay on Philosophical Method*—Collingwood had conceived the analogy in terms too narrow, and in the end, though by no means lapsing into skepticism, he had lost the power of his initial vision and had fallen into self-contradiction. If Chandler's terms were, in contrast, too broad, it was not from a failure of conception. His monograph was the warm-up for a more important book which he now believed himself fully prepared to write.

The prospect filled him with a serenity which must have been apparent at a glance even to strangers who saw him sitting, smiling, staring nearsightedly out the window of the bus he took Tuesday and Thursday afternoons (if he didn't get his days mixed up) to the university. He had the look of a Dostoevskian priest, a look at once amusing and impressive on a pallid, owl-faced, professorial little man in thick glasses. It was as if he had discovered for a fact that, despite the opinion of the daily papers, Dame Juliana's angel was right: *All shall be well, and all shall be well, and all manner of things shall be well.* His office-mate, Ken Roos, a friend from Chandler's graduate-school days in Indiana, spoke of him as "childlike" and often, with an air half reverent, half bewildered, told anecdotes about him at the faculty lunchroom that made him seem some second Thales tranquilly tumbling down well after well. Chandler's wife sometimes teased him too. "Excuse my husband," she would say to friends when he'd lapsed into one of his silences, "he's got it into his head that today's Thanksgiving." It was true. For Chandler every day was Thanksgiving. He loved his teaching: Every book he opened turned out to be closely related to his projected work, and every student turned out to have truly remarkable insights which the student himself, like poor Meno, did not understand. Watching Chandler in front of a class, or hurrying to his mailbox, or trying out a new piece on the piano (Chandler was an excellent musician), one could scarcely help thinking (if one's thoughts were inclined to run in such channels) of Berkeley's joy when he came to see the dreadful Lockean universe from a new angle which eliminated all skepticism, "corpuscular philosophy," and the black pit of atheism. Chandler was infinitely pleased with his shabby little study off the children's room—his Cave of Error, as his wife called it. He found great satisfaction in his sour old pipe, his new, somewhat mulish ball-point pen, his beautiful children, his piano (though the sounding-board was cracked), the remarkable speed and efficiency of the cleaning woman Marie had found. Above all Chandler was grateful for his wife. It was Marie—a pretty, soft-spoken, intelligent girl, once a student of his—who made possible all the rest. It was she who had decided on their coming to Stanford from Oberlin (he was, as she said, a stick-in-the-mud), she who sent out the checks each month, she who decided on buying the house in San Francisco, she who kept up their social calendar—a complicated business, since Chandler was a firm, unsentimental member of numerous organizations for social progress, including a combo which played, free of charge, for groups concerned with advancing civil rights. Without Marie he'd scarcely have known where to turn for pipe tobacco. And she managed it all quite effortlessly, or so it seemed. She even enjoyed it, although she admitted she'd liked teaching high-school English more, before she'd given it up to take care of the children.

And so there was nothing whatever to detract from Chandler's joy or, to put it another way, to keep him from his book. And his joy was, moreover, pure: It was the work itself he looked forward to, not what it would win him in the way of money or prestige. One could scarcely imagine a project less likely to succeed in strictly practical terms: It was to be called *The Uninhabited Castle: An Apology for Contemporary Metaphysics*. He'd been gathering notes toward it for years. Certain sections, in fact, were already worked out in rough draft, for he'd taken the time to type up his lectures when they were relevant.

Unluckily, he found he couldn't begin at once after finishing the monograph. The work on that had left him emotionally exhausted and, because of the hours he'd put in, apparently, had slightly damaged his health. His teaching seemed to take all his time and leave him spent, even shaky. But his serenity held. The necessarily lazy weekends gave him time to notice his family, count up his blessings, and daydream. From his chair in the garden, on the side of Twin Peaks, he could see all San Francisco Bay—the bridge, white sailboats, ocean liners moving in and out. Perhaps when the book was finished he'd visit Japan.

He would acknowledge at the outset the truth of Warnock's observation that the metaphysical castles of the past have not fallen under siege, generally speaking, but have simply crumbled—citadels much shot at and never taken, merely discovered, one sunny afternoon, to be uninhabited. But he would go on to ask just how much that mattered. The question was not whether systems were expendable but whether they were useful at all and, beyond that, whether a well-thought-out metaphysical hypothesis was more useful than the more common sort of thing, "angles of vision" or, more ponderously, "alternative conceptual systems."

However his book might at first be received, it would be recognized at last as important, at least as a minority report. Of this Chandler was confident. He had always been a man who knew his strong and weak points, and he had worked for years and with all his might at filling in the important gaps in his scientific and philosophical knowledge. Compared to the new book, the monograph he'd just completed would be juvenilia—or so he hoped. Happily, since such things can be destructive, he had no particular fears or overwhelming compulsions: If his *Uninhibited Castle* did not work out—if the obstructions that inevitably arose in one's road, when one once got going, proved impassable—he would be sorry, but not crushed. He had labored before on projects which, despite the radiance of their promise, had failed to work out in the end.

But though he knew better than to lose himself in grandiose dreams, he was, for all that, calmly and more or less constantly awake to the possibility of splendid success, a triumph of the kind especially attractive to a man of his particular make-up: the triumph, in a way, of self. "Professor Quixote," his wife sometimes called him, and she was not far wrong. His concern with metaphysics in the age of analysis made him a man born too late for his time, a harmless lunatic all of whose energy and skill went into a heroic battling, by the laws of an intricate and obsolete code, against whatever he could contrive in the way of dragons. His success, if he should prove successful, would not be success in some worthwhile endeavor but merely proof to himself and the esoteric world of his own quite superfluous discipline that he could manage a feat which, as everyone including James Chandler knew, was no longer worth attempting. He would prove, in a word, that an outmoded kind of philosophy was still of great value, in principle, with the result that—to take the most optimistic view—the usual disparagement of metaphysics would be dropped. The result would *not* be, probably, that philosophers would turn once more to metaphysics. Such work was very difficult, and the product—even if it could be shown to be perferable to the scatter-shot results of humbler labors—would not in the end seem worth the greater effort and, worse, the risk of total failure. Thus in plain truth James Chandler's project was one from which any man of sense ought to shrink. Why did he pursue it then? No doubt he lacked the sense God normally proffered even to His philosophers. But perhaps—or so he at times suspected—he differed from most of his fellows in another way as well. He had once come across in a graduate paper, and had copied down in one of his notebooks, a statement which had for him peculiar interest: "The twentieth-century philosopher (if we discount self-pitying existentialists) does not suffer from any profound metaphysical anxieties. Philosophers who happen to believe in God and those who happen not to, do the same sort of work." Chandler himself sometimes believed and sometimes did not, and his indecision troubled him as it had troubled Collingwood before him. Collingwood had written, "For the Christian, as never for any pagan, religion becomes an influence dominating the whole of life; and this unity once achieved can never be forfeited again." Perhaps it was because of this very notion, pervasive in his work, that Collingwood went unnoticed. And perhaps it was this same old-fashioned uncertainty which, disguised by rationalizations, gave Chandler's anomalous project its mysterious luster.

But there was another, more likely explanation. The pleasure in the projected achievement lay simply in the fact that—like the crest of Everest to a mountain-climber, or like a bank to a man inclined to steal—it was there; it might be managed. It was the glow of self in a new shape, in Sartre's phrase, calling to itself from the ground of the future. That was, at times, precisely Chandler's sense of it: a shadow that stood on a hill in the center of a labyrinth. He would reach it, as he had reached it already in uneasy dreams; and it was of no particular significance, as anyone could see, that when he reached the heart of the labyrinth the character of the place would be changed, the shadow gone to a farther hill, a new center, so that he would be forced to pursue again, pursue all the length of infinity, like Spengler's Egyptians, joyful and without hope. For in this—the basis of all his muddle-headed nonsense (but that was perhaps overstating the thing; Collingwood too had made the mistake)—Sartre was wrong: It was not one's past monstrosity that one fled in pursuit of one's finer image, or that was at least not the necessary case. One negated a self one liked perfectly well for a self one liked better and another which one liked better yet in a game of infinite ascension. It was as if (as Chandler had put it to classes) Geoffrey Chaucer were to find himself in grim old Dante's Purgatory. Each ledge would be a splendid triumph, a place too interesting to leave except that there stood, above, still finer ledges. And so if the project he now had in mind did not satisfy him when he finished it—no immediate problem, in any case—then so be it:

One could always turn up new windmills to conquer. However man's view of the universe had changed, the macrocosm-microcosm concept of those wise old Greeks still held: One was, oneself, with all one's kind, the cosmic detonation. Or the cosmic rose, perhaps, as Collingwood had it—an idea as exciting (though admittedly false) as anything Chandler had ever come across. As Collingwood put it:

That history is a process in which tout casse, tout lasse, tout passe, is doubtless true; but it is also a process in which the things that are thus destroyed are brought into existence. Only it is easier to see their destruction than to see their construction, because it does not take so long. May it not be the same in the world of nature? May it not be the case that the modern picture of a running-down universe, in which energy is by degrees exchanging a non-uniform and arbitrary distribution (that is, a distribution not accounted for by any laws yet known to us, and therefore in effect a given, ready-made, miraculously established distribution, a physicist's Golden Age), for a uniform distribution, according to the second law of thermodynamics, is a picture based on habitual observation of relatively short-phase processes, and one destined to be dismissed as illusory at some future date, when closer attention has been paid to processes whose time-phase is longer?

His monograph was just newly out (causing scarcely a ripple in the sea of philosophical thought) when Chandler learned he had possibly a month, or at most only two or three, to live. He had, according to his doctor, aleukemic leukemia, on the verge even now of the blast crisis, an increase in the lawless proliferation of lymphatic-type cells that would swiftly and suddenly shift the white count from its present six thousand to something astronomical, perhaps near 500,000; there was, in effect, nothing to be done.

And so it was settled. The limits of Chandler's identity (It was thus that he put it to himself, fleeing into the comforting arms of pedantic abstraction) were set.

2

HE stood at the window in the doctor's office, Marie in the chair in front of the desk behind him, the doctor in his own chair, carefully balanced, expressionless— all this from memory, for Chandler was not looking now at them but out at the wide street and, a block up the hill, the hospital, white in the sun, the sky very blue behind it. Cars in the hospital parking lot, looking down past the long white railing at the street, glittered sharply, and he had to look away. He glanced at the desk, a row of books along one side, a blotter, a pen set, white and yellow papers.

"About thirty percent of the time we achieve a remission," the doctor said. He had a red face, curly silver hair, prominent teeth. His hands were fat. Marie sat perfectly still, pale, waiting. "After that," the doctor said, "we keep the patient under close observation. You'll need to be hospitalized, of course."

"Why?" Chandler asked. The sound of his own voice startled him like a sharp intrusion from without. He had not realized he was going to speak.

The doctor glanced at him, then down at the blue-green blotter. After a moment he said quietly, as if evasively, "We need to keep close watch, in cases like this. For one thing, the drug we'll use when we try for a remission will have a toxic reaction before long, and we'll have to discontinue it." He lifted the pen from the pen set and examined the bright gold point.

"But after the reaction I won't need to be here," Chandler said. He had an odd, completely irrational sense that winning this point, getting home again, was important. As if he were standing outside himself, watching it all disinterestedly, he saw himself speaking sharply, angrily, like Old Man Pursey at a faculty meeting, or like Chandler's father long ago, arguing about levitation.

"You don't *need* to be here," the doctor said softly, as though he were angry himself.

Marie said, calm, "You said 'for one thing,' Doctor. What are the other things?"

"In cases of this kind we can expect severe anemia, and you'll need transfusions to keep you going. And then there may be other things too. The spleen may swell, pain may show up—"

"But *why* keep me going?" Chandler asked, startling himself again. And still he seemed outside himself, a bemused and dispassionate observer.

"For your family, perhaps," the doctor suggested, speaking still more softly now, playing with the pen. It was painful for him, and in another mood Chandler might have sympathized with the man—if the unreasonable, petulant patient were somebody else.

"True," Chandler said, pouncing on it, "but I'll see less of my family in the hospital, even if you drag this business out, than I'd see of them at home." He found all at once that he was frightened—not frightened by the thought of death; that had not yet taken hold: he had sealed his mind against it as tightly as Noah sealed his ark, or, according to the Schoolmen, the Second Noah sealed up the castle of the saved—but frightened by the godlike authority of the red-faced, healthy, bored-looking man who could listen to him or refuse him, just as he pleased.

But the doctor said, "Now listen, it's a free country. I've given my advice, that's all I can do. If you want to stay out, let Nature take its course—" He waved vaguely.

Marie said, holding her purse so tightly that her knuckles were white, "The doctor knows best, James."

Chandler tried to think, but the silence was intense,

every line in the room very sharp. He could have counted the pages in the books on the desk. At last he said, "How long will it take to find out if a remission's possible?"

The doctor frowned, studying him or perhaps looking through him, and Marie watched the doctor's face. "Matter of days. Maybe as much as two weeks."

He thought about it for a long time, or tried to. His mind was not running. Marie said, "We'll do whatever you say, Doctor."

At last, wearily, Chandler nodded. The idea of dying flooded in.

But even now, alone in the hospital room that looked up at the Sears sign higher on the hill, he could not quite assimilate the fact. He went over and over it in his mind, sometimes very calmly, sometimes in terror, but most often in a kind of puzzled and anxious desperation, as one goes over and over a knotty line of Greek in Plato's *Timaeus*. He himself had written long ago, when he was still young and in excellent health, "A philosopher is not better prepared than another man for the crises in life, for example, the coming of his own death; he is merely prepared to suffer more systematically, which is to say neither to suffer more nor to suffer less but rather to evade in a slightly different way," and lighting on this passage now—he was rereading all he'd ever written— he was surprised to see how right his guess had been. By long habit one assumed that questions, if they were not demonstrably meaningless, had answers: and so his mind worked at it day and night—and failed. Then one morning, the morning of the fifth day, he awakened to find that the question had somehow answered itself. When he tried to articulate the answer there was nothing, nothing whatever, like the void the physicist pictures if the universe, where matter is motion, should stop. It was simply that he had, now, a remarkably tranquil certainty that in three weeks or so he would be dead. He knew, too, exactly what he would do with the time he had left.

He had visited Batavia, New York, only four or five times in twenty years. His mother had visited him in

California on several occasions, but never for more than two or three days at a time. However long she had planned to stay, she would grow restless and homesick almost at once—there was nothing for her to *do* here, she would say, almost in fright, as it seemed to him—and she would leave. She was old now, over seventy, and she had never seen the two younger girls. And so that morning when she came, Chandler told his wife of his decision (making a formal announcement of it, standing at the window in his bathrobe, his hands clasped behind his back), and began to work out his plans for the trip east. He'd wait two more days for the reaction to the drug—he'd learned the name of it by now: tetra-amino pteroylglutamic acid—and then, whether it had come or not, and whether or not a remission set in, they would leave on the first train they could get. She accepted it quietly, sensing that argument would be futile, and she did not stay with him as she usually did—reading the cards, admiring the view of the Sears store, talking about the children, friends, the trouble the neighbors were having with their dog. She said, rather formally, "I'll see about tickets and—arranging things." He said as she was about to leave, "Batavia has a hospital too, after all. Two in fact." She looked at him, and then, falsely, she smiled, nodded, and left. It was after dark when she brought in the children for their afternoon visit. When they came he was feverish and diarrheal—the reaction had come—and they stayed with him only for a few minutes. He was desperately sick all night but better in the morning, merely shaky. In the afternoon the doctor announced a rise in the blood platelets, a sign that remission might be one its way. They would watch him closely the next few days, though of course if the remission didn't hold there was nothing on earth they could do. A trip across the country was out of the question. It was very important that the symptoms be watched, however well he felt just now.

But two days later—on Easter Sunday, a cold and foggy April afternoon—the family boarded the eastbound California Zephyr at Oakland. At Chicago they changed to the clanking, fallen dignity of the New York Central. Sleeping on the train as it hurtled through what seemed empty space, Chandler had terrifying dreams which, afterwards, he could not remember.

3

As the train pulled into Batavia, the children were delighted by everything they saw—the heavy, broad trees just beginning to bud, the iron fences, the old brick and frame houses with their latticework porches and high windows, the muddy Tonawanda Creek, swollen now, in flood season, to within eight feet of the floor of the iron bridge. There were birds everywhere—robins, sparrows, cowbirds, chippies, starlings. Marie seemed less pleased then the children; perhaps she was noticing already the smell of Batavia's water. As for himself, he was beginning to wish he hadn't come.

The feeling had begun to rise in him while the train was still crossing the Amish farmlands of Ohio, and now, as they loaded themselves into the cab they'd found waiting at the end of the platform, the feeling had become oppressive. Too much was changed, thrown into a buzzing, blooming confusion. They had to approach Bank Street by a roundabout route; Jackson was being torn up for sewage repairs. Huge platforms and timbers from which heavy chains and hooks depended had been thrown up at crazy angles the length of the street. Fixing the sewage line was always a job in Batavia. The city stood on a thin earth shell above quicksand. Chandler sat hunched in his corner, his thick glasses close to the window, and struggled to square what he saw with what he remembered. Liberty, like Jackson, was being torn up. The cab moved on, past Polish and Italian grocery stores, hardware shops, and run-down photography studios in old houses where in his day people had lived; it turned north on a wide, tree-lined street where houses that had been white before were gray now, or dark green, or brown. The Massey-Harris plant stood empty and dark, its brick walls black, its windows broken out; and across from the Massey-Harris plant the cemetery seemed at first completely unfamiliar. The lawns were smooth and newly mowed, as they'd always been; the hedges were trimmed as usual; the little Richmond mausoleum with its flat, solid walls and its iron bars seemed no darker, no more severe than it had seemed to him thirty years ago; but even so there had come a profound change. It was like a landscape transformed by a change of light.

Further on, when they were passing houses once more, the driver said unpleasantly, "Nigger section."

Chandler lifted his eyebrows, saying nothing, though normally it was his practice to make clear his angry disapproval. He was stopped, now, by a puzzlement that verged on fright. There had never been Negroes in Batavia when he was a child. But the driver was right. An old woman sat on a porch rocking an old-fashioned cradle with her foot.

"What do they find to do in Batavia?" Chandler asked. His voice was feeble, and he realized he hadn't spoken aloud for a long while.

The driver shrugged. "Breed, I guess." He glanced into the rear-view mirror. "Beg pardon, lady."

Marie smiled.

"Why are you smiling?" Chandler asked, startled. But now she was not smiling, and his question seemed to baffle her. It struck him that perhaps he had been mistaken.

The Negro part was far behind them; the taxi turned left onto Main, heading back toward Bank. They reached the house, oddly narrow and empty-looking, and Chandler stared up at it a moment with a feeling of revulsion before he climbed out to help the driver unload. The suitcase he reached for was so heavy he could scarcely move it, and the driver took it from him without a word. He paid the man grimly, as if for slovenly and dishonest service, and the taxi drove away. Then, for what might as well have been the first time in twenty years, as it seemed, Chandler faced his mother.

She walked with a thick black cane; she was nearly blind; and she had a goiter. She stood smiling, holding out a shaking hand, and as he went to her, herding the girls ahead of him in his embarrassment, he remembered his grandmother in her black lace veil. She had been slighter, more genteel—you'd never have caught her with gray slip showing—but the shaking and the blind old eyes were the same, and he was shocked. As he reached out to touch her he saw that his hand, too, was shaking. She caught him to her and hugged him for a long moment, weeping inwardly, then released him and smiled with tight lips. She turned to the children.

"Beautiful!" she said, bending stiffly to hug them now and patting each of them in turn on the back of the head with fingers like pieces of wood.

Karen, the oldest, said affectedly, her white gloves clutching her patent-leather purse in a way that made one think of what she would be at nineteen or twenty, "Grandma, we're *so* glad to see you again! I simply *love* New York State!"

Marie stood looking on, smiling in a strained way, with her arms folded over her bosom. She had on a gray, California winter suit, and the hint of color on her eyelids matched the material. It all struck him, here in Batavia, as brazen, and he looked away from her quickly.

His mother said, "My, what a little lady our Karen's become!"

Susan, the second, said anxiously, "I'm a lady too, Mommy."

"Of course you are, dear," Marie said, touching her.

"You're all little ladies," his mother said, laughing, "even little Annie."

The two-year-old scowled up at them, as solidly built

as a small boulder, stubbornly unmodified by her frilly pink dress. "No," she said, "no yady."

They laughed, and his mother's shaking hand reached out to her.

"Be careful, Mother," Marie said quickly, with a smile, "she bites."

"Eat!" the child said suddenly, so anxiously and so savagely that it startled them all. *"Eat! Eat! Eat!"*

4

MARIE wanted him to go to the hospital at once for tests to see if the remission was taking hold and, if not, what they ought to do about it. Chandler lashed out at her viciously —as he might have lashed out at a table standing in his way, or a branch in his path, or a snake—making her cry, driving her to the indignity of reminding him that he'd sworn to the doctor in San Francisco that he'd get tests the minute he got here. (This was in the bedroom—his own childhood bedroom, just down the hall from his father's old den—as soon as they were alone. It was afternoon. The sun was on the other side of the house, so that the room was gloomy and seemed smaller than it was and more dingy. Time lay in the room like a visual dimension: Once Chandler and the room had been intimate but now he was a stranger, seeing the place from a new angle, and though every line and every plane, every welt and blister in the wallpaper, the myriad cracks in the plaster in the closet were the same, the whole effect was changed, had become repulsive.) But her crying, her nagging did not impress him in the least. The crying positively pleased him, in fact. It seemed to him that he hated her unspeakably and had always hated her. He saw each feature separate and distinct, and he was sure no power but stupid delusion could bring them to harmony. She'd become what she was: a pointless disposition of teeming atoms, brute Nature spiritless and overwhelming as the sound of a siren outside a music hall. Her ears were small and white, like a dead child's, her eyes were set too far in, like the eyes of an old, old woman, and though her eyebrows were carefully plucked and civilized, one could see by the very shape of her forehead that in their natural state they were shaggy, the eyebrows of a creature at best not quite human.

"Either the remission has come or it hasn't," he said. Even to himself he sounded like a crazy old man, and as the ironic idea of old age touched his thought he added quickly with bitter self-pity, "Either way you'll be rid of me soon enough." She stared, white, more hurt than he'd ever seen anyone in his life, the dingy clutter of the room's dead substance zeroing in around her, as it seemed, and before he could think what to do she had fled down the hall. Chandler stood shaking, horrified at what he'd done—or rather at what he'd *seen,* the vision more terrible than the act—and then, fists clenched, he threw himself on the bed, sobbing, swearing at himself, cursing God as he'd done as a child. Soon, again like a child, he had cried himself to sleep.

He dreamed he was in some kind of cluttered old store, some sort of junk shop that was very familiar and where he felt comfortable and happy. There were bins of battered, moldly books which contained rich secrets expressed in language which, like the scent of unremembered flowers in a garden infinitely receding in time, was always just at the edge of intelligibility. He was close, very close to the meaning of the words: Any moment now they would be clear; and he had nothing to fear: He had all the time in the world. But there was a noise, a kind of music, that impinged upon his consciousness and distracted him, and so he left the books, deliciously conscious that any time he pleased he could come back. He wandered further into the shop, conscious now that he was naked, but neither embarrassed nor distressed, squeezing past complicated old bronze objects that he could not quite identify —large and intricate machines, rickety conveyor belts with slats and holes like something used by Catskill farmers (He remembered the endless rumble of apples tumbling in the sorter and rolling down into cellar bins) but the wooden slats were stained with blood (There was nothing horrible about this; nothing out of the ordinary)—and then, over by a window, he saw his father, sitting on the floor like an Indian basket weaver, smiling. Chandler was overjoyed: He'd thought his father was dead. He'd never seen anything anywhere so beautiful as his father's smile. He was listening to the unearthly music and looking at something, a small, rusty gear—a wheel—suspended, supported by nothing but air, three inches from the floor. Chandler realized all at once that all the queer machines were running and the tiny wheel was turning, spinning at incredible speed, shooting off terrible sparks of brilliant color—yellow, green, blueish red. His father had worked at it all his life, down here in the cellar (It was not a junkshop, he'd known all along). Still smiling, oblivious to Chandler's alarm, his father looked up at him and carefully placed his finger over his lips.

When Chandler awakened, the room was strangely dead and cold by comparison to his dream. It was dark outside, but light came into the room from the hall. Marie was standing beside the bed, a shape unexpectedly large and close. She said, "Do you want to eat?"

He remembered lashing out at her, and the way her face had seemed to shatter when the words struck. Remorse overwhelmed him, made all the worse by the dullness of ordinary reality and by the sad plainness of her kindness to him now. She deserved better, more than brute substance could provide. He reached for her hand. "Marie," he said. She smiled, motherly, and patted his hand. And of course she was right, there was nothing to say, it was done with.

"Your mother's fixed drumsticks and mashed potatoes," Marie said. "She says it's your favorite food."

Chandler laughed, then wept, clinging to her hand. Downstairs he could hear Karen at the piano, keeping the pedal down too long.

"You're feverish," Marie said, touching his forehead.

He nodded. "I'm better though. Much better." He got up.

He was surprised to find how soon his sense of the strangeness of things began to leave him. Memory relaxed its hold and he began to grasp things as they were rather than as double exposures of past and present. The smells in the house were partly responsible—the sharply familiar smells left by years of coal heat and chlorinated water, the scent of furniture polish, and in the kitchen the acrid smell of coffee grounds. At first they were disquieting, too rich with associations; but soon they became agreeable, came even to be reassuring. His mother's voice had the same effect, disquieting at first, then soothing. She couldn't tell them how glad she was to see them, she told them again and again, and, hugging the children clumsily whenever they came within reach, she exclaimed repeatedly at how pretty they were. Karen and Susan, the older girls, looked exactly like Marie, she said; little Anne—oh, there was no doubt of it!—little Anne took after her father.

When the children were in bed and Marie had settled in the living room to read, comfortingly near, where he could sometimes hear her turning a page, he sat with his mother in the big, dark-cupboarded kitchen, as they had often done years before, to drink coffee and talk. Her mind sometimes wandered, and her voice had grown husky —she had once had a beautiful singing voice—but nevertheless as his mother talked, or as she paused briefly to add a line to one of her hundred thousand lists (Things to Do, Letters to Write, Inventories of Cupboards and Closets), the past and the present drew still nearer together. She talked, in her curious singsong, of people he had known in school, sometimes people who had once been best friends but whose names it now took him a moment to place. She had followed their lives. She knew of their failures and successes, their marriages, and in some cases, their deaths. It seemed that nothing could happen to anyone anywhere, or at any rate that nothing could happen to anyone whose life impinged upon her own, however tenuously, without her finding out about it. They talked about relatives, too, and about old friends of the family. "Most of the old names are dying out," she said. "Kirkland, Ingraham, Cary, Brisbane, Brooks. . . ." It was that night that she first mentioned the Staleys.

"I do hope you'll visit them if you feel up to it, James. I know they'd be pleased to see you."

It surprised him that the Staleys were still alive, and he showed his surprise. His mother understood the look, or, if her dimmed eyes did not catch that, she understood his silence. "Oh, they're still very much alive," she said. "Aunt Emma won't know you, poor thing, but Aunt Maud and Aunt Betsy are pert as ever. Aunt Betsy's still giving piano lessons. She's eighty-three years old and still sharp as a tack."

He smiled. He might have known the Staleys would last.

His mother said, whimpering a little because of the trouble she had these days with her voice, "The Staleys have always been long livers, except for Eddie. He was killed in an accident, you know. There's no telling how long Eddie might have lived."

"How old is Emma Staley now?" Chandler asked.

His mother sat very still, smiling vaguely, perhaps thinking. Then at last she said, "They've always been such good people."

He looked down. Without thinking about it, he began to trace with his fingertip a path through the light and dark grays of the formica tabletop. The surface was rough, not as clean as it would once have been (except that the table was new, of course; it was something else that he'd traced as a child—yes, now he had it: the pattern in the linoleum that had been gone from the kitchen floor for twenty-five years).

She said softly, "It's always so restful to see them. They never change. They used to be the richest people in Batavia, you know, and when the stockmarket crashed and they lost most of their money we all thought it would kill them; but it didn't. They went on just as they always had, except that they gave lessons now, and the way they put themselves into it you'd have thought they'd always been teaching children to paint and sing and play the piano." She caught her breath. Her weight made breathing difficult. "Aunt Emma and Aunt Maud have had to give up giving lessons, of course. Emma's gotten very odd; she has to be watched every minute."

"What does she do?" he asked.

"They have a girl living with them," she said, misunderstanding. "Viola, Eddie's daughter." She pressed her lips together, then sighed.

"That's lucky," he said. "They'd never be able to keep up the house by themselves."

His mother shook her head. "She's evil," she said matter-of-factly.

He frowned, feeling weak again. "She's what, Mother?"

"Evil." It was a settled conviction, not open to question, as sure and weary as the turning of the seasons. He looked at her, surprised at this new twist in her character. Her eyes were closed and the corners of her mouth turned down like the corners of an irritable child's mouth. Chandler smiled, depressed, and leaned on his elbows.

At last he said, "What does Aunt Emma do?"

The old woman looked blank.

"What does Aunt Emma do?" he repeated. "You say they have to watch her."

The question upset her, apparently. Her lips pursed and she picked with her fingernails at specks of something on the edge of the table. She reached for the sugar bowl and moved it a little, then began to search vaguely about the table as if for something she'd misplaced.

"I would like to see them again," Chandler said. He raised his coffee cup, rather awkwardly, spilling a little.

"Yes, I want you to, dear. I do hope you will. I want you to see their house too. You remember it, don't you?— the old-fashioned lamps and the chairs and the red glasses? It's all still there." She folded her hands and, smiling absently, her mind far away, looked at the wrinkled skin. "After all these years. . . ." She seemed to forget what it was she'd been saying.

Then, directly over their heads, something crashed, shaking the walls of the house, and he jumped to his feet. When he reached the upstairs bedroom-den, he found his father's huge old cherry-wood secretary lying face down on the rug, the bookcase door broken and pieces of delicate antique glass scattered the length of the room. On one side a crack ran the length of the wood. The three girls howled in grief and fright, and Anne had cut herself. Marie reached the door just behind him, her book closed over one finger. When she saw the ruin, or saw, perhaps, how lucky the children had been to get out of the way, she sank back against the doorpost and wept.

"Who's responsible for this?" Chandler shouted, snatching off his glasses—heaven knew why. He was shaking all over. Anne held her hand out in front of her, trying to keep the blood off her nightdress. He stood helpless, enraged, and, moreover, blind with his glasses off, and he shouted again, "Who's responsible for this?"

"Is everything all right up there?" his mother was calling from the foot of the stairs, her voice like an old wooden cartwheel creaking on its shaft. "Yoo-hoo! Is everything all right?"

5

IT rained during the night, and it seemed to him that he never once closed his eyes but lay wide awake in the at once familiar and mysterious room, staring, listening to the murmur on the roof, the rattle of water in the gutter at the edge of the porch roof just below his window. For hours, as it seemed, the rain fell steadily, as if with a weary satisfaction, falling through the night as the train had seemed to fall through space, plunging unimpeded forever through darkness. As he listened to it his body relaxed to the last nerve and yet grew at the same time, as it seemed to him, increasingly alert—not alert with dread or with hope or indeed with any emotion he could name, but alert, he would have said, like some seed long hidden in the earth, some dried-up tuber: It was as if he could actually feel the remission building up, his strength returning; but of course it was not that. He'd no more be aware of the leveling off than he'd been of the plunge: a ghost inside him, painless, invisible—something from a poem—

> *the invisible worm*
> *That flies in the night, on the howling storm,*
> *Has found out thy bed of crimson joy,*
> *And his dark, secret love does thy life destroy.*

He remembered waking up on dew-white summer mornings in the big old frame house on the Creek Road, six miles south of town, his grandfather's farm. The hired men would be doing the chores, and his grandfather, close to ninety but still erect, energetic, would be out in the garden hoeing or snipping vines, or he'd be beyond the garden in the apple orchard, no coat over his white shirt and wide black suspenders, a cap pushed down on his thick white hair. Along the road and around the garden there were brilliant red poppies, bushes where dark red cranberries glistened, and heavy on the fence and the wire gazebo in the middle of the garden there were roses. Though the sun had only been up for an hour, the snow-white geese would be out in the orchard already; and some of the cows, already milked—and the two or three heifers that ran with the herd—would be working their way up the lane toward the pasture. It was there that he should have gone, not here. But his grandfather had been dead for years, and the farm had been sold. The barns that had once been a clean red were black now, and nothing was left of the house but the rubble-filled cellar, a sunken place half hidden by woodbine and poison ivy and purple nightshade. His father had wanted no part of farming. "Times are changing," he had said, and Chandler's grandfather had accepted it, perhaps even had recognized his own voice in it, looking back to a time still older, a stately white house that looked down over the village of Oakfield, old Senator Chandler's place, his father's. It had burned down fifty years ago, empty, decrepit even then, and within James Chandler's memory the spaced, enormous oaks on what had once been the lawn had been cut down to make way for wheat. And so he had come to his mother's.

But here too his memories were sharp. The walls of time moved outward imperceptibly, and the clear, sweet sound of his wife's breathing coexisted with the noisy ticking of the clock that had stood on the dresser (The clock was gone now, had been gone for years). If one could relax, suspend all thought completely enough, one might slip out of time entirely. As clearly as if she were here beside him, he heard his mother turn in the bed three rooms away. He remembered hearing her turn over at night, sometimes again and again, in his childhood, just after his father's death. It was perhaps the one thing he remembered most clearly from that period—that and the nightmares he'd had. She'd be gone when he got up for school: His breakfast place would be set at the dining-room table, shredded wheat waiting, already broken up, in his bowl, a note under his glass telling him there was grapefruit in the refrige; and on the piano stool, near the front door, he would find his lunchbox, coat and hat, galoshes. From school he would go to the novelty shop, which was becoming little by little, under her management, a book and stationery store. He would sweep and help her close up, neither of them speaking, and then they would drive home, still in silence, and he would practice the piano or do his homework while she fixed dinner. Even while they ate they scarcely spoke. And yet he felt close to her and thought her the most beautiful woman in the world. Sometimes he would pretend to be sick, so that she would come and sit by his bed with her hand on his forehead.

A neighbor coughed, then stillness again. Marie's breathing changed; she was awake. She touched his arm, not from anything so conscious as affection, it seemed to him, but merely to see that he was there. Then, after a while, she went back to sleep. He could hear faint music, a drive-in, perhaps, far away; farther off yet he could hear the rumble of traffic on the Thruway. He could remember his grandmother playing the piano at her place. It was Christmas, and he was very small, perhaps three or four. Her face was white, somehow unreal, and on the glossy black piano there were huge, blood-red poinsettias. He listened to the rain. "Dear God," he thought vaguely, as though he were indeed a child and about to begin his nightly prayers. He let the thought hang in the air and for a long time he looked at it, not judging it, merely looking. He turned on his side and absently kissed his wife's shoulder, then went on listening. Again Marie wakened briefly, then slept as before. *Be patient therefore, brethren, unto the coming of the Lord. Behold, the husbandman waiteth for the precious fruit of the earth, and hath long patience for it, until he receive the early and latter rain.* At last he slept.

6

CHANDLER slept late, and when he awakened he felt better than he'd felt for weeks. His mother, Marie, and the children had apparently been up for hours. He shaved and dressed quickly and went down. The children were out in the garden playing, laughing and talking noisily with some neighbor child. Marie was in the living room reading the mail, which she'd just brought in from the box on the porch. She sat in the middle of the couch, in black slacks and a dark, striped shirt. She had letters strewn all around her and, on the arm of the couch, pictures of someone's children. He picked them up.

"Morning, Rip," she said, not looking up from the letter she was reading.

"Hi. All that mail ours?" The pictures were of people he didn't know, strangers whose imposition he faintly resented, and he put the stack down again without looking at more than three.

She nodded. "It's three days' worth. I had them hold it up in San Francisco."

"Why?"

"I don't know." She shrugged, then looked up. "I thought it would be a nice surprise, coming all at once."

He laughed. Some of the mail, he noticed, consisted of bills—the P. G. & E., the telephone company, the Library Bookstore, Blackwell's. He said slyly, feeling pleased with himself, "You didn't want Mother to see the bills."

She frowned, signaling to him with her eyebrows. His mother was in the next room. Then, shrugging again, she said lightly,

> Have it your way,
> It's just as you say,
> The world is ugly and the people are sad.

He bent down and kissed her on the forehead, then went on into the dining room.

His mother had on a gray housecoat with huge white flowers. It made her look older than ever. Her wrinkled skin was the color of ashes, and the shaking seemed worse today. But the sun was bright, bursting over the dining-room table, and he could smell toast and coffee.

"Good morning, Mother," he said formally, clasping his hands behind his back.

"Good morning, James," she said. "Did you sleep well?"

He nodded and smiled, then said as an afterthought, "Did you?"

She sighed. "As well as usual."

He'd forgotten the old ritual question and was enormously pleased to hear it again. In a minute she would tell him what the temperature was, how the sky looked, what it said in the *Daily News*. When she died it would be the death of an age, a way of seeing; the end of the great Romantic return to Nature.

"It's still cloudy," she said. "I imagine we'll get more rain this afternoon."

He half turned to the window and pretended to study the condition of things. "Mmm," he said thoughtfully, nodding; and the sound of his voice, that particular nod, vividly recalled to his mind the image of his father. "Well, life goes on," he said absently, with a vague but meaningless sadness or, really, weariness in his voice. His father had been dead for thirty years. He glanced at his mother, and her look shocked him. She stood motionless, her arthritic knuckles interlocked, her eyes red, her great, loose lips stretched out, clamped together, and it struck him with terrific force that she was grieving for *him*. Tears filled his eyes and for an instant he was sure he would cry.

While he was at breakfast, Marie came in, poured herself coffee, and sat down across from him. She asked what he thought they should do about that old desk the children had tipped over in the room upstairs. "Is it worth anything, do you think?" she said. "I mean, should we send it out?"

The question triggered the same exaggerated response that his first sight of the ruin last night had set off; but this time he kept himself in hand. He removed his glasses slowly, giving the first rush of anger time to roll away harmless; and then he saw that her question, complicated as perhaps it was with a labyrinth of deeper questions, accusations, self-justifications, could be treated as though it were simple. Marie was no lover of antiques as antiques, yet she did have an eye for quality: She knew very well that "that old desk" was worth something, and she knew, too, that for its memories it was worth something to his mother and himself. But generously supposing that her question was not intended, really, as an open slap at all she found threatening around her—the opposition, say, of her husband's past and her children's future—or at any rate supposing that if it was a slap it was not fully conscious—one could treat the question as meaning simply, "Now that you have considered the objective and subjective value of the desk, should we count what happened last night significant or not?" Chandler said calmly, "I think we could get it fixed."

For a moment she looked puzzled. "Well of-course we'll get it fixed, James," she said then, crossly. "What I meant was, should we send it to one of those places in New York or can we get it fixed somewhere in Batavia?"

"Oh," he said hastily, looking down.

"I'm sure we could get it back in a month or so," she said. "But if they have good cabinetmakers in Batavia—"

"Let me see," he said, thinking back, or acting the part of a man thinking back; he wasn't over his embarrassment yet. "I think there *is* one good one here. Maybe I'll run by and see him this morning."

"You don't want me to?" She asked it very casually, but her eyes were anxious. Like his mother, she had a grayish look, as though she'd been sleeping even less well than he'd thought.

"No, I'd enjoy it," he said. It was true, of course, that she could do it better. It was she who did the buying, paid the bills, changed lightbulbs, repaired whatever broke down in the house. Chandler was one of those people, as Marie sometimes said, who could fall down a manhole on his way from the bedroom to the kitchen.

"Well, if you really want to," she said, dubious.

"Anyway, I'd like to look around the city." He reached for another piece of toast, then looked about vaguely, unaware that what he needed now was butter. She pushed it toward him.

"Would you care if the children rode along?"

"I could take them," he said. "Originally, though, I meant to walk."

She looked at him, startled, then nodded and resigned herself to it. She would take no chance of crossing him as she had when they'd first arrived, it seemed. His remorse swept over him again, but now as before there was nothing one could say.

His mother, who had been listening from the kitchen, came in to suggest that the children go shopping with her. Marie would be able to take a nap or write letters or read. And so it was settled. He finished eating, then went up for his coat, the new, fur-collared czar's coat, as Marie called it. Marie settled at the dining-room table to catch up on her letter writing. She'd always kept up a voluminous correspondence with old college friends, relatives, people she had taught with. His mother, when he left, was sitting in the kitchen, breathing heavily, frowning, making her list.

It was a bright, cold day, and as always in such weather, Chandler was in high spirits. He walked rather slowly down Bank as far as North, and he found that walking tired him hardly at all. But the cabinet shop he remembered on the corner of North and Bank was gone, replaced by a grocery store. He was not surprised or discouraged. There would be others. He turned left and walked as far as Ellicott, past the house where William H. Coon had lived once—in his highschool days Chandler had accompanied the old man's solos for flute—and past the School for the Blind. The brick buildings of the Blind School were no longer trim and new: Matted, dead ivy vines darkened the walls, and the white paint on the doors was peeling. The playground and park across from the Blind School had lost about half their trees—elms, probably. All over New York State the elms were gone. He turned down Ellicott, heading back toward the center of town. He paused to rest from time to time, but it was strictly precautionary. He felt perfectly strong—stronger than normal, if anything.

He walked down Main as far as Jackson without seeing any sign of a cabinet shop and, more surprising, without seeing a single soul he knew. There were people everywhere, but they were strangers—indeed, not Batavians at all, perhaps people from Buffalo, he would have said. Batavia had been, in his day, a farmers' city. Feedstores, farm-machinery places, a plow factory, the Massey-Harris plant, movies, grocery stores, saloons; a city of Welsh, Irish, English, a handful of Germans, an Indian or two, and across the New York Central tracks (gone now to the edge of town), Italians. But the people who milled around him today were something else. They were of every conceivable extraction, for one thing; and for another, their dress, their speech, their abruptness—even queer, trifling details like the way they patiently waited for the WALK sign—marked them people of the city, a new breed. With a part of his mind he was pleased by the change. Even if it meant destruction—Main Street widened, the trees pulled down, mansions turned into restaurants—it meant progress too. Chandler's own father, neither brutal nor simpleminded, had considered Italians an inferior breed; and the guilt had hardly been all on his side. A man could know as much as he had any way to know; it was nonsense to ask more of him. What Chandler's father had known about Italians was that they were strangers with strange ways: They talked too loudly, laughed too much, drank wine, made too many friends too soon; they lied, imaginatively, glibly, like grown men with the minds of children; they flirted with one another's wives—even, at times, with a white man's wife (they were never, to Chandler's father, white). When Prohibition came they opened garages and brought in alcohol in the radiators of new cars, and with the money they got they opened pool halls, bowling alleys, roller rinks—strange and obscurely dangerous entertainments. If some of them lay outside the pattern—the quiet, gentle old man who collected rags and junk, the Marcisis with their grocery store—they lay outside it because, in effect, they had risen above it. They had seen the value of the higher culture, or, knowing where acceptance lay, they aped their betters. Whatever the exceptions, the rule held good: Italians were not quite human. And the proof was simple. If a man named Baker or Brown or Smith walked down South Jackson Street at night he was asking for trouble, and he got it. On the other hand, an Italian could walk wherever he pleased, and *they,* who were civilized, would merely watch him from their windows and, if he loitered, telephone the police. Except that that was an unfair way to put it; the fear of the older Batavians was blind, but not completely unintelligent. Sometimes a loiterer was dangerous, and if a non-Italian did not seem especially dangerous even when he came up onto your porch, it was because you knew him, or knew his family, or anyway knew exactly where he lived. Nothing on earth could resolve the thing but time, and after a while time had done it. It was good, and Chandler was wholeheartedly for it: One noticed at once, here in Batavia—though not when one was in San Francisco—that a name was Italian; but one made one's assumptions on the basis of the face, not the name. The two cultures were as much one as two cultures could ever be without every man's sacrificing his pleasure in happening to be his father's son. It was good, even beautiful, and it was worth the cost of the comfortable, narrow old brick street, the trees, the mansions. In time, almost inevitably—only the death of earth could stop it—there would be peace between races as well, and nations; and the beauty of what had happened here would be raised to the billionth power.

Except that it was *not* all right that the narrow old brick street was gone. It was good, but it was not all right. There was not a trace of the comfortable old country town, nothing. Or if that was too strong, there was nothing that didn't stand out like a death's head, a Victorian gable singing *Memento mori* above a cheap, glossy storefront. He recalled, suddenly, Collingwood's phrase, *a process in which the things that are thus destroyed are brought into existence.* What was it, exactly, that was being built? Not even the brotherhood of man, because there were always new waves of strangers: "Nigger section," the driver had said, with a kind of laugh, as though he were showing a dirty picture. They too would be assimilated and would assimilate, but then there would be still other strangers, if not strange cultures then strangers of some other kind—Nature is never spent—and the city would expand, all cities would expand, and the glossy storefronts too would fall, leaving only, here and there, a windy Sears to sing *Memento mori*. He remembered: *A lawless proliferation.*

"Something must be certain," he said aloud, thinking vaguely of the unpleasant strangers on the sidewalk around him. "I've nothing against you, you understand, and I grant you your inalienable right to the pursuit of happiness. Nevertheless—" He remembered again, suddenly, the garden and the orchard on his grandfather's place, the geese walking in the trees. And he remembered in the same instant, as if the two were connected, Walter Proctor, Negro sociologist and trumpet player with the CR Combo, wiping egg from his sleeve. Chandler had never gotten rid of that momentary shock of outrage and guilt, though he'd written about it later for *Dissent.*

Walking along with his head bowed, his hands behind his back, brooding on mutability, he did not see the pit in the street until almost too late. He stood precariously balanced, one weak hand desperately gripping the sawhorse he had nearly knocked down on some worker's head. Someone caught hold of his elbow and pulled him back. A boy. "You ok, mister?" he said. Chandler nodded, too upset to speak, and the boy studied him, squinting like a Jewish tailor, then smiled, shrugged, and turned away. "That's quicksand down there," an old lady said, to his right. He nodded. "Yes, I know. Close call." "Then again you might have hit one of them pipes," the old lady said. The idea seemed to please her. She said—and he noticed only now the distinct, upstate-New York twang—"You must be new around town." He thought about it, savoring the irony, then nodded humbly. "Yes, I am." "More people coming to Batavia every day," she said. She sighed. Chandler smiled. Then, tipping his hat and turning from her, his knees weak, he made his way around the long trench very carefully, without looking down.

It was not until he reached the door of his mother's house—he'd decided to take a taxi back—that he realized he'd forgotten all about his search for a cabinet shop.

"Any luck, Q. T. Hush?" Marie said, smiling, guessing at once that he had forgotten.

"All sorts of luck," he said solemnly. "I narrowly escaped being swallowed up by quicksand."

"What?" she said, alarmed.

"However," he said, "as Providence would have it, I was preserved."

"Oh," she said. "Oh well," she said then, with mock disappointment. She kissed him on the cheek and took his coat, which he was in the act of hanging on the doorknob.

7

CHANDLER had always had dreams from time to time. They were often in beautiful color and so vivid that he could remember them for days. Almost invariably he saw himself in his dreams as heroic: He was always discovering and ingeniously interpreting priceless old documents long believed to be lost; sometimes he discovered the secret of the universe and lectured on it to cheering thousands in what seemed, when he recollected it later, a kind of pidgin Greek; or sometimes, after a trip to the movies, he dreamed of chasing thieves across city rooftops. He enjoyed his dreams, both at the time he dreamt them and afterwards. It amused him—though it did not in the least surprise him—that a man like himself, outwardly reserved, timid, scholarly, should have in his heart such grandiose desires.

But lately the character of his dreaming had changed: His dreams were often nightmares, these days, and they became increasingly convincing. And here at his mother's house he had nightmares worse than any he had met with since his childhood. These dreams concerned his children, or rather concerned, in the usual confused way, his mixed love for and resentment of his children, his anxiety over what would become of them but also a certain jealousy based, as he reasoned it out, on his fear of death and his consciousness that others would live on.

On the second night he spent in his mother's house he dreamt that he was awakened by an insistent ringing of the telephone. A voice he didn't have time to place urged him to hurry to the railroad bridge. He threw on his coat— an old military coat with a revolver in the pocket—and hurried out into the bright, dead, heavy sunlight. He ran through this sunlight and soon came in sight of the bridge. High on the bridge, their familiar light-colored coats clearly outlined against the pinewoods beyond, he saw his three small children walking along on the ties. He called to them but they didn't hear or else refused to look in his direction. He ran after them and as he ran he realized (with a pleasing sense of the power of his intellect) that the children were blindly oblivious to a terrible danger, the train which, he somehow knew, was just around the bend. He drew near to them at last and called to them again. Anne, the one who had his face, turned and smiled. He realized abruptly that he had made a mistake: It was not Anne but an old, old woman with a toothless, wizened face like the face of a monkey. She had been expecting him. Her mouth was full of blood. He glanced down to see what time it was, then remembered, in sudden, stinging terror, that his wristwatch lay where he had left it, at home on the dresser. The old woman began to smile, her head tipped back to keep the blood in, and she reached out to stroke his cheek. And now he felt, together with terror, a horrible, obscene delight.

He didn't mention the dream the next day, but he had great difficulty getting it out of his mind. Once, as he was helping his wife unpack the last of the children's things, he happened to glance up and see his youngest daughter watching him and smiling. She was bent toward him, her hands on her knees, more intensely *there*—more real, he would have said, than anything in the room around her, like a figure inside the mind. Before he knew why he was on edge, he commanded sharply that she go away somewhere and play, and it made her cry. He was sorry at once and lifted her in his arms and promised to take her to the park this afternoon; but even as he held her tightly, pressing his cheek to her hair, he could not entirely rid himself of the dream.

Later that day something even more distressing happened. As he sat looking through old papers in the room that had once been his father's—the ruin of the secretary stood in the corner waiting for the cabinetmaker Marie had promised to call—he was conscious of the children's voices coming up to him from the lawn below. Gradually his sense of well-being left him: The children were talking about him. He heard the oldest, Karen, saying:

"Mother says we're not to bother him."

"Why?" Susan asked. "He's not doing anything."

"Just the same, we're not to bother him." Then, after a moment, "It's because he's sick."

"Why isn't he in bed?"

"You'll find out when you're older." There was another silence, and then, coldly, matter-of-factly: "He's going to die. I heard Mother and Grandma talking about it."

Chandler sat still, his forehead on his fist, and the feeling of the nightmare was back. He got up, weak all over, and went to stand by the window. They stood below, in their light coats, looking up with ancient, solemn faces. He covered his eyes with one hand and waited, and after a moment he was calm again. It was true that they were only children; they loved him and they would miss him. What was he asking? He was, after all, a grown man. He thought of his own father. "Oh God," he prayed, "please. . . ." But it was empty; one could not resuscitate

God after all these years. Even if it was all true—and he'd never been perfectly sure it wasn't—one couldn't turn on belief again now, merely because it would be comforting. It came to him that the children were no longer there below him. Had he imagined it, perhaps?

That afternoon he did take the children to the park. He was happy as he pushed them on the swings and on the merry-go-round, admired their daring on the jungle gym, or stood ready to catch them at the foot of the slide. One moment, above all, stuck in his mind afterward. Anne was up on the slide, just ready to slide down. She stood balanced, smiling, unable to get up her nerve. Karen and Susan stood on the platform behind her, smiling too, patient and superior. Their hair moved a little with the breeze, and above them stretched clean blue sky. Anne came hurtling toward him, still smiling, but frightened, holding out her arms. He caught her and fell back, pretending to be knocked over by the impact, and as he lay legs-up in the sand, his glasses cocked up onto his forehead, the laughter that came down, ringing, from the sky was so strangely, so unspeakably beautiful that he had the sense of having stepped unexpectedly from one world into another, having slipped away out of time and into the boundless.

That night he had another nightmare. It was morning, and opening his eyes, he saw that the sun was shining in pleasantly; however, he felt uneasy. Then he realized that Karen and Susan were leaning down towards him, wide-eyed, to whisper something into his ear. There was an old woman in the bedroom with Anne, they told him; then they straightened up and waited to see what he would do. He knew that he must leap out of bed and get the old woman out of there, but his muscles would not work. He tried to think what had happened to him and realized after a moment that perhaps it was all a dream. But it was not a dream. He lay wide awake in the spare bedroom in his mother's house, Marie lay sleeping beside him; he could hear his mother and father—their words muffled, just barely intelligible—in the kitchen. A bird—a nuthatch—moved upside down on the budding branch of the elm outside the bedroom window, and on the lawn a beautiful horse was nipping at a corner of a book. A group of bearded men stood waiting to hear his decision, squinting at him, worried, chewing thoughtfully on the knuckles of their right hands. He could not move or speak. He strained with all his will to wake himself, and suddenly the room was dark, or dark except for the lighted dial of the clock.

The following morning, for the first time in two weeks, he thought of going back to work on his writing. It was in a sense a mad idea: It was unlikely that he would live long enough to finish anything of any significance at all— indeed, he had nothing in mind to write, at the moment; his book on metaphysics was obviously out—and his working on some trivial little problem, his meticulously reasoning out steps in an argument that would probably never be concluded, would keep him from the few important things he still might do with his life. There were old haunts he wanted to see again; there were changes in weather he wanted to watch very closely, for once; and he wanted to spend long hours with Marie and the children—take them to the movies, read to them, go to church. And yet he was tempted. It was what he could *do,* after all, the function that defined him.

Still uncertain whether or not he ought to go back to work, Chandler, with his wife's help, moved his books and papers into his father's old room (It had been his wife's idea to bring them) and arranged a place for himself, just in case he should decide to get busy again. By mid-afternoon he was well on his way to committing what little time he had left to grappling with the problem of memory, a problem that had often attracted him, for technical reasons, in the past. He knew very well that he hadn't time for a job of that sort, but perhaps he'd begin on it even so, affirm the absurd. It was chance that stopped him.

Among his books was one with which he had worked in graduate school: *An Analysis of Knowledge and Valua-*

tion, by C. I. Lewis. From page 317 to page 336 the pages, heavily marked in blue and black ink—as was the rest of the book—had been torn down the middle from top almost to bottom. It had not been an accident. Surprising though it might seem to an outsider, in the light of all his later writing, Chandler had reached, that night long ago, what might have been a turning point. In the middle of his reading he had leapt up in fury, tearing the book and hurling it away, and when pacing in his room was not sufficient, he had thrown on his coat and had rushed out into the snow, bareheaded, only sneakers on his feet, to walk. It was all double-talk—he'd fumed—a kind of insanity, an elaborate system of wheels spinning free, producing, achieving nothing. Lewis spoke of certainty: "hard kernels," "givens," "a certain complex of sensa or qualia—what Santayana calls an 'essence'"; but what had Santayana to say, himself, of essences? that "every essence is perfectly individual," that "essences are universals," that "the multitude of essences is absolutely infinite," that "all essences are eternal," and that *"essences do not exist."* He had come to the edge of the city, and here where no buildings blocked the path of the wind, the storm churned in godlike anger. Willows down near the frozen lake crackled and whipped and seemed ready to break. Up above, flaws of snow-filled wind rushed blindly over the drifted hills into darker hills beyond. The sight of all that violence and desolation had checked him. He had turned back and had gone to an all-night diner for bacon and eggs. He had listened to the talk of truck drivers, and their supreme good sense, their unmistakable joy in life—even if it was all illusion, the trick of the moment—had astounded him. And so he vowed he would have no more of word games: He would seize existence by the scrotum, would return to the existentialism of his simpleminded youth. For if Heidegger refused to ask ultimate questions, refused to acknowledge that the answers to one's immediate questions might well be involved with larger answers, at least such a man could say, like Gide's Thésée, *J'ai vécu!*

And so that night might well have been a turning point.

But as it happened, in less than a week he was back on epistemology. The very superficiality of the thing attracted him. Also, he was better at it than most of the graduate students around him; it would mean a future, a job, like anything else. And Chandler had defenses now. He had learned a stance. Not only in his writing but in his thinking as well, he would be reserved, clever, disinterested, a master of technique. For that week he had fallen in love. He could not even remember her name, although he could picture her clearly even now. A girl very much like Marie, unbelievably innocent, naïve, though of course Marie was no longer that, in some ways. No doubt the other girl had also changed by this time. One could in no way prevent it, even in oneself. One could only watch the changes, control them to whatever extent one could, not struggle against them unless one could win, seize them. *Sheer plod* ... something ... *sillion shine.*

On what he recognized himself as a foolish, melodramatic impulse, Chandler now, standing in his father's study, completed the job he'd started fifteen years ago— finished tearing the pages out of Lewis. Then, feeling a new vitality, he went downstairs to look for excitement. The children were away playing at a neighbor's house, and Marie, who had a slight headache, was taking a nap. His mother was reading her lists.

He remembered very little, afterward, of the nightmare that came that night. He remembered standing in the children's room, listening with all his might, and remembered hearing something at last, a swishing sound, perhaps the sound of a skirt. He struggled with someone on a rooftop—dimly he recalled a dry, skull-like face, long hair, the scent of an old cedar trunk left for years in an attic—and then he felt himself falling and felt a burning pain shooting through his knee. When he awakened, early the next morning, he was cold and stiff. The window, which opened onto the porch roof, was partly raised, and when he got out of bed to close it, pain shot, once again, through his knee. In the bathroom he discovered with amazement that his face and chest were scratched and bruised. He sat weakly on the edge of the tub, shaking, trying to think. He jumped up all at once and hurried to the children's room. Warm sunlight splayed over their blankets. They were sleeping quietly.

8

HE was reading Marcus Aurelius, studying the queer strain of terror throughout the *Meditations*. It was a thing he'd never noticed before and something about which, as far as he knew, no one had ever written. Was it simply something he projected onto Aurelius? Would he find it, given his present state, even in the *Crito?*

The chattering of the children broke his train of thought. They were calling for him, wanting him for something. Marie was shushing them, and his mother was saying, her voice irritatingly sweet, "Don't you want some nice warm ginger cookies?" The chattering turned to whining. He snapped his book shut angrily and jumped up. They cringed away as he came into the living room, and Anne began to cry. "We wanted to show you," Susan wailed. Karen broke in quickly, "Daddy, we saw something *you* never saw." He hesitated. Marie was staring at the floor with the stupid, washerwoman look she got sometimes when he behaved, as she would put it, irrationally. Shame mixed with his anger. He stood watching helplessly as Susan and Anne wept. "Now wait," he said, "what did you want to show me, Susan?" It took him a long time to get the crying stopped, but at last the children were sunny again and eager to lead him, hobbling a little on his bad knee, out into the street. Marie called them back from the porch and insisted that Chandler take his hat and coat.

April was nearly over, and after weeks of cold and wet a mock summer had set in. Children were playing marbles on Washington Avenue, and dogs ran in and out of the shrubbery in great excitement, as if they'd been penned up all winter. He carried Anne on his shoulders and silently prayed that it wasn't much farther. Susan skipped along sideways, to his left, telling him that she had been the first to see it. Karen walked backwards, ahead of him, leading the way. She was beautiful, walking in the sunlight. Her blond hair was incredibly fine, and her eyes, like Marie's, could seem at once completely happy and yet reflective, remote. At the edge of the park that opened off Ellicott Avenue they all stopped and Susan pointed. Triumphantly, wonderingly, she cried, "There!" He could not tell at first what they meant him to see. Then he realized that they meant the game on the lawn below. He had seen it many times before, but today he saw it through their eyes, and he too was impressed.

Down in the center of the bowl-shaped park, Blind School students were playing their queer form of baseball. There was a bell inside the ball, and on the ground there was a string to lead the runner around the bases. When a batter managed to hit the ball, the fielders would stand motionless, listening, then would dash after the jingle crazily. Sometimes they collided with each other, running full tilt; once one of them ran into a tree. Chandler winced but continued to watch, fascinated, bending forward slightly.

"What are they doing, Daddy?" Susan asked.

"They're playing baseball," he said. The bell tinkled softly, far away but clear, like a sleighbell, or like a coin rolling on the street.

"They're blind, aren't they?" Karen said solemnly, with a trace of affected compassion.

He nodded. He watched the batter, a squat, gnomelike boy with white hair and, as it seemed to Chandler, shadows in place of eyes. The boy stood very still, his head queerly tilted, listening. The pitcher swung the ball around and around, and the bell jingled merrily, innocently. Then the pitch came. The batter swung and connected solidly:

No one made a sound. The ball went high over the pitcher's head, a bright patch of white, a nagging, innocent jingle. The fielders stood motionless, listening. It was high over the center fielder's head now. He began to run. Chandler barely controlled an urge to shout. It was all, for some reason, incredibly moving—the absolute silence of the players, the rocklike stillness of all but two: the batter wildly stumbling around the bases, sliding his hand on the guide string, the center fielder plunging headlong after the soft, teasing jingle. Then something very disturbing happened. The ball came to rest and was silent. The center fielder came to a stop, his head bent forward and tilted; behind him, the runner hesitated, ran three steps more, then stopped. Absolute stillness. Slowly, like children in a trance or like people moving underwater, the players on both teams began to move in the direction of center field. Just beyond second base they got down on hands and knees and began to grope in the grass, soundlessly, mechanically, as if without hope.

Karen started off to help them. Chandler called to her. She looked back at him, puzzled. "But I can see it, Daddy!"

"Stay away," he said.

"But Daddy!"

"Stay away!" It was almost a scream.

He turned away, starting toward North Street. After a moment he heard Karen following him. "Where are we going, Daddy?" A complaint. He glanced back at her. The blind players were still hunting in silence for the ball.

"Let's see what else there is to see," he said too cheerfully. He wanted to be around the corner, out of sight of the place.

Infuriatingly, she stopped and stood pouting, looking at the ground. She did look like Marie, he thought glumly.

"Do we have to walk very far?" she asked. Susan stood behind her, a smaller image of the same recalcitrance. Anne was terribly heavy in his arms, and his legs were shaky. It was hard to breathe.

"You don't have to walk anywhere. You can sit right

down where you are for the rest of your life." Then, because all at once he saw not only Marie but also himself in her pout and, looking at the image of himself, was amused—and obscurely sorry for Marie—he smiled and relented a little: "We'll bring your meals to you."

She came up even with him and, though she would not look at him, seemed prepared to walk at his side. Susan asked to be carried. "Susan—" he began; but Anne, it turned out, wanted to get down. Susan was so heavy he was afraid of falling, and at last he talked her into walking with the others.

Behind them, the blind players were still on hands and knees.

9

OAK STREET was deserted. The large old houses with their long, banistered porches and fenced-in gardens had gone shabby while he had been away. The street had been widened: Lawns were foreshortened; many of the trees were gone. On the front porch of what had once been a doctor's house—Chandler could not remember the name —sat a still, solid old Indian woman. There was no one else in sight, and there wasn't a sound. It was as if the street had been depopulated by plague. He heard piano music. He turned casually to see where the music was coming from and realized with a start that he stood in front of the Staley house. He pursed his lips and stood reflecting a moment, so that Anne looked up at him expectantly. He recalled that his mother had hoped he would visit them. And then he remembered, *Emma's gotten very odd.*

"Karen," he said, "do you know the way home from here?"

She looked at him sulkily.

But he would not be put off. It was perfectly ridiculous, the thought that had seized him—or no, not thought but superstitious alarm: the old woman in his dreams, the mysterious dream that had been real.

"Listen, it's very easy. There's something I have to do."

She didn't need his directions, but she didn't want to leave. "Why can't we come in with you?" she asked.

He kept his temper. "Perhaps you can, tomorrow. But right now I have to go in by myself. Please, Karen. Run along now. Maybe when I come home we can all go out to a movie." And then, losing patience, he turned from them and started toward the porch. When he looked back they stood where he had left them. He resolved not to look back again. He knew well enough that Marie would say he was being irrational. So he was. He wouldn't think about it.

"Daddy!" Susan cried out.

It electrified him, but he saw at once that there had been no hint of alarm in her voice, and he controlled himself and pretended not to hear.

In the act of reaching for the doorknob, he stopped. His hand hovered a moment, then drew back. Aunt Betsy was giving a lesson, and it had been one of her rules, in the old days, that friends and students come in without interrupting. It was thirty years, though; it might be presumptuous, mightn't it, to assume that he was still on the same familiar terms? Besides, Aunt Emma wasn't well.

He stood a moment looking at the door mat; then, on an impulse, he moved to the right along the porch to peek in through the music-room window. The piano top was up, hiding the student, but he could see Aunt Betsy. She might have been sitting there all these years, giving lessons one after another, whispering curses under her breath, growing more immense and more pale by the week on the party sandwiches her sisters brought in on a tray whenever they found the time to make them. All three of the Staley sisters had given lessons in the old days. Aunt Maud had taught singing, Aunt Emma had taught painting, Aunt Betsy had taught piano. They had liked to say they were poor as churchmice, but Aunt Betsy had a music room equipped with two Steinway grands and a Steinway upright. Certainly Aunt Betsy as he saw her now—"aunt" because his mother and the sisters had been friends—did not seem a woman crushed by poverty: Bloated and pale and erect, her hair blue-white, she sat like an ancient queen among her pianos.

"She's looking at us, Daddy," Karen said excitedly, right at his elbow. It was true. The old woman was calmly returning their gaze as though there were nothing unusual in the least in being stared in at from one's porch by a girl and a middle-aged man in thick glasses.

"Get back to your sisters," he hissed. Then, turning to Aunt Betsy again, Chandler smiled nervously and bowed, touching his hat. Then he went around once more to the door. He thought fleetingly of hurrying off down the street as though he had got the wrong house. The three children were squatting now at the foot of the walk, the two younger girls listening intently as Karen whispered to them. He knocked.

His knock brought not one of the Staley sisters but a younger woman, a girl. She had a round, pretty face, or pretty except for the wide, flat lips. Her eyes were green as emerald, and for an instant Chandler stared like a fool. He touched his nose then, and looked down. When he introduced himself and explained his errand she smiled brightly—too brightly, somehow—and held the door for him. She was the niece, Viola, she said. She had often heard her aunts speak of him. As he started through the doorway she said, "When I heard your knock I thought it must be a salesman. You should have walked right in."

He looked down again in a half nod, smiling, embarrassed. "I should have, yes. I'm sorry."

When they reached the outer parlor, the waiting room

for Aunt Betsy's students, the niece put her hand on his arm, stopping him, and said, "I'll get Aunt Maud. I won't be a minute." He was startled all over again by the green of her eyes. He couldn't tell whether a thing so unnatural was beautiful or terrible. She crossed to the double door opposite and was gone, leaving him still in his light coat, his hat in his hands. The young woman's eyes continued to molest his thoughts.

The house lay silent; then, behind the closed double door to his right, the music lesson started up again. He let his head fall to one side and listened, grateful for the distraction. *The Spinning Song.* He waited for the child's right hand to miss the B ♮ in the middle section, and when the correct note came and the first theme had safely returned he felt relief.

The parlor seemed smaller, more crowded, more cluttered than he had remembered it, but nothing was changed. Ball-and-claw chairs, gloomy, dark, flocked wallpaper, silver jars of artificial roses. *The Old Mill,* one of Aunt Emma's oils, hung in its usual place. He crossed to look at it. He had looked at the painting often in his childhood. He had been quite fond of it. He had to smile now to think that he had once been so easily impressed. Every blade of grass, every leaf, every stone was tortuously rendered; every form had its precise shadow; and, light or dark, every detail had the same gloomy luminescence, deep, rich color obscured by layer on layer of varnish. One could see that the young Emma Staley had painted with feeling. In the sky, dark, mountainous thunderheads; below, ancient cypresses huddled together, pitted rocks, churning white water, the crumbling remains of the mill. All was motion and decay: It seemed to rot before one's very eyes. The varnish was a network of cracks; the painting might have been hundreds of years old.

All at once, without warning, even as he stood inwardly laughing at the painting, the old mood rose in him again: He felt a sudden, surprising unrest, a vague, ardent thirst for the past, for wilderness, for freedom, for heaven knew what—a paradoxical sense of intense dissatisfaction with himself and, at the same time, a kind of vaulting joy. He stood perfectly still, his head on one side, his eyes closed to slits, and he explored what he felt, the sensation he would have said he'd outgrown and forgotten long ago. Indeed, it occurred to him that perhaps what he felt now was after all not emotion but its shadow, a violent waking of memory, a kind of waking dream. His family had lived on Liberty then, though once his mother's people had lived up on State Street and his great-grandfather on his father's side had lived in a mansion. The Staley house, to which Chandler had walked from school every Thursday afternoon for his music lesson, had in those days represented all that one might with luck achieve —nice things, manners, dignity, a kind of power—and at the same time all that he himself might for obscure reasons —his glasses? was that all it was?—be excluded from. He felt himself a visitor there, set apart, like a visitor to a museum, removed from the secret life of the place. *The Old Mill* was at that time the only oil painting he had ever seen. He'd stood fascinated, as a child; and the reason, it struck him now, was this: He'd known nothing then of the stock Romantic tone, and so he'd assumed that Aunt Emma had painted just what she saw, and that what she saw—he had seen it himself in his earliest childhood, at his grandfather's—was a world that only people like the Staleys knew how to enter, or perhaps reenter. He'd believed in magic, in those days. The old angular comb on his grandmother's dresser had a past that he was always just on the point of divining.

He smiled and turned from the painting. There was nothing more to it than that, however sudden and passionate the upsurge of feeling. And yet even now that he had accounted for the sensation, his mingled pleasure and dread did not quite leave him. The yellow sunlight that filtered through the yellowed lace curtains and splayed on the faded, threadbare rug seemed the light of his childhood. He remembered all at once, quite vividly the blind children in the park.

He gave a violent start when he saw the boy in the

corner. He'd evidently been sitting there all the while, his hands folded on his knees, his music stacked neatly on the floor beside his chair. The boy stared up calmly from his place in the shadowy part of the room, his expression so open, so unguarded that one might have thought he was appraising not a man but some lifeless thing—a colorful cigar paper, an unusual plant, a carved statue in an exhibit case.

Chandler smiled abruptly. "Hello. What's your name?"

"James," the boy said simply.

"James?" Chandler said, "why, that's my name, too."

"James St. Clair?" asked the boy. He seemed perfectly prepared to accept it if it was so.

"No, Chandler, I'm afraid," Chandler said, laughing. He felt queerly relieved, but the boy only smiled politely. Chandler remembered vividly now how it felt to sit waiting in the shadows, going over one's lesson in one's mind, dreading Aunt Betsy's whispered curses.

At last the niece returned.

"Would you like to come with me?" she said. "Aunt Maud's thrilled to hear you've come. It seems your mother's her dearest friend in the world." She laughed with what was apparently meaningless and habitual sarcasm; and he said, "Yes, thank you." Then she noticed his coat and came a little closer. "I forgot to take your coat, you poor man! Here you've been standing all this time! I guess I'd forget my head if it weren't screwed on!"

Chandler smiled and excused it awkwardly as she helped him out of the coat. She carried the coat back to the entryway, talking all the while, lightly complaining that it was hot enough in this house even without a coat on; no doubt it got more difficult, as one grew older, to keep up one's body temperature. Aunt Betsy, she said, kept the thermostat at ninety all the time, and even that wasn't enough: She had an electric heater going full blast in the music room. The niece hated to think what it was doing to the pianos. Then she was beside him again. As they started toward the living room she smiled at the boy in the corner and said affectionately, "Hi, Peter." The boy looked at her. "He's only seven," she said, tilting her head to look at Chandler, "and he's almost through the third John Thompson book."

Chandler studied her, puzzled, vaguely uncomfortable, but the niece did not notice. Uneven notes hung in the air behind them, a Czerny phrase. After a moment the phrase came again, high in the treble, the notes this time clean and hard and certain, as if struck from thick, cut-glass goblets.

"My name is James," the boy said distinctly.

For just a fraction of a second, the round, innocent face of the niece changed, and Chandler was at once certain that the boy was telling the truth. "That's odd," the niece said gaily, perfectly composed again when she'd closed the door behind them, "why on earth do you suppose he said that?"

Chandler smiled, baffled, and shrugged, then squinted at the girl, his hand over his mouth.

10

THE parlor in the Staley house opened onto the dining room; to the right, through the wide, oak-beamed arch, lay the living room, a long, gloomy cavern with old, red and yellowish wallpaper, a fireplace at the far end set between high, oval, stained-glass windows. If the laws of life and death hung fire here in the Staley house, waiting upon the will of the three old ladies, then the living room was the center of the mystery. A rug that had once been blood red but was now faded and shabby flowed the length of the room; the chairs were done in red velvet, tasseled, fringed, antimacassared, rising precariously on gryphon legs which gripped glass balls in their claws; a faded, indistinct tapestry covered much of one wall, and on the opposite wall, in heavy, oak-leafed frames, hung two more of Aunt Emma's oils. There were milkglass vases and bowls on the table by the sofa, on the mantelshelf, and on the spindly little desk below the tapestry; the lamps in the room were white china. Aunt Maud, wearing arm warmers and a lap rug, sat close to the fire. She turned her head to greet him. Here yes were shockingly sunken.

"James Chandler," she said softly, holding out her hand to him.

He took the hand and nodded, smiling, and said, "It's good to see you looking so well, Aunt Maud." He glanced at the niece, who smiled and nodded as if to encourage him; but it seemed to him for an instant that, despite her smile, he had in some way annoyed her. The old woman squeezed his hand, and he was surprised to discover what strength she had in her fingers.

"Dr. Chandler teaches at a college in California," the niece said, bending down to Aunt Maud's ear. It was odd that she knew that. Chandler had not mentioned it.

Aunt Maud smiled vaguely, and the niece bent closer to say it again, shouting this time. The old woman nodded and said with an absent look, "How kind, kind." Then: "Don't you think it's chilly in here?" she said, looking up anxiously at Chandler.

He half nodded and smiled as though he too were deaf, and he reflected on what answer he ought to give. The niece, meanwhile, went around her aunt's chair and bent down to poke the fire as if in rage.

Little by little his awkwardness left him. Leaning toward the chair where the niece had now seated him, the old woman asked about his parents and asked about friends he hadn't seen since gradeschool, and she listened eagerly, pertly, to his answers although he was sure she caught very little if anything of what he said. He answered expansively, nonetheless, conscious of feelings he would want to think back to later. It pleased him to be talking again of the past, and it surprised him that he should find it so extremely enjoyable to play this game of empty forms, communion as pure gesture. He heard distant piano music and thought fleetingly of the other James, back in the music room, playing for Aunt Betsy.

There had come a lull in the conversation. At last Aunt Maud said thoughtfully, looking down at her lap, "I can't tell you how thankful we are that Viola can be here with us." She glanced over at the niece, seemed to consider, then looked back at her lap. "We hardly knew her when she was little, you know. After Eddie sold his half of the store to Mr. McIvor, they moved away to Illinois. It's a sad thing, don't you think, to move away from your own home?"

Chandler bowed his head, smiling absently, and touched his chin.

"A child should grow up where people know her," the old woman said. She sighed. "But Eddie thought he could make more money there, poor boy. We lost everything, you know. We were poor as churchmice."

He nodded.

Her face brightened, and she exclaimed, rather wildly, "We've had to live by our wits!" She smiled, her mouth open and her eyes too wide, waiting for him—it seemed —to laugh.

"Aunt Maud," the niece said, apparently guessing what was to come.

"Come here, young man," Aunt Maud said, crooking her finger at him, "put your hand on my stomach." She moved the lap rug down.

Before he quite knew what was happening, Chandler had obeyed. The niece's eyes opened wider, but her horror and humiliation left her speechless.

"Now," Aunt Maud said, pressing Chandler's hand firmly to her abdomen, "watch." She let out, he would have said, every particle of air in her body; then, slowly, she inhaled. The soft, dead flesh of her stomach turned to muscle under his fingertips and little by little her stomach, then her chest, filled with air. Her trunk became grotesquely bloated and as solid as a truck tire. Then at last she released his wrist, her eyes closed tight, oozing tears, her mouth still in its ghastly smile. He was half prepared to hear her sing a clear, sweet high C. But she breathed out again without a sound. Chandler shook his head slowly, his hand on his mouth. The old woman said feebly, completely spent, "That is the secret."

"Beautiful," he said; and then at once he was flustered, the word was horribly wrong.

"I don't allow myself to do that very often," Aunt Maud said, and her voice was still weaker now.

"Thank God for that," the niece said with startling violence. Then, quickly, as if to keep Chandler from sitting down again, as he was just now on the point of doing, "Have you come for the whole summer?" The anger was still in her voice.

"I expect so, yes," he said, nonplussed. "Marie and the children—" He let it trail off. It was foolish of him to have left them out there on the street; foolish of him to have come, for that matter. Suppose they were to wander off? Bank Street was not far, but they were only children after all. Suddenly he remembered the sewage excavations and, down in the pits, quicksand. But that was more than a mile from here. "I'm afraid I had better be running now," he said. "I only meant to drop in for a moment. I hope I haven't tired Aunt Maud."

"Not a bit," the niece said lightly, grimly, waving it off, and again the hint of pointless sarcasm was there. "But surely you can stay long enough to join us in a cup of Ovaltine?" She seemed to find the very thought revolting.

"No, really, I'm afraid," Chandler began, but the old woman cut him off. She seemed to have sensed rather than heard that he was preparing to leave. She sat more erect in her chair, with a frightened look, and she said, "You won't go without saying a word to Emmie, will you?"

"Please, Aunt Maud," the niece said sharply; but the old woman seemed not to notice.

"Emmie'd be terribly sorry to miss you," she said.

It was hard to know what to do. It was clear that the niece was dead set against it, but it was clear, too, that Aunt Maud was very anxious to have him look in on

Aunt Emma; and to put the thing bluntly, that was what he had come for, wasn't it? "I don't know—" he said, looking down, adjusting his glasses with one finger.

At the sign of his weakening Aunt Maud grew still more insistent. "Viola, run see if Emmie's awake."

"Now Aunt Maud, you know better," the niece said earnestly, leaning closer and shaking her finger as if at a child. Then, turning to him, her eyes like fire over copper: "I'm afraid Aunt Maud doesn't quite understand the situation, Dr. Chandler. I'm awfully sorry, and I can't tell you how embarrassed I am, but the truth is that, well, Aunt Emma is very sick."

Now, for some reason, Aunt Maud seemed to be hearing every word. She began to shake, and there was fury in her eyes. The muscles of her face tightened, and then all at once she began to cry out, "Emmie! Emmie, come in here a minute!"

"Aunt Maud!" the niece shrieked. "Oh my God, Dr. Chandler, this is terrible!" And then soothingly, only half controlling her fright (but was it fright? Chandler wondered; was this, too, an act?), "Now Aunt Maud, you be nice and quiet for Viola, be a good, good girl or Aunt Betsy will have to come scold you."

But Aunt Maud would not be stopped. She was screeching it now, her eyes brighter than an owl's, her talons gripping the chair-arms ferociously; the hunch of her back seemed not age but malice: "Emma! Emma! Emma!"

Aunt Betsy seemed to hear none of it. She was playing a duet with her pupil, three rooms away, one piano giving out sweet, soft, faltering notes, the other chiming fortissimo with the soul-shattering precision of a clock. Chandler stood with one hand raised futilely in the air, uncertain which of the women most needed calming; and then both the screaming and the pleading stopped at once. He too heard it: the sound of an animal scratching at a door. Their eyes instantly showed him the place. Beside the desk, on the wall to the left of the fireplace, the wall where the long tapestry hung, there was a door he had scarcely noticed until now. The doorknob turned as he watched, but the door would not open.

"You've locked it," Aunt Maud exclaimed, half rising from her chair.

The doorknob went on turning, and then the scratching came again. The girl covered her face with her hands and stood hunched over, trembling strangely, as though she were in pain. Abruptly, as though all the powers of darkness had suddenly leapt from the fire to torment her, she turned and fled.

"She's locked her up like a dog," Aunt Maud said, falling back again limply, as gray as wasted earth. "What are we coming to?"

11

THE scratching went on, quiet, nagging, and it seemed to Chandler to come from every part of the room, from the chairs, the lamps, the fireplace, the stained-glass windows, the paintings on the wall. It numbed him. What made the sound intolerable was not that it marked a human being locked up in a room like an animal but that it marked something manifestly *not* human, something as mindless as a wind, or water wearing away at stone, matter grating on matter in the dark of space.

And then Aunt Betsy was there, with the girl behind her. The girl stopped at the living-room doorway and remained there, her shoulders hunched and her hands clasped just below her chin, like an Oriental.

Aunt Betsy showed no sign that she saw James Chandler in the room but crossed directly to the locked door, turned the key in the lock, and opened the door inward. Then she turned back to the niece and simply looked at her with no expression whatever, and yet the look was, unmistakably, a command. The niece went in quickly, her face set, and the door closed. Then Aunt Betsy came to Chandler, as expressionless as ever—weary, perhaps; her mind on things which had nothing to do with any of them—and gave him her hand. She was taller by a foot than Chandler, and though her head, her hands, and her feet were small, her body was immense. Bowing awkwardly, holding her limp hand (One would never have guessed what incredible power she had in her fingers), Chandler felt like a child before her. Her skin was absolutely white, her hair a luminous white with a bluish cast. Her look was as vague as Aunt Maud's but it was a different vagueness: It was as though her mind had penetrated some ultimate secret and remained there, fixed, like a butterfly on a pin. He thought of the white-haired blind boy he'd seen on the lawn.

Aunt Betsy was less abstracted than he thought. "It's good to see you, James," she said. "I saw in the paper that you were home."

"Oh?" Chandler said, surprised.

"I imagine your mother put it in. It would be strange if she weren't proud to have you back."

He smiled, nodding, and thought to withdraw his hand. "I suppose it would be, yes."

She folded her arms on her bosom as she'd always done long ago when he began his piano lesson. "I'm glad you remembered us. Maud's so pleased to have company now and then." When Aunt Betsy glanced at her, Aunt Maud came alert and smiled timidly, evidently taking care to show her undeviatingly good behavior.

"We've had a wonderful talk," he said. "It's been a long time."

"Yes it has. Do you keep up your piano?"

For a fraction of a second, the direct question threw him into panic. It was as if she had asked, as she'd asked so often, "Did you practice?" Then it came to him that, yes, certainly, he *had* kept up his piano. How odd that she could still, after all these years, frighten him out of his wits! He said, "I've tried to do some playing, yes." Then, with a boldness he'd never have expected, he added: "I was afraid of your curse."

The pun escaped her. Perhaps it was not as open as he had thought it, in the brief excitement of his childish insolence, or perhaps, thoroughly adult, she was simply not interested. "Good," she said. "It's always a waste not to." He saw that her mind was again on something else. He turned, on an impulse, and saw that the niece had come out of the room and stood near the door, sullenly watching.

"You'll want to see Emma again, I'm sure," Aunt Betsy said. If her voice had been expressionless before, it was more so now; and all at once he understood her tone: She was indeed, as his mother would say, a lady. She was braving it out as she'd braved out all those piano lessons—he'd never guessed until this moment how thoroughly she had hated them—sitting perfectly erect and calm, speaking precisely and tonelessly: "B ♮"—and inaudibly, she thought, swearing under her breath.

"Please, if you'd rather—" he began. But it was too late. Aunt Emma had come.

He'd had no idea how completely he had prepared himself to find Aunt Emma the mad old woman in his dreams. But he had been wrong. She was beautiful, almost more beautiful than she'd been when she was younger. She was a tiny, china-doll-like person dressed from head to foot in black: a black shawl of the kind his grandmother had worn, a long black dress, black shoes and stockings, and, oddly enough, black gloves. Her face was like a girl's: trusting, gentle, innocent. She looked at them all with the same friendly curiosity, as though she had never seen them before but was very much inclined already to like them. The niece—grudgingly, it seemed—guided her to Chandler and said, her tone dark with hostility, "Aunt Emma, this is a dear old friend of ours, Dr. Chandler." Aunt Emma smiled, fascinated, but she did not say a word or offer her hand.

Chandler said softly, "I'm glad to see you again, Aunt Emma."

She merely smiled as if caught up in some enchantment, locked by a spell in unearthly innocence.

Aunt Betsy said, "James used to be a great admirer of yours, Emmie."

Aunt Emma turned in the direction of the new voice and smiled as before.

"That's true," Chandler said quickly. "In fact, just this afternoon I found myself impressed all over again by your painting—*The Old Mill*."

She turned gracefully, as if inquiringly, to the niece.

"He likes *The Ruined Mill*," the niece explained coldly. The old woman's smile did not change.

"That's always been one of my very favorites," Aunt Betsy said. "Emma outdid herself there." She spoke heavily, somewhat wearily, as though the play had begun to bore her.

"But these are nice too," Chandler said, nodding toward the two on the living-room wall. They were very much like the other one, but one was of a waterfall, the other of a sun-dial in a kind of park.

"Emmie always had a wonderful feeling," Aunt Maud said, apparently guessing the line of conversation from Chandler's glance at the paintings. "We were always sorry she wasn't able to pursue her studies further. According to Nina Mason Booth, Emma had an unusual natural flair. Nina was a very famous artist, you know. One of the Masons. She once did a cover for the *Saturday Evening Post*."

Chandler nodded.

"Those were Nina's actual words," Aunt Betsy said, "an unusual natural flair."

Without warning, Aunt Emma reached up and touched Chandler's cheek very lightly with her dry, cold fingers. Chandler instantly recalled the similar gesture of the old woman in his dream, but he felt, now, no fright or revulsion, only a slight embarrassment and then a gentle surge of pity. It was as though it were indeed the spontaneous gesture of a child.

Once again the thought of his children waiting out in front burst into his mind, and he remembered again the real though admittedly obscure and remote dangers. With a calculated look of alarm he drew out his watch and glanced at it, though to tell the truth he had no idea what time it was when he'd come and therefore no notion how long he'd stayed. "Oh!" he said clumsily, "I didn't realize—" They observed his little act with the detachment of kindly gods, except for the niece, who glared, in fact almost leered, with open scorn. He saw in terrible clarity how awkwardly he had managed it. How would they have handled it? How would Marie?

Aunt Maud said, her voice feeble but the tone supremely gracious, "Must you? Why it seems you only just got here!"

"No, really," he said.

"Well, it's been wonderful to see you," Aunt Betsy said. "I hope we can see you again sometime when we're not all in such a flurry. Do you plan to stay long?"

"Probably a month or so," he said calmly.

"Then you'll be able to come to Aunt Betsy's recital," the niece said with a senseless, grim smile.

"Now, Viola," Aunt Betsy said, weary and aloof, "I'm sure James has far more important things to do."

"On the contrary," he said quickly, relieved to find among all the uncertainties of the social moment something sure, a date, a physical occasion, to fix upon. "I'd like nothing better. When is it?"

After an instant's hesitation, Aunt Betsy said, "It's the sixth of May, next Thursday. We're having it at the Y.W.C.A. again this year. I do have one or two students you might be interested to hear, actually. Especially a little Indian boy named Peter Tree, Charley Tree's son. Charley has a music store here in town. That's since your time, I think. It's where the photo shop used to be."

Chandler nodded, standing tipped forward a little with interest.

"Little Peter's the quickest student I've ever had," she said. "You know how it is with those people, they surprise you sometimes. Peter's seven, and he's already finished the third John Thompson book."

His glance at the niece was involuntary. Her round,

sullen face showed nothing at all. She looked, for just that instant, very much like Aunt Emma, absolutely innocent and blank.

"I'll look forward to hearing him," Chandler said. Then, turning to Aunt Maud, "It's been good talking to you, Aunt Maud. I hope we'll see more of each other." She spoke of how much she'd enjoyed his visit, then released him, and he turned to Aunt Betsy and uncertain whether or not it was expected, took her hand. "I can't tell you how glad I am to see you again," he said. Aunt Betsy smiled, completely detached, as it seemed to him, neither pleased nor displeased. "Thank you for coming," she said. He turned to Aunt Emma, and he knew all at once that she had been watching him all this while with her gentle, fixed, mindless smile. He said, "It's been good to see you too, Aunt Emma." She merely smiled as before, and when he was ready to withdraw his hand, she did not release it. He was startled at first; but then he saw— though not with anything like certainty—that it was his own behavior that was odd, not hers; she merely meant to walk to the door with him—though she probably no longer knew why one did such things. He bowed and smiled again to Aunt Maud and began to move tentatively toward the dining room. Aunt Emma came with him, smiling, holding his hand. Aunt Betsy and the niece watched with solemn, anxious-looking faces, then followed.

At the double doors that opened into the outer parlor, Chandler paused, nodded his farewells again, and made another move to withdraw his hand. Aunt Emma held the hand in her own as tightly as before, smiling sweetly, even radiantly, as though it were a moment of great significance. He nodded to her again. Her smile brightened still more, and then, surprisingly, as though she had no sense of what the gesture might mean but found it pleasing, she returned his nod. It dawned on him—and he felt foolish to have blundered so before the old ladies, assuming they'd noticed—that Aunt Emma meant to accompany him all the way to the front door.

Aunt Betsy said, "Emma, dear—"

Aunt Emma's left hand came to his arm, the right hand still in his, and she went through the double doors, a step ahead of him, drawing him along. The room was empty now, but in the music room, which stood open, there was a little girl. He walked with Aunt Emma past the high-backed chairs where he had waited for lessons as a child, past the lamp table, past the painting. Her hand on his arm reminded him of something, only a vague impression at first, then a clear memory. He thought of Helen Wiess, the girl he'd been fully prepared to marry once, long before he'd met Marie. He remembered dancing with her, or, more often, watching her dance with friends of his while he played piano with the band. He would watch her, and if he lost sight of her he would watch intently for her dress. Girls with pastel dresses and shining hair, innocent faces, a room filled with graceful, patterned motion—the patterns of separate couples and also a larger pattern which he, on the raised platform, could never quite catch before it changed into something else, like the patterns starlings made in flight or the changing shapes of clouds. Aunt Emma's gloved hand held his fingers lightly and he might almost have forgotten her hand was there, and yet she guided him surely. Beyond the glass of the door he saw his children sitting under the tree, down near the street, and with a start he remembered his coat and hat. "Excuse me," he said, pulling back slightly, "I nearly forgot—" But the pressure of her hand was insistent. He glanced behind him. Aunt Betsy stood with her hands folded at her waist and looked vaguely troubled, and the niece stood at her elbow watching him narrowly.

"I'm afraid I need my coat and hat," Chandler said.

The niece gave a startled nod, then hurried over to the coat closet to her right. Aunt Emma stood waiting, a hint of confusion around her eyes now, and when the niece came with the coat and hat, Aunt Emma reluctantly gave up Chandler's hand. The niece helped him on with his coat, watching him oddly, as if ferociously, all the while, and handed him his hat. He held the hat in both hands, turning it round and round and looking at the band. Aunt Emma's look of confusion was still there, clearer now as Aunt Betsy drew close.

"It's been good to see you," Aunt Betsy said with finality, slipping her hand through Aunt Emma's arm.

Chandler reached for the doorknob, and Aunt Emma caught at his sleeve. Her smile was intense and forced. He said to her vaguely, "Thank you so much," and opened the door. As he'd known she would, however fiercely he'd denied his knowledge, she made a move to come with him.

"Now Emma, Mr. Chandler has to go home," Aunt Betsy said firmly.

The old woman looked up at him with wild eyes.

"Just go ahead, James," Aunt Betsy said. To Aunt Emma she said, "Mr. Chandler will visit us again just as soon as he can." Chandler started out the door, but Aunt Emma held him.

Abruptly, viciously, like a mocking child, the niece began to laugh. Aunt Betsy stiffened and turned to her, her nostrils flaring, but the niece would not stop. "Viola!" she said firmly. Then, in the same voice, "Viola, go to your room."

Instantly, exactly as though the old woman had slapped her, the niece stopped laughing. She stood motionless, as if suspended in space; then, hiding her face in her hands, her elbows straight out, she turned and fled.

"God damned stupid bitch," Aunt Betsy whispered, looking heavenward. Then, composed again at once: "I'm sorry to subject you to this, James."

"Not at all," he mumbled, bowing to evade her eyes. He felt suddenly nauseous, as though he stood on a rickety bridge high over a turmoil of shifting water and sand, or as though he stood on nothing at all, a scaffold of questions. Was the whole family insane? Had the girl been sane when she came to them? Did Aunt Betsy really not see it?

Aunt Emma was clinging to his arm with both hands, and her lips were trembling. "I've been good," she whimpered. "Father, I've been *good*."

It made him start. In his mind he saw, more real than

the entry room around him, the old woman seated beside her bed, fully dressed, even to gloves—even, perhaps, her hat on, her bags packed, for the niece had for some reason gone to her before bringing her out to the living room. He saw her sitting erect and prim, waiting for a long-dead father—or God? was that it?—waiting for *him,* whoever it was, to lead her away from her overpowering world of old mills and waterfalls and sundials of mossy stone.

Aunt Betsy drew her sister back firmly. "Good day, James," she said.

Now Aunt Emma was backing away, still whimpering, forming the words with her lips: *I've been good.*

Chandler stepped out quickly and closed the door.

12

AT the foot of the walk Anne and Susan brightened and stood up to greet him. Karen got up more slowly, her face sullen, accusing him. Her legs and arms were thin, her neck too long; she looked like the childhood pictures of Marie. In a few more years—a matter of moments—she would be painfully beautiful.

"I'm sorry," he said seriously, for Karen's unspoken accusation seemed for obscure reasons bitterly just. At once, Susan's smile turned into a scowl: Only now that he admitted it did it occur to her that he might be guilty and that she might have the right to punish him.

He smiled, both amused and depressed by Susan's change of heart, and he placed one hand on Susan's shoulder, the other on Anne's. Karen stood leaning against the tree, aloof from him and solemn, and Chandler was moved almost to tears by his sudden sense of how vulnerable she was. Had the Staleys' niece been like this once, before her father's death? And yet it was all right. It would be all right.

Anne said crossly, "Wanna sucker."

He tilted his head, studying the tough little image of himself. Then, looking over at his oldest: "Shall we go get some ice cream, Karen?"

"No thank you," she said coolly, avoiding his eyes.

Susan and Anne brightened and Susan began to clap. "Ice cream! Ice cream! Daddy, I want strawberry."

"Karen, *Karen,*" he thought, all at once unable to bear the fact that she would in time forget him, would live on despite his annihilation, growing beautiful without him. Perhaps she would grow beautiful in terrible ways, like Aunt Betsy, or like the poor wretched niece whose every word was a stove-lid over anger: she'd become a lady, no more a true lady than the niece or Aunt Betsy—or Marie —but something as true and good as any Platonic form, a lady like one of those trees that found out its shape among rocks and sand along the Pacific. And then some night at some college dance, standing on some patio overlooking broad lawns and hedges, sidewalks, far-off streetlamps, she would say with a laugh, if that was the shape her beauty took, or with a pout, or with unaffected nonchalance, "I never really knew my father. No doubt he screwed me up in the usual ways." It was hideously unfair. He'd loved her, he'd been good.

Then, helplessly, he laughed. She frowned, as if to say, What *next?*

"Karen," he said, and he intended to say "I love you," but he'd said her name in the wrong tone, the tone of a father to a sulking child, and he couldn't finish as he'd meant to. He said instead, "Susan and Anne would like some ice cream. Are you going to keep us all from it just out of spite?"

She said, "Go ahead, if you want it so damn much."

He bent toward her in fury. "What did you say, Karen?"

She pouted. "Nothing."

He squinted at her, bending down more, his hands pushed deep in his coatpockets now; but her anger was so much like his own childish flare-ups of temper that he could not keep up the heat of his indignation.

"I love you, Miss Chandler," he said all at once, surprising himself. It struck him that, simple as it was, it was something he had not said for a long time.

She frowned up at him, puzzled, then looked down the street, her head tipped forward.

"And ladies don't say damn, is that clear?" he added sternly.

After a long moment she nodded. Then she said, "I suppose if *they* want some, *I* might as well too."

"Right," he said, serious.

She turned her face to him again and studied him for a long moment. "I believe I'd rather like vanilla," she said. "Strawberry is for children."

Her manner was impossibly pompous, and she was trying very hard to please him, and the whole world was hopelessly mixed up.

In the Staley house behind him, some child—the girl he had seen in the music room, of course—began to play the piano. *The Spinning Song*. The almost inevitable wrong note came and then, abruptly, silence. "Son of a bitch," Aunt Betsy whispered in Chandler's mind, and he looked up in terror at the awful justice towering above him. She reached out violently to the treble and chimed out the passage with lightning speed and unearthly power, transmogriphying the instrument to some splendid, dreadful, heavenly machine. Chandler shuddered, hunching his shoulders, absentmindedly touching his hat.

"Carry me," the two-year-old commanded.

"No, this time you walk," Chandler said. It would take every ounce of strength he had, he was suddenly aware, to get to the ice-cream parlor on Washington.

She threw herself on the sidewalk, executing a tantrum. Karen and Susan stopped to wait for her, but hardly seemed to notice.

"Annie, you get up and walk," Chandler said. He

gulped for air. Depression, anger, fear, God knew what filled up his chest like a fluid.

Karen said mock-solemnly, as if mimicking someone, "In my opinion you should take off her shoes. That's what Mother does. Then when she kicks the sidewalk she'll hurt her feet."

He began to laugh, without meaning to. Then, abruptly, he kneeled on the sidewalk and reached out toward Annie to touch her, though that was not why he had kneeled. His groping hand did not find her, and Susan began to giggle. "Stop it," he whispered. Was this what it was going to be like? he wondered in terror; was this—the time itself? Though he could feel the ground under his knees and fingers, he still seemed to be falling, turning over and over as he fell. It was as if the earth itself were falling, as if he had suddenly come awake to the tumbling of the universe in its void.

One of them said, "He's bleeding!"

High above him, Karen said—or a voice he recognized as Karen's but a voice infinitely older, infinitely more gentle, and yet frantic, as though it were indeed the voice of a child—"It's all right, Daddy. Just rest a minute." He could feel the sidewalk moving, changing, dancing under his hands. She touched his face, gently, with indescribable sweetness. He caught at her hand and clung to it.

PART TWO

1

HER room was dark, as usual, the shutters closed—in the dimness, a clutter of shabby paperbacks, clothes on chairs, three stockings over the mirror. Here as elsewhere in this house it was hot and dry, but Viola Staley had no wish to escape it: She had been lying—or acting: It had nothing to do with lying, really—when she'd said it was her aunts who needed heat. She, too, was unfit for Nature—especially just now. Spring, for her, was intolerable. It had always been: She could remember huddling against it as a child, feeling violated by sights and sounds and smells—not only the stench and racket of a neighbor's gasoline lawn mower but even the sick-sweet scent of trees, the music of birds, the movement of clouds above pines. Her mother said that she'd hardly spoken or cried until she was three; and Viola knew that that was surely right. When she'd seen her father in his casket, when she was six years old, she'd felt envy, not grief (or at any rate so she remembered it), and when the nun at her side had said her father was happy Viola had answered "Yes, I know" with such conviction that the other two nuns had looked startled. She had wanted more than anything, in those days, to be dead, or if not dead, a nun, then, cool and gentle and remote as a star: She would stand alone in the church at night, the room cool and holy, and she would pray, and her heart would fill with joy, a sense that she and the dark sanctuary were one—she and all God's creation, one —united as finally and absolutely as an actress and her audience, or musician and instrument and hearer—and she would know she was going to faint. She had fainted often: not just in church but anywhere, once in the middle of the street when a car was coming. Perhaps she had liked the collapse of light around her, the sense of release. Her mother had said, long afterward, that Viola had fainted from holding her breath and had done it on purpose. Perhaps it was true. She'd been strange as a child, certainly. She could see it in the pictures in Aunt Betsy's album. She seemed to remember her childhood clearly, but looking at the child in the pictures, especially the eyes and the carefully tilted head, she knew there was a great deal she had forgotten.

She'd been violently religious. She had read every book she could get about saints and martyrs, and she'd haunted the church and its lawn like a troubled ghost. Six months after her father died, her mother had changed to the Methodist Church (inexplicably at first), the church her father had belonged to. It hadn't taken Viola long to see through it: It was because of the books Viola read. Her mother had been frightened—and for no reason, Viola had realized. It was all a kind of game she'd been playing, a part in a story; and her mother's act repelled her. Her mother was stupid, then! That memory of seeing through her mother was the most significant in Viola's life, it sometimes seemed to her now. It was like a rebirth, like a kind of conception in which she became, miraculously, both the parent and the child: a moment to treasure, for it marked the beginning of her freedom. But in dreams she would sometimes see herself, even now, in a golden casket with a polished glass lid, and faceless nuns would surround her white, still corpse. It was very moving to her, and poetic.

She sat against the pillows on the bed with her knees drawn tight to her chin and the covers pulled up around her. When she heard the children's screams in the street she shut her eyes tight and waited, but the screams still came, and she could hear Aunt Betsy still pounding the piano, oblivious. Her mind cleared, and she jumped up —she was fully dressed—and crossed to the window. The light outside struck like a fist, and she covered her eyes.

She couldn't see them, they were down the block, but their screams were nothing ordinary—an explosion of sound she could not disentangle in her mind from the brilliance of the day. Something terrible had happened. She hurried out, her fists clamped under her chin like those of a person dashing outdoors in the dead of winter.

At first she thought he was dead. She wanted to scream like the children, but strange to say, she rose to the crisis. She ran back into the house and demanded the car keys from her aunt. She pulled the man's limp body into the car, got the children in, and drove to the hospital. (Like a dream, she thought. The trees flashing by to her right and left seemed to glow from within, every line too distinct, like trees seen through binoculars at Letchworth Park—thousands of them; her stomach would go queasy as the binoculars swept from cliff to cliff, over the checks in the grayblue shale and the boiling water, down in the gorge, along the narrow walkways; and she would feel as though she were falling already. Her father had said, "Viola!" and she had opened her eyes wide, suddenly awake again. She'd told him she was smelling the mist from the waterfall. That night she had screamed in her sleep and he had come to her bedside.) Two men—doctors perhaps, or attendants of some kind, she couldn't tell—lifted him onto a table and wheeled him away. There was blood on her dress, and she fully realized only now that his nose had been bleeding. "You all right, miss?" one of the men said. She nodded. She was shaking so violently she couldn't light her cigarette. Match after match went out or burned her fingers, and at last she crushed the cigarette, hurled it away, and covered her face with her hands.

Someone touched her shoulder. "He's still alive, ma'am," the man said. "Has anything like this ever happened before?"

"I don't know," she said. "I hardly know him."

The man looked at her forehead as though she had some mark there, the ashes they put on your forehead on Ash Wednesday. He was young, a man with a bright, tan face and no chin. Behind him the hallway fell away, blazing, past glossy walls and doors and tables with wheels, an old man sleeping in a yellow chair.

"It looks like pernicious anemia," the man said, merely to be saying something.

"His name's James Chandler," she said. "Rose Chandler's his mother. She's in the phonebook."

He went on looking in a friendly, interested way at her forehead, then suddenly looked down at the green and white tiles of the floor. He had on sporty shoes with thick crepe soles, and for some reason they carried, for her, a personal insult.

"Would you like to sit down, miss?" he said.

She shook her head. She thought of asking him to light one of her cigarettes for her, but the request would seem lunatic; even the need for a cigarette might seem lunatic to him—cancer, heart disease. The thought made her furious, suddenly. What business was it of his? Absurd calculations leaped up in her mind and she could not check them: She would offer *him* a cigarette: She would take one too, and he would light it. But no. She said nothing, afraid she had lost all control. Then abruptly: "Please, do you have a cigarette?"

He looked at her forehead as though the question were long and abstruse. It struck her that he was busy diagnosing her the way Aunt Betsy would, sorting out the pieces of her brain on a stainless-steel tray. ("You spend too much time in your room," Aunt Betsy said. "It isn't healthy. What do you do there? Read, I suppose. Not healthy." But it was.)

"Well?" she said fiercely.

He blinked. "Sure," he said.

Her anger turned inward, as always, and she said with fury intended for herself, not him, "Oh forget it. I need a cigarette like I need a hole in my head." She laughed loudly. The smell of the blood on her dress blanked her mind for an instant. It smelled like chicken's blood.

The man touched his chest, where the cigarette pocket would be if he had a pocket in the white thing he wore. He looked down, his chin wrinkling into his neck, and remembered. He said, touching her shoulder again, "Just a second, I'll get you one." He turned and rushed off.

She was afraid all at once, without the vaguest sense of what it was that frightened her. In the same rush of emotion she saw the three children standing white and still by the desk. They looked dead. They shouldn't be here, she thought then, it's too horrible. She went to them, her body in perfect control again now though her fear still crackled in the air around her, and she herded them down the long, blindingly sunlit hall toward the glass doors at the end.

"Where are we going?" the oldest one said.

"We have to get your mother," she said.

The smallest one was crying, and the older two had hold of her hands and were leading her, almost dragging her along. They were only children, and yet they seemed sure of themselves, knew what to do. It made her feel more helpless and futile than ever.

"I want my daddy," the little one wailed.

"Be quiet," she said ferociously. "Everything's going to be all right."

Her voice stopped the child's wailing. She looked up at Viola in horror, and Viola said in desperation, "Please, hurry. We have to run."

"Come on, Anne," the oldest one said. She clamped her lips together and said nothing more.

Then they burst out into charged, ripe air; and to Viola the scent of trees, grass, stirring life was like ether striking the brain. The huge blue Buick, Aunt Betsy's car, sat waiting where she had left it by the hospital wall, half in sunlight, half in shadow. It was a solid, unspeakably respectable car with an expression of arrogant and brainless malevolence, like Aunt Betsy herself. Now Viola's fear centered on the car. She hesitated only an instant—as if a wave of heavy air had checked her flight, then had fallen away—and then she ran to the car with the children, helped them in roughly, and darted around to her side. She had to use both hands to steady the key into the ignition lock, but she managed it at last and turned it.

Nothing happened. She tried again, staring, but something was wrong. She had forgotten something, she knew, but her mind was in turmoil and she couldn't make out what it was she'd forgotten. She kicked at the emergency-brake release—it was free already—then tried the key again. Still the car would not come to life. The oldest girl sat perfectly motionless between her two sisters, her arms around them. All three of them sat watching like dolls some child had propped there. Viola bit her lip and closed her eyes for an instant. Her terror made her nauseous.

"The car won't go," she said. "We'll have to walk."

The children got out obediently and she ran around to them.

She tried to think how far it was to Rose Chandler's place, but it wouldn't come. Any moment now the hospital would know she was gone. She picked up the smallest child in her arms and began to run with it along the walk that passed around the side of the building and slid away past trees and shrubs and wide lawns to the street. The older ones ran beside her, a little behind her, solemn. The sidewalk and street seemed to flow with them like a churning, brown spring flood down the long, bright corridor of sick-sweet, sticky-budded trees, gaping porches, windows. Every car that came up behind them, gleaming like a hearse, was after them, she was sure, but each one passed. They came to the house.

The woman who came to the door stood staring a moment (the blood-wet place on Viola's dress was as cold as ice now), then caught the children to her. "What's the *matter?*" she hissed.

"Your husband," Viola said. "I took him to the hospital."

The woman caught Viola's arm and held it with terrible strength. Her eyes had dark rings and her lips were white. "What hospital?" she said. "Which?"

Suddenly, as though she had finally reached home, Viola sobbed.

"Genesee," she brought out.

The woman looked at her. "Just a minute. Let me get my mother-in-law."

Viola nodded. "Yes. Thank you. Please."

2

SHE could not have said when or why it was that her terror turned into a different emotion equally intense, a kind of joy. The new emotion, like the old, came over her as if from outside, and without a flicker of thought she gave herself up to it, or became it, or stood within it oblivious to it, like a painted image in a church. Only if someone had asked her what she felt would she have stepped back enough from herself to have known. The feeling came unannounced and unguessed, like a sickness in the blood or like fresh spring rain outside one's window in the middle of the night. And it came, also, as if from inside. It was as if she'd achieved an escape from herself, becoming all that lay around her, that and more. The feeling was already there when James Chandler's wife came back to the living room, putting on her jacket as she came.

"Mrs. Chandler," she said, reaching out as if to touch her, though they stood ten feet apart, "I've frightened you when I never should have." Then, with sarcasm aimed at herself, though no one would have known it: "I must have been hysterical or something. The doctor said your husband's all right. I should have told you right off."

The woman looked at her blankly, pausing for a second.

"I'm really sorry," Viola said, "I mean really terribly,

terribly sorry. I don't know what came over me. I've probably frightened your poor children half out of their wits." She looked down at the awful mess on her dress front and held her hands out helplessly. "It all happened so fast. I knew you'd want to be there, and I came straight here—I ran all the way." She laughed again, more fiercely this time. "In fact, I left the car at the hospital. I guess in all the confusion I—forgot it!"

The woman didn't smile. She seemed hardly to hear. Behind her, Rose Chandler came in from the kitchen wiping her hands on a dish towel, her face twisted as if to give muscular support to her weak eyes.

"It really *is* all right, Mrs. Chandler," Viola insisted. "I know it looks perfectly horrible, but it's only some kind of anemia."

Chandler's wife nodded. "Thank you." She passed toward the porch. "Thank you for everything." She bit her lip, dry-eyed and grim, and it came to Viola that the thing was more serious than the doctor had guessed. She opened her mouth to ask a question, but there was no way to ask it. Chandler's wife nodded goodbye and left, mumbling again, "Thank you."

"If there's anything more I can do—" Viola called; but the woman didn't hear. She hurried out to the street, slid into the dingy black car there, and drove away. Clouds of smoke rolled up from the exhaust and glowed in the sunlight, then slowly stretched out, as if reaching for the thick, glowing maples along the walk. Viola stood staring after the car for a full minute after it was out of sight. The exhaust cloud remained, a long, still ghost between two trees. There were enormous red and yellow tulips blooming already in the yard beyond. *Poor thing,* Viola thought, *Lord, don't let her have an accident on the way!* She wrung her hands. Her emotions were churning too violently to allow her knowledge of what it was she felt, and moreover a part of her chaos of emotion was something she could not admit to but must angrily denounce: The truth was, she was glad he had fallen to the sidewalk, bleeding, glad she had been there, glad to feel his cold blood on her dress. Like one watching a liner sink or watching a new motel burn down, Viola felt intensely alive, favored by the gods, and her secret awareness that she was glad made her cheeks and forehead burn with shame.

Still wringing her hands, she stepped back into the living room, closed the door, and turned to the old woman. "He's just left the house," she said at once, speaking rapidly and loudly, her diction precise, as always—the diction of the stage. "He'd stopped by to visit Aunt Maud and Aunt Betsy. It was so good of him. They were both so pleased. He'd just left, and then we heard the children screaming. He must have had a fainting spell. The poor children—" And now, though her joy was as strong as ever, roaring inside and all around her, she was terribly sorry for the children. They were so awfully young, she thought; there was so much ugliness and sorrow in the world! And what must they have thought, running down the street that way, a woman they'd never seen before, their father lying, perhaps dead by now, in the hospital? But she'd make it up to them somehow, yes; she'd make everything all right again if it was the last thing she did.

His poor wife, she thought again three minutes later (washing now and changing into one of young Mrs. Chandler's dresses—a blue shirtwaist that fit her as though it were meant for her). And his poor, poor mother! But she would stay here and help—take care of the children, run errands, minister to their needs. She was bristling with energy now, almost trembling. How lucky it was that someone had been there! How sad it all was for everyone! She partly filled the tub and put the bloodstained dress in to soak. She watched the way the blood moved out into the water. When she came downstairs again his mother was still as pale as flour, as white as the flowers on her dress. The children were really so incredibly good, she thought, waiting there quiet as mice in the kitchen.

"Let me fix you some tea," Viola said. "Have you had your lunch?" She forgot to listen to the old woman's answer. She started in toward the kitchen, and slowly, vaguely, the old woman turned and followed.

She fixed the children Coca-Cola and jelly-and-peanut-butter sandwiches, knowing that that was what all children liked and that they probably never got it except on special occasions. In the refrigerator she found mint and chocolate imitation ice-cream and scooped it out on the only dishes she could find—flat, chipped kitchen plates with painted flowers on them from the cupboard above the sink. *"There* now," she said, bending primly over the table. When the children were eating, talking together in subdued voices, correcting each other at every third remark, she set about fixing tea. She found tea bags—and also the breakfast bowls she'd been after before—in the low cupboard to the left of the counter (In the upper cupboard there were cereal boxes, jams, boxes of Jell-O, salt shakers, a sugar bowl, syrup—she'd have to remember all that, if she was to be temporary mistress here) and a cheap dark green teapot without a lid, in behind the cereal bowls. It was a bright, warm kitchen, fairly small for so old a house, and she liked it infinitely better than the huge, cold, mortician's room at her aunts'. Sunlight burst in through the little oblong window over the counter and splayed on the dark-wood cupboards, the new gray formica tabletop, and the floor in a churning, dusty shaft. It made her remember fixing breakfast for her mother at home. She fixed tea now in the finicky way her aunts insisted on having it done, rinsing the teapot first with boiling water, then running the tea-water over a slice of hot lemon. It always irritated her that her aunts' tea had to be made in this foolishly complicated way, though that was the way she herself preferred it, but today she performed all the ritual with care and felt joy in her knowledge of just how it had to be done. Rose Chandler all this time had said not a word.

Viola said, making cinnamon toast now, "I'd never seen Mr. Chandler before, you know, but it's a funny thing, I knew him the minute I saw him. It was really so *strange.* I'll never forget it as long as I live. I heard him knock, and when I answered the door—you know Aunt Betsy's rule about friends of the family just walking in so they won't disrupt the piano lessons—" She paused a moment, hunting for butter in the refrigerator, her left hand holding the door open, her right hand over her heart. She found it in the refrigerator door, on a tray with a switch labeled *Soft–Hard,* exactly like the tray at her aunts'. "What will they think of next!" she exclaimed. Then, loudly: "Well! When I answered the door the first thing I thought was: Why, you don't need to knock— just as if I knew him, and a second later it even dawned on me who he was, before he'd said. Those thick glasses he wears, I imagine. Someone must have mentioned them. Still, it was almost as if I'd been expecting him all morning." She thought of him lying on the long white table and quickly put it out of her mind. She laughed. "It makes you shudder when you think about it, you know? We got along just beautifully, as if we were the oldest friends in the world. Aunt Betsy was giving a piano lesson, and Aunt Maud's gotten deaf as a stone, you know, so Mr. Chandler and I did all the talking. It's really amazing how much he knows, don't you think? But I suppose that's natural in a college professor. Actually, I expected him to be more—I don't know—remote, or something." Viola laughed brightly all at once, as if remembering something. "We got talking about my singing lessons, and he wanted to see my breath control. It was really very funny. I was awfully embarrassed, naturally, but he was so serious about it, sitting there with his head tilted, and the light blanking out the lenses of his glasses. I finally got up my nerve and showed him my breathing, and it was really quite amazing, he told me just exactly what I was doing wrong. He was better than the teacher I went to in Effingham." She laughed again suddenly, curving her shoulders forward and raising her fingertips to her heart. "Everything's so clear when Mr. Chandler says it. I'll bet he's a perfectly marvelous psychology teacher."

The old woman said as if she hadn't been listening, "How was he when you left?"

Viola shook her head, folding her hands under her chin and looking down at her plate. "I don't know. The doctors didn't seem to think it was serious, and I'm sure they know what they're doing, but just the same—" She remembered the children and stopped. The oldest sat studying the lights on her spoon, her head bent forward over her plate, and Viola knew she was listening to every word.

"Wouldn't you like to go outside and play now, girls?" Viola said. "It's a perfectly beautiful day out. It's just like summer."

The oldest looked up. After a moment she said, "Will Mother be coming home soon?"

"Just as soon as she can," Chandler's mother whimpered. "You be good girls and do as Viola tells you. Karen, you be sure the gate's shut so Annie can't wander off."

The youngest child said, lighting up but speaking softly, as if she thought she might be contradicted if she were heard, "Ouseye. Go ouseye now." She climbed down from her chair. The older girls got up more reluctantly and followed the youngest to the door. The middle one turned the knob and cautiously pulled the door open, giving her little sister time to back out of the way. It opened onto a cluttered back room where there were cans and boxes and African violets. A smell of cleaning materials came in. The younger two hurried straight to the stairs that led down to the back door, but the oldest girl hesitated, holding the kitchen door open. She said at last, only partly looking at Viola, "Would you like to come out with us after a while?"

Viola smiled, startled, caught between pleasure and fright. "I'd love to," she said too sweetly. "I really would. I'll just help with these dishes first, ok?"

The girl smiled and all at once she was beautiful. "My name's Karen," she said.

"That's a beautiful name," Viola said. The girl waited, expecting something more, and Viola added nervously, "I think it's the prettiest name I know."

Karen hung fire an instant, still waiting, then smiled, prim. "What's *your* name?" she said.

Viola jumped and said "Oh!" then laughed, as if angrily. "It's Viola. I'm sorry."

"That's a pretty name too," Karen said politely. Then she was gone.

. . .

It was while they were washing the dishes that Mrs. Chandler told Viola that her son was dying of leukemia. He might go at any time. "Good God," Viola said, turning to look at the woman. Her horror was real, unmistakably; but whether it was horror at what she heard or some older, more complicated emotion that rang in her tone, you could not have known for sure. Their eyes met, and what struck Viola, that first instant, was not the shame of it but something quite different. Looking at Rose Chandler's face—the red netting in her eyes, the bulging goiter, the folds of sickly flesh falling in upside-down *v*'s from the inner corners of her eyes and the wings of her nose—it came to her with terrific force that the old woman was—she hunted for the word and found it:—beautiful. She looked away from the old woman's face to the gray, soapy water in the gray-white sink, and the intensity, almost holiness of the moment faded. "I'm sorry," she said softly, clinging as if for dear life to the feeling that was slipping from her. "I'm terribly sorry." The old woman said nothing, and Viola went on staring at the water. In the drama she played she could not make herself turn and look at the old woman again, and it was not fear that prevented it, or embarrassment or anything of the kind, but awe. It was as though the gray, heavily lined, slightly shaking face were sacred, and Viola Staley not worthy to see it. Then she remembered the children. "The poor children!" she exclaimed, turning, once more raising her fingertips to her heart. The anguish in her voice, like her horror before, was real.

Mrs. Chandler nodded, not trusting her voice to speech.

"It's terrible to grow up without a father," Viola said. "I know." She spoke sincerely, but she felt unclean. She could not have said exactly why it was terrible that her own father had died when she was six—for that was what lurked, disowned, in her mind. But for all Viola's sense of impurity, the remark comforted them both.

They had a bond, and Viola felt herself Rose Chandler's friend. "Good grief," she said, "I promised the children I'd play with them!"

The old woman turned slowly to squint at the clock on the wall above the stove. "It's quarter to two," she said, a sharper whine in her voice now. "The little one should take her nap."

Viola nodded, hanging up her apron. "I'll bring her in."

An awkward silence fell between them. The old woman wanted to say something but couldn't quite make up her mind to it.

Viola said, "Thank you for telling me about Mr. Chandler. I want to do everything I can, make it up to them."

The old woman looked at her with distaste, then nodded. Then her look clouded. She smiled unhappily. "It's so good of you to be here," she said. She leaned on the sink with one hand and reached for the back of Viola's hand with the other and patted her fingers clumsily. "You're a dear, good girl," she said. She began to cry.

As soon as Viola could escape, she went out to look after the children.

3

VIOLA stayed that night at the Chandlers' house. She'd called Aunt Betsy to explain, and Aunt Betsy had agreed —coldly, distantly—that that was best. Chandler's wife was still at the hospital. She'd phoned a little before suppertime to see how things were and to say that if everything was all right at home, she'd stay on at the hospital for a few more hours. She'd protested half heartedly that Viola need not spend the night, that James's mother could manage the girls without too much trouble; but when Viola assured her that she was glad to stay, Marie said no more, merely gave instructions for the children's taking of their vitamin pills and hoped there were still diapers left for Annie. If there weren't, there was a wash in the Bendix down cellar that Viola could run through and put in the drier. Everything would be fine, Viola said. She and the girls were having a wonderful time, there was nothing to worry about. And so it was settled.

It had taken them no time at all to forget their fear of her. All that had happened this morning at the hospital they had reinterpreted by now. It was something they'd all been "through" together. Without Viola's even speaking of it, Viola's interpretation had become Karen's, for Karen, almost from the first, was in love with Viola. Karen was eight, Viola nineteen. And Karen's feelings influenced the feelings of her sisters: They became jealous and thus contenders both for Karen's attention and for Viola's.

They showed Viola around the house and yard, introduced her with pride to the neighbor children, told her long stories about San Francisco, where Karen had been in the third grade. "I don't go to school here in Batavia," Karen had said. Her tone was ambiguous, as if she couldn't decide whether to be proud or heartbroken and would like to be told exactly why they didn't have a school for her here. Viola had said only, "Maybe when things are a little more settled—" and had let her sentence trail off. She'd been aware that she was skating on very thin ice. Luckily, Karen had decided not to pursue it, perhaps as conscious as Viola that the first wrong turn would lead them to her father's dying.

It was moving to Viola that the children should have so quickly forgiven her loss of control this morning. How happy this family must be, she thought, if such quick adjustments were possible! She loved watching them, talking with them, though ordinarily children distressed her. The girls' sense of the safeness of things was infectious. At the same time, she envied them almost bitterly. There was something make-believe about her own people—her mother, her aunts—something more unreal even than the tea party of the girls and their dolls. However clumsily she held her Chatty Cathy with its matted yellow hair and its idiot eyes, its legs defaced by scrawls in red ink, Annie held her doll as though it were a child. The effect was unmistakable, as it seemed to Viola, though it wasn't something Viola could have explained. The Niagara Electric man who came whistling along the side of the house to read the meter was a man playing at being a gasman, the man at the drive-in where they went for cokes was a waiter playing at being a waiter, but the chunky little play-mother *was* what she played. She showed her doll the pictures of chickens on her nesting blocks—"See bird?" she would say "See piddy bird?"—with such infinite gentleness that there could be no question of its being a game.

They were splendid children, actually splendid, all three of them—literally angels—and it excited and frightened her a little that they chose to like her. She'd sat on the porch, part of the afternoon, with their grandmother, talking (in her quick, nervous way) and watching them; and she would feel so pleased that she'd actually flush when sometimes, riding by on a neighbor child's bike, the middle one, Susan, would look up at her and wave. Like Karen, she had a square face and dimples, blond hair, and large blue eyes; but Susan was more boyish than Karen—at once more boyish and more feminine, in a way: It was Susan who climbed on the garage roof, went so high on the swing next door that Viola had to look away, and stood up on the seat of the bicycle, fell in a heap, and tried it again; and yet it was Susan, too, who brought her "God's little treasures," as she called them (something she'd got at Sunday school in San Francisco)—a violet, a round, white rock, the stiff flat carcass of a sparrow she'd found in the street. She was the quick one, in certain ways. They had a book of

prehistoric animals—Viola had read it to them after supper—and Susan could name them all. And she was the
curious one, as well. She wanted to know why the ptero-
dactyl pterondons died, what the world was like before
there were seeds, how long it took for men to change
from tiny, rodentlike creatures to what they were now.
She wanted to know if horses and men were tiny at
the same time, and whether they might not still be, somewhere, tiny men—like Tom Thumb—and tiny horses.
Anne, too, was boyish, but boyish in a different way. In
looks, despite her chunkiness, she seemed to Viola an
angelic little girl—brown hair as light as gossamer, a face
as pretty and delicate as any there ever was on earth—
but her looks were the sly trick of an impish god. Anne
was a bulldog in clever disguise. She had, for certain kinds
of things, a perfectly amazing attention span. Her grandmother had hundreds of stories to prove it. Deprived of
the Rice Krispies box, she said, Anne would search
through the house for a chair or stool she was big enough
to move, would drag it from one end of the house to
the other, would wait for her mother to turn her back,
and in what seemed a split second would have the Rice
Krispies poured out on the floor and would be dancing
in them, solemn faced, as though she took no pleasure
whatever in God's gift of a wicked imagination. Viola
herself had seen her stalk her grandmother's cat for a
full half hour, watching the beast more patiently, more
craftily than would any dog. When at last she sprang—
missing, luckily—it was with an expression so earnest that
one would have believed she fully intended to eat it. To
Karen, of course, both sisters were, in their boyishness,
beneath contempt. She was of a very knowing age, but
Viola, without really thinking about it, sensed that that
was not entirely it. Karen had probably been knowing
all her life. However rough the games they played,
Karen's dress was always immaculate, her hair always
pressed into place, neatly barretted. She had notebooks,
ring binders, which she prized more than life and which
no one but Karen herself might touch—except for Viola,
Karen explained, because Viola was her friend. In a tor-

tuous hand that would one of these days be elegant, she wrote stories concerning Moppit the Dog and Missy the Cat, the Balloon Man, and a certain Wealthy Princess. They were—or so it seemed to Viola—really excellent stories, unlike anything she'd ever seen, with startling touches—the balloon man's faint unhappiness, for instance, at taking money for his balloons, or his choice of the little orange balloon, when all the rest were gone, for himself. And yet despite the great difference between the three—the eight-year-old, the six-year-old, and the two-year-old—they sometimes played beautifully together. They played house, when Anne could be made to play house; or, sitting on the front porch steps, they played school, Karen the teacher of course, Anne the problem child who, if she could be persuaded to, sat in the corner. They fought sometimes, naturally, but even their fighting seemed to Viola clean and healthy. She remembered again that their father was dying, and her mind seized on images of candles, tombstones, a hearse shining in the rain, tall women in black. She concentrated on the images in her mind, and after an instant, as if choosing her response, she thought: *Horrible!*

She tucked them into bed at nine o'clock with the only fairy tale she could remember at the time, "Sleeping Beauty." Half an hour later they were, like model children, asleep. She stood in the hallway looking in at them, the youngest with her feet sticking out through the bars of the crib, Susan sleeping corner to corner on top of the covers, one arm thrown out at a queer angle, as though she'd fallen there from her bike, Karen sleeping demurely, like a real princess in a bed without a bean. Suddenly, fiercely, Viola thought: *I love you.* And the words took in not only the children but also their grandmother downstairs, and the man in the hospital, and his wife. All at once it was more than a vague spiritual hunger that she felt, it was a desire almost specific enough for words. She wanted time to stop.

She went downstairs and said, "The children are asleep."

The old woman was setting the dining-room table for

breakfast in the morning. "Good," she said. "It's been so nice for them, having you here."

Viola scarcely heard her. Her heart beat lightly and rapidly, and she knew that in a moment she was going to be afraid again, perhaps do something strange. The house was incredibly quiet. The sound of a spoon being gently placed on the tablecloth was startling.

"It's beautiful to see children sleeping," she said very softly.

The old woman said, "They're dear, sweet girls."

"Are the doors locked?" Viola said.

"I locked them a little while ago." Then: "It's chilly out. The thermometer's down to thirty-four."

Viola crossed to the front door and tested it. It was locked, as the old woman had said. She kept herself from going to try the back door.

"I'm pooped," she said suddenly, though *pooped* was a word she hated.

Chandler's mother turned her head to stare blindly, perhaps irritably, in Viola's direction. "Why I bet you are, poor thing," she said. "There are clean sheets on the bed in the den—that's the room next to the bathroom."

"Thank you," Viola said quickly. She could not trust herself to say more but merely nodded, remembered to smile, then fled up the stairs. She closed the door of the bedroom-den and did not stop to hunt for the light but hurried over to the window and opened it wide. Cold air leaped in at her and she stepped back. She closed her hands over her bosom and hugged herself against the cold. She had left her cigarettes downstairs on the arm of the couch and, much as she needed one now for her nerves, she did not even consider going down for them. "What's the matter with me?" she said aloud. "What's *wrong* with me?" Then something quite frightening happened. She saw, standing six feet from her in the dark room, a woman. The woman stood motionless, staring at her coldly as if from another time and place— an erect, pale woman with sharp, glinting eyes, a neat, shirtwaist dress, dark hair. When Viola raised her clasped hands to her chin, the other woman did the same, and only that instant did it come to Viola that she was looking at her own image in a mirror. She shuddered, but the absurd fear that had come over her would not leave at once. Then she thought: *The dress.* What had chiefly tricked her was not the darkness or the unexpectedness of the mirror but the unfamiliar dress, young Mrs. Chandler's. But it had not only tricked her, she realized now; it had awakened her—or almost awakened her—to something she had not known about herself. She tried to see clearly what it was that she'd glimpsed, but it wouldn't come. She saw that her face was twisted now with the effort of trying to grasp whatever it was, and she laughed.

She undressed quickly, hanging up the dress, throwing her own clothes carelessly over the chair by the desk, then stood for a long time naked before the open window, biting her lips together. The night was enormous and threatening. It was like the vaulted roof of some huge old church in a dangerous state of disrepair—the stars, tiny holes letting daylight through. A bird flew over, just above the Chandlers' garden, his underside lighted by the glow from the back room, and for an instant Viola believed it was a bat.

When all her body ached from the cold, she closed the window and went to the closet to look for some kind of robe. The only thing she could find that would do was a man's overcoat. *His,* she thought. She remembered laughing in the entryway at Aunt Betsy's, when Aunt Emma had wanted to leave with him, and she remembered his look of astonishment and distaste. She could hear as plainly as she'd heard it then Aunt Betsy's unforgivable *Go to your room.* She felt again her excruciating shame and anger, and she clamped her hands to her face. But she would never see him again; he was going to die. Then, calm, she put on the coat and went down the hall to the bathroom. Her face in the mirror was pale and puffy around the green eyes, as if she hadn't been out in the sun for years. She thought of the girls' faces, then of the old woman's, Mrs. Chandler's. It struck her for the thousandth time that her own face was like

Aunt Emma's: As years passed it would grow simpler and simpler, more and more blank and meaningless. In sudden horror she remembered the car. It would still be there, since Aunt Betsy would think she had it here. Or perhaps by now the police would have taken it. Perhaps they'd already phoned her. Aunt Betsy would promptly phone here, of course, and Rose Chandler would answer and would tell her that Viola had gone up to bed. They'd talk about Chandler's visit there—about how she'd crazily locked Aunt Emma in her room before letting him in. Had Aunt Betsy phoned already? Had the phone rung and Viola missed it?

As she passed the head of the stairs she hesitated, then bent over to listen. The old woman wasn't on the phone now, at any rate. She went to the children's room and looked in. Still quiet as a tomb. She went to the room that was hers for the night, hung up the coat, and crawled into bed. The sheets and pillow were freezing cold, but she hugged the pillow to her small breasts with all her might. She heard the old woman coming up the stairs, slowly, slowly. "Good night, dear," the old woman called in a high, thin voice as she moved past the door. Viola shut her eyes tight and clenched her teeth. *Please,* she thought. *Dear God, please!*

The faces of the children rose up in her mind, and she strained toward them. She loved them, and they loved her, too, and it was good to be here, good. *I said, My name's Viola, and she said That's a beautiful name. And she said, My name's Karen. That's a beautiful name, I said. My name's Viola.*

The night was full of shouts and clicks and rumbles, far off but painfully distinct, and the room was charged with the scent of budding trees.

4

NEITHER conscious nor unconscious, hovering between the two, Chandler's mind constructed visions, dreamed, engaged itself in hair-splitting arguments made out of meaningless sounds—a door closing, a fan turning on, the murmured conversation of two technicians standing above him. None of this would he remember later, and yet it was a terrible time for him. He saw, at one point, an enormous, lead-gray sky full of blackbirds turning and turning like a wheel around a hub. A moment later he stood against a drugstore wall surrounded by a shouting, milling crowd and blurry placards, gray-white faces convulsed with a rage too vast to have anything at all to do with the docile, stubborn, merely human marchers who had triggered their fury. Beads of sweat popped out on his forehead and sometimes the muscles of his face would contract. The worst of it lasted for less than fifteen minutes. As the new blood supplied more oxygen to his brain, his mind began to work somewhat more smoothly. One would have thought him a healthy man except that he was unnaturally pale. He was moved, asleep, to a private room on the second floor, a cupboard of a room with a bed, a dresser, a toilet, a window, a small gold plate on the door: *In Memory of Mrs. Amos Byrne.* He was given a sedative and strapped to his bed.

Marie Chandler was left waiting a long while in the doctor's office. She stood—though she was not aware of this—exactly as her husband had stood in the doctor's office in San Francisco, looking out at the street. But she did not see sharp images, as her husband had; her eyes brimmed with tears. A blur of budding trees, the vague outlines of houses, indistinct and vaguely comforting movement on the gray of the street: cars, bicycles, a bus.

When she heard the doctor coming she wiped her eyes and turned to face the door. He was a tall, balding man with a small gray moustache and one gold tooth, and when he said hello, his voice was strangely gentle. The hello was clipped, as though he were English, or Canadian perhaps.

She said at once, firmly, "My husband will want to get home again as soon as possible, Doctor."

He raised his eyebrows. "Your husband is a very sick man, Mrs. Chandler."

She nodded. "I know. He has leukemia."

The doctor studied her, considering not her husband's state, she knew, but hers. He said, "He's been diagnosed, then?"

"In San Francisco, yes, We talked it over with our doctor there, and we've agreed that it would be best for him to spend as much time as possible at home." She became aware of a faint hostility in her tone, a fierceness that this doctor had done nothing, so far, to deserve.

He touched his moustache with the knuckle of his first finger and looked at the floor. "Your husband's blood is extremely thin," he said. It was the voice of a quick, impatient, emotional man who had taught himself by years of practice to keep himself casual and detached with his patients. He had a temper, Marie Chandler knew without thinking, that might snap in an instant at some piece of stupidity in a staff meeting or when he caught a nurse not minding her p's and q's. "The slightest little cut—even a scratch from brushing his teeth—could be the end of him. And he's weak."

She waited.

"Here in the hospital we could keep him going maybe twice as long as he'd last at home."

"But why keep him going?" she asked sharply. The

words came to her as if from some play she'd read. The doctor squinted, and she explained quickly, "He *wants* to be at home, you see? Even if you drag this business out, he'd see less of his children here at the hospital than he'd see of them at home."

The doctor slipped his fingers down into his suitcoat pockets and went on staring at the floor. "Mrs. Chandler, you're not being realistic, are you?"

Suddenly she was angry—at his question perhaps, his laying the responsibility on her. Her heart beat lightly, and a small white circle of pain came, low in her throat. She said, and her voice was suddenly hollow, as though the room had grown immense, "We have to do what he wants."

"Listen," the man said quietly, "outside this hospital he'll be dead in a week. Do you hear me?"

Her body went cold and she had to reach out to the windowsill for support. She whispered, "In San Francisco they said—"

"A week," he said, watching her.

Marie closed her eyes and tensed her body, fighting off terror. She said, "We have to do what he wants."

The doctor came to her now and put his hands on her arms. "We'll talk to him," he said.

She nodded. She looked at his face and saw that he was tired.

He said, "Can I take you to his room?"

"Yes, please," she said.

He patted her right arm gently, as though she were his child, then guided her to the office door. "I'll have them bring up some coffee to you," he said.

She nodded again, then hunted in her purse for a Kleenex and blew her nose. She was intensely aware of the aluminum chairs they passed in the hallway, the long, curved desk, the black rubber pad on the elevator floor. The air was heavy with the scent of plants and alcohol, and the nurses' uniforms were unnaturally white. A fat man in pajamas and a black hat and coat watched them as they approached her husband's room.

"He'll be asleep for a while," the doctor said. "The

straps will come off this evening, probably, when we're sure there's no immediate chance of his hemorrhaging again. Would you care for a magazine?"

"Thank you, don't trouble," she said.

Her husband lay white and unbelievably still. She touched his hand, where it lay outside the covers, strapped to the bedside.

"You'll be all right, then?" the doctor said. He smiled and managed to make it sound as if he himself had no doubt that she'd be all right, and she knew she would be. She nodded, and he left. Five minutes later a nurse came—a beautiful Indian girl who spoke very precisely and formally, as though she'd learned all her English in college. She put coffee and a tattered *Atlantic* on the dresser. Then she too was gone. The room became large and empty.

5

SHE stood for a long time looking out the window, seeing nothing. She didn't know whether or not one was free to smoke in a patient's room. Probably not, she imagined; at any rate, she'd found no ashtray on the dresser, and hospitals always had hundreds and hundreds of rules, like prisons and churches and banks. She put the idea of a cigarette away in a kind of box she kept in her mind— the literal image of a box, an image she'd picked up in childhood from *Peter Pan* (though she no longer remembered where she'd got it)—and closed the lid and locked it. The desire for a cigarette would not return for hours. Watching her standing at the window, motionless, her head tilted, her arms folded, you might not have guessed that only an hour and a half ago her husband had escaped death by the skin of his teeth and that next time—a week now, perhaps two if he stayed in the hospital—he would be finished. That too she had locked away, almost successfully, in her box.

Everyone who knew her said that Marie Chandler's self-control was perfectly amazing. She, for her part, was puzzled and faintly annoyed sometimes that other people were not similarly strong. But she deserved less credit than she and her friends supposed, or at any rate deserved credit of a different kind. She had a quick mind, but quick because it took shortcuts, a mind energetic but facile. If she never lost her mental footing or sank in the quicksand of abstruse speculation, it was chiefly because she never planted her feet very firmly. She skittered over the surface of things, sculled with the wind, judged the right or wrong of a point on some such grounds as whether or not *The New Yorker* would be likely to mock it. When her husband argued with friends at the table— on capital punishment, for instance, which everyone in San Francisco seemed to be against except James Chandler—it never entered her mind to wonder what she really believed. For her the important fact was that her husband was making a fool of himself, speaking pompously, a little cockily, with the glint that sometimes came to his eye when he'd had a martini or two too many, and quoting Plato in Greek—which instinct told her was grossly unfair, a little like bringing in religion—or disparaging Nietzsche as "another German," though everyone they knew admired Nietzsche and in fact Ken Roos had given James that Walter Kaufmann book for Christmas. And so Marie would say out of simple embarrassment, "Oh, James doesn't mean what he says, you know. He just likes to take the unpopular side." Everyone would laugh with relief, and most of them would believe Marie was right, including Marie herself, for the moment. And indeed Marie's embarrassment was righter, more philosophical, James Chandler knew, thinking back, later, than his own dead-earnest talk. He knew as well as any man, in his saner moments, that proclamations and flat, unexplained contradictions of other men's views, the assertions of the great man who (as Hegel said) imposes upon the world the task of understanding him, have no place whatever in human affairs—unless it be the comic stage. If one cannot stoop to common grounds, one is better off keeping still, like the unknown god. Momentarily blind to his own guilt, Chandler would be so furious he couldn't speak again until dessert.

Marie's mind, as she herself knew, was not theoretical but practical. It never occurred to her to wonder what she really believed for the simple reason, as she'd put it to her husband once, that belief was obviously of no practical use. Once in a burst of rage Chandler had called her a "damned pragmatist," and she'd been so hurt by the tone in which he said it that she'd taken the trouble to look it up and had even read a book on the subject, *Pragmatism,* by William James ("Henry James's brother," she would always explain). She'd been greatly impressed —it was the only philosophy book she'd ever read from cover to cover—and long afterward, in such a way as to keep hidden from him her reason for wondering, she had asked her husband why "people" berated pragmatism so. "Because pragmatists have no character," he'd said gaily. (He'd happened to be in high spirits. His lecture had gone well that day, and his graduate assistant had told him he was inspiring.) "It's one thing to be a blind man baffled by an elephant; it's another to be a stupidly complacent blind man who doesn't in the least mind thinking the rump of the thing is the beast itself. A pragmatist is a spiritual eunuch *ex nativitate,* which is to say a vulgar, soulless creature not to be trusted in a room with decent people's daughters." "I ask questions and you play word games," she'd said. "All right," he'd said, humbled, patting her hand in that childlike way of his, which always annoyed her, "it goes to show I'm a pragmatist myself." And then he'd launched into a long, long lecture—waving his arms—on something about how pragmatism went after Truth, which is unknowable (but Marie *knew* that wasn't right), by redefining the term.

"I give up," she'd said wearily, cutting him off. "I didn't ask for a treatise!" For days after that she could hardly stand the sight of him. But then, characteristically, she'd forgotten all about it, because he *did* love her, obviously. (It was the week he'd started skiing lessons because she'd complained in a moment of annoyance—over something else—that every time they went to Mt. Shasta he spent all his time in the cabin reading books.) If there was something seriously wrong with her it was wrong with lots of other people too and he'd simply have to put up with it. *She* put up with plenty, God knew. And that was true.

Admittedly—though this never entered Marie Chandler's mind—her theory of the uselessness of abstract theory did not work very well. What James called "moral questions" did sometimes come up, especially at school, where many of her students were "sociopathic," as the counselors said, and the English papers she received were sometimes alarming revelations. But the occasions caused Marie no special difficulty. If no handy cliché seemed to satisfy her emotional dilemma, she turned—unaware that she was doing so—to her husband for a ruling. He would talk at great length, apologetically, sitting on the side of the bed (It was always at bedtime that difficult questions gelled in her mind), his hands lying limp in his lap. He knew his talk embarrassed her and he quickly became embarrassed himself. She would carefully follow all he said for a while, but then, seeing that it wasn't really at all to the point (and to tell the truth, Chandler really did make these occasions an excuse for bringing up curious ideas that she wouldn't listen to at other times), she would turn off her mind and would merely bask in the soothing endlessness of his talk, that and his physical presence, until at last he came down to cases and told her what she should do.

But Marie Chandler and her husband were not basically dissimilar. They were both, in the loose sense, idealists, though Chandler had words for it and his wife had only poems. (Despite Chandler's courage, Marie was not a pragmatist but a mute of sorts. Not a poet herself but only an infallible reader, she acted by one code and talked, if she was forced to talk, another.) Both Chandler and his wife operated, as Chandler would have somewhat pedantically put it, not by the law of utility or by the regularian principle—the dangerous generalized purpose of doing things of a certain kind on all occasions of a certain kind—but by the religious principle of conscience. R. G. Collingwood once wrote, in a passage James Chandler was fond of quoting, "Man's world is infested by *Sphinxes,* demonic beings of mixed and monstrous nature which ask him riddles and eat him if he cannot answer them, compelling him to play a game of wits where the stake is his life and his only weapon is his tongue." Both Chandler and his wife knew the truth about the sphinxes, and neither of them was on their side. But Marie was one of those people who are forever hoping that perhaps the game can be played not by wits but by intuition, which is to say, one of those beautiful and good artistic people who fight courageously on the side of mankind and always get eaten in the end. What is more, she knew it. She frequently presented theories on why she loved her husband—theories to be found in any decent popular short story on the subject of marital fidelity: that he was a good, gentle man; that he wanted "The kind of life she wanted," that is, the same kind of house, yard, children, Friday-evening entertainment; that he was good in bed. But she knew that her theories were false. She loved him because he was what she was too inhibited to be, quietly and vulgarly independent: He answered, however inadequately, by his wits. If her own strength lay in her always avoiding all dangerous waters, to shift the image (She could banish the thought of smoking from her mind because she was no more a confirmed smoker than a confirmed Presbyterian), she did not mistake her strength for omnipotence. She loved him because he was stronger than she was, and she could love without self-abasement because in the shallows, whatever it might be in the depths, James Chandler's well-caulked ark was worthless and, worse, ridiculous. She loved him like a mother; that is, she worshiped him, on one hand, and, on the other, forgave him for faults she doubted that anyone else could possibly forgive.

Standing at the window, her face drawn, she waited for some sound from her husband, some outcry or request —anything. There had to something she could do. The most trifling effort—wiping the beads of sweat from his forehead—would mean a good deal to her now. An image of desert came into her mind, wasted earth spilling over cliffs toward a becalmed sea. She controlled her fancy, but stranger thoughts came then: superficially placid thoughts like quiet smalltown streets over quicksand: plans for her life afterward, as hollow and formal and numb as funeral arrangements. She'd go back to San Francisco. She could think of no real reason, but that was what she would do. Another vague picture came into her mind, the high school where she'd taught for two years in Iowa, when she was finishing up her B.A. at Grinnell. (She'd lived in Iowa most of her life. Her parents still lived there, in Fairfax, near Cedar Rapids. That was the kind of school she liked best—a big, new, efficient building on a hill overlooking prairie-land, students who came from good corn country, fat Czech children (hundreds of them, bursting into the world like mushrooms) whose parents spoke broken English and sent in vegetables and kolacky "for teacher" and intensely, angrily demanded the absolute best for their children and had no idea before hand what was best. Except of course that there were no schools like that in San Francisco. Still, she had come across good enough students at John Muir in San Leandro, even in her *R* sections— Remedials or, as she had preferred to call them, Rats or, sometimes, Reptilia. (This with amusement, for they were not to her—as they were to her principal—dangerous or inscrutable, "a sickness of civilization spawned in the human gutter." He had been afraid of them—a prissy, gutless man, a eunuch and a lisper; but she, even when they shocked her she had never been afraid of them—seriously afraid, that is, any more than she would be seriously afraid of a Hampshire boar or a bull or a mean rooster.)

She bit her lip to white, and tears came. She did nothing to fight them. One never had quite enough time (she thought); time was everything! James, being a college professor, spent only ten or twelve hours a week in the classroom, and though it was true that as long as his health held out he had worked every night until two or three in the morning, the work he did at home was his own, his play. Apparently people cared more about whether or not there is really something there when you look at it than they cared about whether a boy became a civilized human being or a thief.

In her anger (for indeed Marie had talked herself into anger) she glanced over at her husband's bed, and for an instant her heart stopped cold. He looked dead. He lay with his mouth open, his eyes not completely shut, the whites peeking out. There were bits of dried blood in one nostril. His right arm, strapped to the bedside, was worse than all the rest. It was bare from the elbow down, the flesh white under the hair, the fingers limply curved. The sight made her sick for a moment, and even as she thought how much she loved him, she had a sinking sensation in the pit of her stomach, as though in her heart she knew she was lying and wanted him safely dead. She went over to him and stood watching his chest move. *I do love you,* she thought. Abruptly, she leaned over and kissed him on the mouth. The lips gave under hers and his breath was bad. She straightened up quickly, thinking nothing whatever, her eyes tightly closed. She touched his forehead gently. It was cold. It was always unnaturally cold or unnaturally hot these days. *I ought to get myself something decent to read,* she thought. She hated the *Atlantic*. (It occurred to her only now, in fact. But she always had, it seemed to her, even in high school, where her teacher had made the class buy it for the "serious fiction.") She glanced around, located her purse on the chair by the dresser, picked it up, and walked out into the hallway. She met a nurse who was just on her way in to see him. A plump woman, bright red hair.

"He's asleep," Marie said.

The nurse smiled, showing dimples and very white rodent's teeth, and her eyes twinkled. "Good for him!" she said as if it were something rare. Marie felt suddenly jealous of the nurse, as though the nurse had said something *she* ought to have said; but it wasn't that, of course; something more complicated.

"It seems like hours since anybody's come in to look at him," Marie said.

"It's a regular beehive around here today," the nurse said, twinkling again. "I'll just run in and have a look at him now. Could I get you some tea?"

"I was just going down to the—"

"The nurse nodded. "Good idea. I wish *I* could!" And then, with another nod, she went in and closed the door.

Marie stood looking at the doorknob uncertainly for a moment, frustrated and upset, as if someone had completely misunderstood her motives, then opened the door and put her head in. "Do you know what time the doctor will be coming?" she asked timidly.

The nurse flicked out her wrist and looked at the watch she wore on the inside of it. "Probably a little past six," she said, showing her dimples and teeth again. "It's quarter to five now."

"Thank you," Marie said. She remained in the doorway, but the nurse had turned away again. The nurse moved the pillows under his head and put her fingers on his arm—like something dead—and read his pulse. When she finished she said brightly, "Would you like to wait outside?"

Marie nodded, touching the collar of her blouse, then obeyed. She leaned on the wall beside the door. Down the hall from her a white-haired nurse pushed an empty wheelchair into the elevator, then held the door, looking hurried and cross, while an old woman with no teeth came down the hall and got in. A man in a brown business suit came out of the room three doors from Marie and walked toward her, holding a paper and putting on his glasses as he came. He nearly bumped her with his right elbow, and when she said "Excuse me," he glanced at her briefly, saw that he didn't know her, and went on, reading as he walked. For the next two minutes no one came near, though there were people at the far end of the hall, around the desk, laughing and talking. Then the nurse came out and smiled as if surprised to see her.

Marie said, "Is he—"

"Everything's fine," the nurse said. "Coming along just beautifully. In an hour or so we'll be taking that nasty old strap off."

"When is he likely to wake up, do you think?"

The nurse shook her finger and laughed. "Now just you let Nature take its course. You go get yourself some tea and a nice bowl of soup."

Marie nodded. When she thought of the nurse's words later, *Let Nature take its course,* she would flush with anger, but just now she felt only an indefinite remorse—a kind of hunger—and a sense of slight disorientation. She thought all at once of Viola Staley, and sharp, unreasonable indignation flared up in her. She ought to have been there herself when it happened, not some stranger. His nose had bled. No doubt he'd looked a mess, sickening. It wasn't right that a perfect stranger, a girl, see him like that. She walked quickly, furious all at once and in tears again. The elevator dial pointed to the four, and she turned impatiently to the stairs. She went down the stairs quickly, almost running, but at the first-floor landing she stopped for an instant and closed her eyes tight. *I do love him* she thought. *I do!* She gripped the aluminum railing tightly and stood motionless a moment longer. Then, calmly, swiftly, she went down the hall to the coffeeshop.

6

THOUGH the room was crowded, one face stood out for her at once, long before any of the others separated themselves in her mind from the general background. The man was staring at her in a curious, frightening way, and she remembered that she'd seen him staring at her earlier this afternoon, when she went into James's room with the doctor. She gave him only a glance, then slid onto a stool at the lunch counter and looked straight ahead, her face burning, her hair rising on the back of her neck. She accounted for her immediate sense of him by the first explanation that entered her mind: He must be sick with something that affected his mind. He looked it, certainly. He was enormously fat, with a large head, and he wore a black, expensive hat and a black, expensive coat. Underneath he had on pajamas and on his feet bright red, lumpy slippers. His face was lumpy and horribly scarred on one side, as if he'd been burned, and his eyes were huge and far apart.

He stood not ten feet away from her, smoking a crinkled, dirty-looking cigarette and studying her critically. She realized, seeing herself through his eyes, what people looked like on counter stools, the buttocks squashed and rounded, the back curved, the head pulled up at an unnatural angle. A shudder went through her. The horror of it was that one couldn't even retreat or change one's position, display oneself at a better angle; it was as if the man's demonic look had fixed her forever, transformed her into an object, something as dead and alien as the tired-looking apple pie on its brown-white plate on the shelf behind the counter. She did not need to look again to know that his eyes were still on her.

Then the waitress was there for her order—a lady with a sapphire ring on her little finger. Marie was nonplussed for an instant; all the room seemed to have gone subtly wrong. Then it came to her—she'd seen the sign as she came in, and there was another on the wall in front of her—that the counter was run by volunteers from the Hospital Auxiliary—wives of doctors, probably, or church ladies; Batavia society.

"Tea," Marie said. Then abruptly, as if as an intentional affront to someone, "No, coffee. Black. And I think a hamburger."

"Onion and tomato?" the waitress said, polite but indifferent. She pronounced it to-*mah*-to.

Marie nodded. She glanced over her shoulder and saw that the man had vanished into thin air. Then, to her horror, she saw his black hat slide onto the counter beside her, and she smelled the smoke of his cigarette. There was something odd about it, a smell like—what? The smell was freighted with associations, but whether good or bad she could not make out. For the split second in which the cutting edge of the smell pierced her consciousness she seemed to slip into an instant's sleep, or, perhaps, an instant's awakening. She felt, for just that fraction of a second, suspended in space, and it was as if the stranger was within her or was in some way herself. But the next instant she was collected again, and it came to her like a joyful revelation that the man could not sit down beside her; there was no room.

"Lots of food energy in tomatoes," the man behind her said suddenly, loudly. His voice was unctuous, as high-pitched as a woman's; but it was not definitely unfriendly, and there was enough embarrassment in it, even fear, perhaps, to give her some feeling of safety. He leaned toward her, stinking like a goat, smiling, but failing to meet her eyes. "It has been found by experiment that a tomato plant can develop enough root pressure to lift a column of water 384 feet." He chuckled or, rather, giggled, then wet his lower lip with his tongue.

He *was* mad; there was no doubt of it. Marie thought a moment, then put on a smile and turned to look at him. "Is that true?" she said.

He shrugged, with a confused and helpless look, like one suddenly pulled down from splendid heights, and her fear of him evaporated. "Science," he squeaked, as if in awe and bewilderment. "What is Truth?"

She laughed, but though she was calmer now, the laugh was sharp. "Clearly you're a philosopher," she said. "Only philosophers talk idiocy like that!"

The fat man took on a still more eager, still more frightened look. "Then I know you! We're ancient friends!" he exclaimed. "To tell the truth, I wasn't sure of it until just this second. He he he!" He had a quick, mincing way of talking, like an elderly homosexual, a man who might molest little boys. Now that he had his hat off she saw that his head was huge and egg-shaped and perfectly bald. It came to her that the man must have some grotesque disease, some growth swelling inside his brain. If you cut through the skin, she had a feeling, it would all be black inside, like one of those puffed-up ears of corn on her father's farm. She looked away, but the man prattled on.

"You see I don't know your husband in the flesh but only by reputation. That is to say. I've read him with interest. In point of fact, I once appeared opposite him in a magazine, the, uh, the uh—" He wet his lips and looked at the ceiling, sliding his middle finger down his thumb as if to snap it, but achieving no snapping sound. "I forget the name of the journal," he said, wetting his lips again, smiling weakly. He removed the cigarette from his mouth, fumbled with it, dropped it, bent down to get it. He bobbed up again with the cigarette in his mouth and said, ashen-faced: "I used to publish quite regularly.

"You *are* a philosopher, then?" she said.

Now his face was dark red, so dark that the sudden

change alarmed her. "Oh no. Not really. Not actually. Here, let me give you my card." He hunted through his coatpockets, looking down, his eyes bulging more than usual. He came up with a card between two fingers and offered it to her, his hand shaking violently, on his lips an idiotic leer. It said:

JOHN HORNE
Attorney at Law
"Quidquid tetigit ornavit"

There was no address, no phone number. Marie turned the card over as if to find an answer of some sort printed upside down on the back; then, unwilling to admit that she couldn't make out the Latin, she smiled and nodded. "It's very unusual."

"Yes, yes it is," John Horne said. "*I* think so, at all events." He looked startled, as if by a pain in his stomach. "Oh!" he said, "perhaps you mean my writing for philosophy journals, stepping out of my own place to worry other men's kingdoms. Yes, that's unusual too." He seemed painfully embarrassed by his supposed mistake.

"No, I meant—" she began; but she let it go. The hamburger came. She couldn't eat it. They looked at each other, and the silence that had fallen between them expanded.

"Well," he said, his eyes lighting up all at once, his whole fat body striking at the word as though she, or someone in his mind, had finally asked him exactly the proper question. "I saw his name on the foot of the bed—on the chart, you see (I wander about at my liberty here, at least as long as no one is looking—ha ha)." He went pale for a second, covering his mouth with his fist. "I saw his name, 'James Chandler,' and I thought to myself, I've encountered that name! It rings a bell! Then I thought, the philosopher! But you see I wasn't sure it was the right James Chandler. A relatively common name, you know. I couldn't think how I was going to find out, and then along you came, and—" Again he went pale, as if shocked at his own daring.

Marie said quickly, "You mean that remark about tomato plants was part of—" She broke off, studying him, prepared to be alarmed.

He giggled nervously again. "It didn't even fit, to tell the truth. I'm sure you noticed. There's no relationship whatever between root pressure and food energy. Or none that I know of. Of course I may be wrong." He looked confused for a moment, then appeared to have straightened something out in his mind. He tilted his head, beaming. Marie returned the smile, then looked down at her hamburger.

"I've offended you," the man said at once, touching her arm. "Forgive me."

She had a dreadful premonition that the man was going to kneel, right there beside her stool, in the middle of the coffeeshop, and when she glanced at him, she discovered to her astonishment that he really was about to do it. She caught his hand in the nick of time. "No!" she cried. Her mind raced. "I'm not offended at all. I'm touched. Honestly, I'm touched."

"Touched?" he said, still prepared to kneel.

"By everything," she explained vaguely, snatching the first thing that came into her head. "By your remembering. And your looking me up."

He smiled, his wrinkled, gray face sagging. She withdrew her hand.

She said, "You see we're strangers in town, or anyway I am, and it's good to see someone a person can talk to." She forced another smile, brighter than the last.

His soft, fat hand came to her arm. "It's a trying time for you," he said. His eyes filled with tears.

Marie Chandler's whole body revolted against the feel of his hand on her arm, and all her puritanical Iowa soul cried out against the intimacy of the man's compassion; but though his touch burned her arm like fire, all sensation rushing to the place like a garrison to a breach in the wall or white cells to the point of infection, not a muscle flickered. He was weeping now, yellow tears seeping out and washing down the scarred misshapen ledges of his cheeks, and all along the counter people looked at the incredible man and herself. It couldn't have been much worse if he had kneeled. She was aware of wanting to cry with frustration, and almost at once, even before she knew why she was doing it, why it was all right to let herself do it, she allowed herself to weep too.

"I don't know what I'll do," she said. Abruptly she covered her face with her hands, and the weeping turned into sobbing. It was the first time she'd spoken the truth aloud.

"Poor dear," the man said, deeply moved. "You poor, poor girl." He put his arm around her, whispering, "There, there; there, there." The gray-haired woman looked at her, then away, and beyond the gray-haired woman two men leaned together and said something.

She reached out blindly for her purse and gathered it to her, then slid from the counter stool and made her way, fighting her sobs, to the door. The man stayed behind, and as she fled down the dizzy length of the first-floor hallway, she was alone. At the end of the hallway she stopped, blocked by high, wide windows looking down at the parking area below and the entrance to the emergency rooms, unreal in the yellow of late afternoon. There was nowhere more to go. Then it came to her that to her right, just off the hallway, stood a waiting room, almost empty at the moment—a dimly lighted, comfortable place with green leather chairs, magazine tables, reading lamps, only one of them on just now. There was no window. Two women, an old man, and a child sat along one wall, not talking. Marie sat down in the darkest corner of the room, as far as she could get from the others, and rifled through her purse for Kleenex. She blew her nose and wiped her eyes, then began to sob again, for once more the words had come into her mind— *I don't know what I'll do*—as though it were the words themselves, not the fact of his death, that had power. The child whined and the mother scolded him. When Marie looked up, the fat old man with the scarred, bulged face was standing there—it was as if he'd come up through the floor—separated from her by the low, magazine-cluttered table in front of her chair. The sight of him sobered her, and she said with a nervous laugh, "I forgot to pay them." She nodded in the direction of the coffeeshop.

"It's all right, it's been taken care of," he said. His lips had a loose way of coming together and parting as he talked, as though there were no moisture at all in his mouth. He had his hat on again, and he had another crooked, crinkled cigarette.

"I'm sorry to behave this way," she said. "I'm just all nerves these days." She blew her nose.

The man merely stared, uncomfortable. Again and again he wet his lips as if to speak, then thought better of it. Then, after a quick, angry glance at the others in the room, he leaned toward her.

"Listen, I know how you feel," he said. His eyebrows were lifted, and his eyes were larger than ever. "And I know there's nothing anyone can say. But I want to tell you something, Mrs. Chandler, if I may." He sucked excitedly at the stub of his cigarette, but it had gone out. He glanced at it, then got out cigarette papers and a can of Prince Albert. (That was why the smell was familiar, it came to her. When she'd first known him, James had smoked Prince Albert in his pipe.) John Horne rolled a cigarette as he talked, his eyes going repeatedly from the cigarette to her face and back, his whole manner frantic, for he spoke with feeling. What he had to say was very confused, or so it seemed to Marie, and his expressions, his gestures, his tone, all seemed something made up, not life but some sort of stage performance—a sad-clown act, or one of those monologues in a Beckett play at the Actors' Workshop. And yet, strange to say, as he talked she began to see clearly again, sort herself out.

He said rather loudly, as if in defiance of the silent group behind him:

"You must understand that this is a difficult thing for me. I've never been good at talking with people; in fact it's only very recently that I've begun to try it at all." He glanced over his shoulder, making sure the others were minding their business. One of the women, a buck-toothed, stupid-looking person, looked straight at him a moment, then down. Horne wet his lips with his tongue and hurried on. "For years I didn't have the courage to say 'Good morning' to the man I bought my newspaper from. I'd actually practice it on my way there sometimes—he had a stand right in front of the office-building where I worked—I was in Buffalo at the time—and it would make the sweat pop out on my forehead. I'd try it first one way and then another, 'Good morning, Mr. Populos,'—this cheerfully, like a shopkeeper—'Good morning, Mr. Populos,'—more casually, mind on other things—'Good morning, Mr. Populos,'—an undertaker. Even mere practice was terrifying. It was exactly like standing on a bridge, playing in deadly earnest with the idea of jumping. When I got to the stand I'd go blood-red with fright—no, shame—and I'd say nothing. I was probably the most timid creature in Buffalo, New York. But because of a cat (I'll explain all that at the proper time), I conquered myself. I cannot speak, I simply and positively cannot, but I do it." He puffed at his cigarette as if hungrily, then drew a piece of toilet paper from his pocket and wiped his forehead.

Marie sat rigid, drawn back from the man's deformity, his smell, his words, as from an adder.

"I know how ludicrous all this sounds, Mrs. Chandler. You can't imagine it, born Venerian as you are, with the moon in a fortunate aspect, Calliope for a godmother, Tisiphone busy with lesser creatures; but the plain truth is, however absurd, that speaking this way, for a man congenitally shy (whatever his arrogance, you know), is directly equivalent to—" He hesitated, flustered, hunting for an image. "To marching with the Negroes in Birmingham, or burning oneself alive to preserve one's religion, or infecting oneself with some deadly disease for science. You find these comparisons comic, no doubt." He laughed, goatlike, to show that he too saw the comedy. "But you see, I consciously choose to speak, difficult as it is for me, and I choose not for my sake—certainly not for my own comfort—but for the sake of, as it were, mankind. Suppose Charles Dickens' Scrooge had not been sent those dreams and had not been miraculously transformed, but suppose he had come by the process of reason to the conclusion that it was his duty to be unselfish. Think what it would have cost him to become the Scrooge of Dickens' final scene! Every smile would be agony, every gift to the poor a piece of his own heart. And so, in a word, if what I say seems ludicrous—" He paused; then, softly almost a hiss: "But does it count without a change of heart? *That's* the question. Is it possible for a man to be reborn?"

His lips began to shake, and he couldn't go on. Abruptly, like something mechanical, he sat down in the chair nearest her and removed his hat. He began to shake all over. The child came near and bent down to look up at him as he might have looked at a sleeping lion.

Marie Chandler sat very still. She had no choice, she knew, but to get up and go to him, but she was like a victim of abulia, or like a person in a nightmare, unable to move. Little by little his shaking began to pass. At last the old man seemed calm. For a long time neither of them moved a muscle; then Horne got up. The child fled back to its mother.

"I'm a ludicrous creature," he said with a wide, ghastly smile. "Not entirely human, really. Some sort of mutation that will never catch on. It says on my card 'Attorney at Law' and *'Quidquid tetigit ornavit.'* Both statements are bitterly ironic, at least from a certain point of view. From another point of view—but I'll come to that. I'm a law librarian, in point of fact, for a large and complicated firm of people whose first names I know only by hearsay. In all my life I've never dealt *in propre persona* with an actual case. All strictly theoretical. I hunt up precedents, I theorize, I reason, I commit thick books to memory—mostly indexes alphabetically arranged: Aamram, the State of New York *versus.* A caricature of the modern condition, my life. Spectator of spectators. But that's all of very little interest, of course. I realize that. I mention it only by way of background, so you'll understand the seriousness of what might otherwise seem quite preposterous, that my one significant relationship, the only significant relationship in all my life, has been (and I make no apologies for it; the fault has not been entirely mine) with a cat." He got out his materials to roll another cigarette, lit it, and began to pace back and forth as he talked, almost running at times, at times stopping abruptly, snatching a puff at his cigarette, wetting his lips, mopping his head with the toilet paper he carried for that purpose. "Human beings must have significant relationships; it's the *sine qua non* of the existence of the species. You hear biologists talk about the adaptability of man: how the first primitive human being when he came from the trees couldn't run at all compared to a deer, or see very well compared to an eagle, or hoist things up like an elephant, or bite or scratch like a wolf or a tiger, or keep warm in winter like the polar bear, or swim like a fish, or fly like an eagle, and yet in a short while he learned to move about faster than sound, see galaxies thousands of light-years away, move mountains even in the absence of faith, kill his enemies by ICBM's, walk in comfort in Antarctica, search out the oceans, and fly up as far as the moon. Very adaptable, no doubt about it." He hesitated a moment, glancing in terror at the silent group behind him, then hurried on again, as if to stop would be to end. "But I'll tell you the truth, being a theoretical person committed, like biologists, to celebration of the trivial. All that rushing and seeing and hefting is only the *way* we stay alive, not the reason for it. The reason is purely and simply self-love, the greatest power in the universe. And the true measure of human adaptability is man's power to find, despite overwhelming arguments, something in himself to love. It's not a thing to be scorned or to reprimand children for; a thing of beauty! Because at its root self-love is awe: Man looks at himself and says, 'Great God, what a splendid thing!' Not vulgar egotism; nothing of the kind. Splendor! Honest and forthright recognition of the best there is in Nature.—Unless we're mistaken.—And I'll tell you the proof, a brilliant insight I had when only a very young man, and in fact an insight I later wrote up. (I used to write up all my insights, in those days, and I'd publish them and await the results; such was my mania, I confess it. I wrote it up and published it as an answer to logical positivists, who would cure us of philosophical curiosity—'*cure*' us! So one of them actually puts it. A group which in those days I sadly deplored. And do yet, though I may be wrong; I may not have fully understood them. Always that chance.)" He paused, staring at his cigarette with his bulging eyes. "The proof, as I was saying—an incredibly obvious thing, yet persistently misinterpreted by foolish people—though possibly they're right and I'm wrong, of course—, foolish people who . . . Where was I? Ah! . . . who are always afraid of human freedom (and no amount of article writing will change it; I've learned that much, at least. Articles merely awaken one of the weaknesses in one's own position)—the proof that self-love is awe, as I was saying, is the fact of love. Serious. Perfectly serious, my dear Mrs. Chandler. Any psychologist will tell you that what we love in the *alter*—you notice how it puns on *altar?*—is our own projection. 'Only God can love you for yourself alone,' as the poet saith. A beautiful truth, an inspiration! But stupid people twist it and transmogrify it, which is to say, make it monstrous. They call it a matter of self-delusion: I fall down before the projection of myself and worship it as I symbolize it in someone I do not in fact love at all or know or feel, even, indifferent to. They identify it with onanism and other equally revolting things. But they misunderstand, if my own interpretation is correct. Self-love is in fact religious awe in the presence of the mystery of life represented in oneself. A mystery too vast to get hold of—infinite, changeable, everlastingly capable of unexpected developments (I might mention a piece in the *Daily News* this very morning about a man who swam close to Niagara Falls to save some child he didn't know. They got back alive, and he told the reporters, 'I never knew I'd do such a thing.') So great a mystery—" He paused again, apparently having lost the thread. He blinked rapidly, his loose lips pursed. Then, excitedly: "The mystery of life! A thing so majestic requires our worship, and a thing so complex can only be worshiped with the help of symbols. *There's* why people fall in love, or make up religions, or turn themselves into philosophers. It's why we invent our Draculas and Frankenstein monsters. (Only by logical abstraction do we separate one kind of mystery from another. *Mon semblable.*) You have heard it said that *Cogito, ergo sum.* But I give you a new law, which is *Sumus, ergo amemus,* or, conversely, *Amamus, ergo simus.* The most ignorant boy will lie down and die for his ignorant girl, unless of course he's got less religion in him than a common dog. And let it be added, despite certain risks, that the commonest child of Cerberus will on rare occasions lie down and die for its human master, though not, as a rule, the reverse." He paused. "Though perhaps under certain circumstances —" Then: "If you push me to the more or less logical conclusion, that dogs are worshipers of life, like ourselves, I reply that only seventy-five million years of evolution— or forty-five, perhaps; I forget—distinguishes Herr from Hund. But I leave these things to veterinary science—I mention all this, however, only as background."

Two well-dressed teen-age girls came in and sat down, to Marie's left. They began to talk, very quietly, flipping through magazines.

Horne blushed and seemed to shrink from them as from something preternatural. He even stepped away a little. He ground out his cigarette in the ashtray on the table in front of Marie and promptly rolled another. When he had the new cigarette lighted, he straightened up once more, but this time he did not pace. He stood with his head tipped far to one side, his left hand in his coatpocket, and smoked, getting himself in control by a terrific effort of his facial muscles. At last he said: "The striking feature of human adaptability—have I said this already?"

She shook her head.

He jerked his head in a nod and returned to his formal pose. "The striking feature of human adaptability is man's adaptation to his own unspeakable ugliness. I speak as a grotesque myself, from a family of grotesques. The point might not occur so forcibly to a person like yourself, more fortunate by birth. I learned very young. It was pointed out to me by relatives, by playmates, even by my mother, indirectly. My father had a metal plate in his head—a brilliant civil engineer in his earlier days, tradition holds, but prematurely kicked by a horse, which left him addled and also cantankerous. A difficult person to love. He beat my poor mother and me half to death— we had to call neighbors in sometimes. But he meant no harm, you know. It was just his way. As for my mother, poor soul, she had muscular dystrophy. It took supreme effort and great contortion to lift up a coffee cup. She stands immortal in my mind—I say it with devotion, as God is my judge; indeed, I say it with devout admiration—she stands immortal in my mind with her tongue clamped firmly between her teeth and her kindly blue eyes crossed. We had very few visitors. The house settled slowly around our ears, with no one able to take care of things, and my mother looked forward to the resurrection of the body. She always wore carefully ironed dresses, though ironing was hard for her. (I merely mention the point in passing.) Also she always wore gloves and a hat—with white and red berries on it, symbolic of Holy Purity and Martyrs' Passion—when she left the house. Ironically enough, my poor ill mother was knocked down in the street—my word of honor—on three separate occasions: Once by the Father, presumably, once by the Son, and once by the Holy Ghost. She could never make it across before the light changed."

Horne stood silent for perhaps a full minute, lost in anguished thought, perhaps still delivering his monologue and unaware that he had ceased to speak aloud. Then he said:

"I came to be attracted, for obvious reasons, to the discipline of Law. A metaphysical problem, really, the problem of justice. I graduated from Buffalo U. at the top of my class—a matter of record—and settled down to life of a legal librarian, an occupation which perfectly suited my character, involving, on one hand, a justification for endless, altogether pointless thought, and involving, on the other hand, just enough need for nice distinctions and just enough contact with reality (at third remove) to keep me relatively safe. Most of my waking hours I spent among the books of my employers; for sleep I returned to my two-room bachelor apartment above the Hyde Street Market.

"Time passed; I never dreamed of marriage; I grew older and fatter. I lost my youthful confidence, what little I'd had. I thought myself the forlornest of men, a genius crushed by the force of circumstances. And then something happened to me which changed my life.

"Lying in my solitary bed one night, I heard what I thought was a prowler in my kitchen. I lay there for possibly fifteen minutes, shaking like a leaf, my head pulled down inside my covers, too terrified to think. Then something made me realize that whatever it was I had in my kitchen, it was not, at least, human. I thought at once of the murders in Rue Morgue, then of the possibility of rats. At last, with more courage than I'd have thought I possessed, I got up and tip-toed in to see. I snapped on the light. There on my kitchen table stood a gigantic yellow tomcat, a veritable tiger. His back went up and his jaws parted ferociously, but I wasn't afraid; in fact—it's uncanny, when you think about it—the very first words I said were, 'Well, so it's you!' I stepped between him and the open window, and he hissed like a cobra, those terrible-snake-toothed jaws wide open. But I hesitated for only a moment. In a flash, I had the window closed, and he was *mine!*

"You never heard of such a battle of wills as ensued in the months that followed. He befouled every inch of my apartment—purposely and maliciously, according to a carefully worked out plan. He refused to eat, with the notion of killing himself and leaving his death on my conscience. Whenever I came anywhere near him, he hissed. Sometimes in the middle of the night I'd awaken and find him staring at me with his yellow, dusty, unblinking eyes, thinking, I am firmly convinced, of fratricide. But he finally decided to eat my food. He began

to befoul my rugs somewhat perfunctorily and sometimes he would even turn, as if absentmindedly, to the
kitty litter. At the end of six months we had established
the terms of our truce. That was as far as it ever went.
Armed truce. I began to let my fellow being wander
nights, and he, being old, elected to come back for his
food. He eventually came to consider the room I happened to be sitting in faintly preferable to a room in
which he would be forced to sit alone, as long as his
position was significantly higher than mine. (He invariably perched on the top of my bookshelf, just below the
ceiling.) But we were not friends, not at all. We were
of different species. That's very important, from a cat's
point of view. Right to the end—we were together for
three years—he'd strike out like a rattler if I dared to
reach up to pet him. When he died, of poison, I believe—
he was never a popular cat with the neighbors—I buried
him in the yard behind Mr. Jensen's store, under the
stump of, I believe, an oak. It was only after Tommy's
death that I realized the significance of what had happened."

He came closer now and bent down toward her. The
eyes of the group followed him. There were others now,
looking in from the hall.

"I had lost something, Mrs. Chandler. Which implied
that I had had, all along, even before I met him, something to lose, which implied in turn something more,
something as yet undiscovered but capable of being lost—
something in myself, you see, something to be seized,
brought to birth, requiring only my self-annihilation. I
became a believer in that great spirit in whom we live
and move and have our being. I saw my way clear at
last to accept, in principle, the resurrection of life."

He was silent for a moment, his lips trembling. Then he
said: "Life can be resurrected, Mrs. Chandler. Do you
understand me?"

She shook her head.

He leaned still closer. "All the vast array of Emblems
tells us that life can rise again! Isn't that so? Is it possible
that my reasoning is fallacious?"

She closed her eyes. She felt cold and unnaturally calm, as if dead, and an image of gray, rolling hills and a golden Iowa sky came into her mind. She made herself think of San Francisco, and what came to her was the hill on Duboce between Buena Vista and Castro streets. Once she'd come down it with her husband when both of them were slightly drunk. The nose of the car seemed to dip into space, and below thousands of feet below, lay all the lights of the city—the yellow of the bridge, and Market Street, an explosion of reds and blue-greens where the theaters were, the clean, white lights of a billion billion windows.

"I'm not sure I know what you're talking about," Marie said suddenly, getting up from her chair. "But I have to get back to my husband. He may be awake by now."

"What I mean—" old Horne began anxiously. His fingers were shaking, and his eyes were wide and—she would have sworn—malevolent. The others were looking at him now as if in alarm.

But Marie had no time; she'd stayed away too long already. She threw him a quick, false smile and mumbled, "Thank you. I *do* appreciate . . ." She slipped around him and walked down the hallway rapidly, her high heels clicking like shots.

7

Most of the first afternoon, James Chandler was under sedation and strapped in his place; if physical movement were kept to a minimum, the danger of renewed hemorrhaging would be comsiderably decreased. His white count now stood at roughtly 100,000. His temperature was subnormal, but not significantly so. Watching him sleep, one would not have thought him seriously ill—certainly not as ill as the man three doors down from him, who lay in agony with a broken foot.

Toward dusk natural sleep supervened. He awakened briefly, as dark came on, when a nurse, the Indian girl, came in to see how he was. Marie did not happen to be there at the time. He lay calm and comfortable, watching the girl work, assuring her with some cheerfulness, in answer to her oddly polite, apologetic questions, that he felt quite well and that, no, he would not blow his nose or do anything terribly strenuous at least until morning. He asked about his glasses and something to read—Dorothy Sayers would be just the thing—and she promised to do what she could about rounding up both. There was a library of sorts, she said, on the main floor. He might be well enough to go down tomorrow—in a wheelchair if he was still feeling weak. The doctor would be in any moment to tell him exactly how much he could do and how soon. She was gone from the room not more than two minutes before she returned again with the doctor, a genteel old Canadian who had very little more to say than the nurse had said. It was just as well, as far as Chandler was concerned. He was tired and in no mood for making decisions. The nurse's name, the doctor said, was Miss Sundown. She was a Seneca princess. "A very old Western New York family," the doctor said with a wink. The girl concentrated on loosening the strap that held Chandler's arm, apparently embarrassed. Innocently, without thinking, Chandler said, "I should be unfastening *your* straps." In horror, he recognized what he had said as soon as it was out, and his face must have shown his extreme confusion, for it was clearly at that that she laughed. "Do you really think we should free him?" she asked the doctor, still laughing. Chandler closed his eyes, still painfully embarrassed but feeling, nevertheless, peaceful and happy. He thought what an excellent name it was, Sundown, and how much finer this doctor was than the one in San Francisco.

"Your wife's here, by the way," he heard the doctor say (It was as if the man were speaking to someone else, far off). "She's having a bite to eat, I imagine." He pressed Chandler's stomach. "Any pain?"

Chandler shook his head. Before he knew it, he was asleep.

Like any dream, it was a conscious creation, an imaginative work of selection and arrangement; but what gave the dream its peculiar flavor was the fact that he was conscious moment by moment of his mental activity in putting it together. He had the conviction, as he dreamed, that he was creating an artistic masterpiece, that writing it down sometime afterward he would find it another *Kubla Khan*. It was not, alas. In fact, he was so ludicrously wrong that he laughed with delight, thinking back afterward to that sober, grotesquely inflated opinion he'd held as he dreamt. He remembered the story of Oliver Wendell Holmes's dream of the ultimate secret of the universe: *A faint odor of turpentine pervades it all*. But even as Chandler laughed, something came to him, or rather hovered in the periphery of his inner vision, so to speak, an idea that he could not quite catch hold of, but one that was right—that much he could feel—some insight that might be, at least for him, revolutionary. He tried to focus his mind on the thing not quite visible, all the muscles of his body slightly tensed and ready to pounce; but the insight would not come. He would have to retrace his steps, he decided, and find somehow the spring that would release the idea again, his mind coiled and ready this time to seize the intruder itself, not merely the faint emotional charge that signaled its nearness.

He'd been thinking when the intruder came, he recalled in a moment, of the various components of the dream: medieval color symbolism from Bonaventura, touches from Collingwood and Hobbes, a sentence from William James, another from *Burke* . . .

It came again. *Burke,* he thought. He repeated the name again, like an incantation, and each time he repeated it that charge was there, incredibly faint, growing fainter, infuriating, like a memory that would not come— but not a memory, exactly. What? "Burke," he thought again. But the spell had lost its power. His mind stood irresolute a moment, precisely like a hunter who has heard the whisper of the lion behind him; then, warily, every sense on a razor's edge, his mind moved on. There had also been elements of his past and still others from his present situation, in particular that strangely ambivalent feeling, which, entered so many of his dreams these days, about his daughters. He hesitated. He sensed that he'd almost triggered the thing again with the thought of his daughters; but he found it was a false alarm, perhaps merely a mistaken hunch that the thought of his daughters would do it.

The dream had begun in annihilation, one more ludicrous attempt of his sleeping head to resolve the problem that was constantly with him, the problem of death, this time by denying the thing it opposed, consciousness itself. He had eradicated all the world, a reasonable enough solution, however impractical in fact; and then like Dostoevsky's ridiculous man—or like Descartes—he had systematically re-created all he had formerly denied.

But all that was the wrong track. *Burke,* he thought. Nothing.

He was bitterly tired. He let himself slide into vague thoughts about the past.

Chandler had lived on the farm with his father, his mother, and his grandparents for three and a half years; then his father had moved the family in to Batavia, to the white-shingled house on Liberty, and there too Chandler had lived (he would guess) for about three years. After that the family had moved to Bank. Chandler's father—a tall, lean, long-nosed, gloomy man—had a profitable business by now and was thoroughly happy in his way. He worked long hours at the store (a second-class novelty shop in an attic in Richmond, snug little retreat from the world, which specialized in ingenious,

childhood, Chandler had been deathly afraid of the three horses on his grandfather's farm. They were not especially large horses, nor were they, as far as he knew, especially mean. But sometimes at night, lying in his bed as a child, he would hear the horses laugh. The laugh was utterly without humor, godlike in the sense of inscrutable and unanswerable. He would look out his window at the garden and the orchard, the highway to the right, to the left the ghostly dew-white field where the horses nickered. Once while he watched, one of the horses lifted its head and stared directly at him, as if with monstrous scorn, and showed its teeth.

He forced himself back to considering the dream.

It had begun in some indefinite kind of place, fog hanging everywhere, above him, below him, all around him, motionless, He waited for a long time, but to his great satisfaction nothing happened; there was only silence and the queerly dazzling gray of the fog; he was neither warm nor cold. Then, as though the recognition that he was neither had tipped the balance, he was cold. He became aware of occasional blooms of colored light: a sense of color, then grayness again, then color again, then grayness. He watched silently, careful not to move a muscle, prepared to be terrified. It was not an illusion; he saw them clearly, deep colors of the sort one sees in old stained-glass windows, but he could not make out and actively had no wish to make out what the colors were or even where they were. Each time they came, they were brighter.

Little by little he became aware of something else, some trifling disturbance of emptiness, a point of focus, and the more his mind shied away from the place, the more undeniably the place was there. He crept closer, moving on hands and knees without a sound, and at last he made out dark lines in the fog. Shapes. It was, he discovered, some kind of machine, a queer construction of rotted wood and rusted wire, much too intricate and much too large to grasp in a single mental act. In what seemed the center, in a kind of chamber framed by what looked like the disintegrating remains of an intricately carved rosewood clock, there stood, or rather hung, supported by nothing, a wheel. It turned a little as he watched, and a sound came, something remotely similar to a muffled roll of drums. When the wheel stopped, the sound stopped. After a moment it turned again—circling slowly. He put on his glasses and studied the turns of the wheel with care, smiling and nodding at each full revolution, and counting: *One, one, one.* Again the wheel stopped, and then once again it started up. This time the wheel turned on and on, faster and faster, by some law of its own, and the rumbling sound was louder and closer, and he knew that it was the clatter of things in motion. He saw them coming, three lights in the distance, one of them gold, one of them scarlet, one of them golden green. It was too late to stop them, and they were enormous, with great rolling eyes and flying manes, their necks clothed in thunder, glory of their nostrils terrible, and they swallowed up the ground with rage. He began frantically to dismantle the machine, using the pieces to make a fence, and he finished it just in the nick of time. They reared up, then stopped and stood above him, trembling with power, laughing scornfully, eating the fence with a terrible noise and slobbering as though he had made it all of apples. One was gold, one was scarlet, one was green, but he could not see clearly which was which; they seemed to keep changing. Now the fence was entirely gone, and he lifted up his arms to protect his glasses. Then someone said (It was a sly old woman who was somehow in dangerous league with him; she caught his left hand in her clawlike right and raised her own left hand to the horses), solemnly, feeble as she was, as though pronouncing the completed word: *There's the same thing I saw before again!* Suddenly, magically, he was released.

"But who was she, the old woman?" he asked himself now. Had he really dreamed of her before, or had she entered the dream only this moment, in his reconstruction of it? Suddenly the dream that had seemed so clear to him before seemed obscure. She, at least, had not been his doing. Or rather, since of course he *had* put her there, she was the one element in the dream that he'd introduced without understanding—indeed, without even needing: She had nothing to do with the rest, and he himself might as easily, and more properly, have delivered that final magical phrase, the affirmation of consciousness which hurled him into life and, therefore, death.

But no, no of course not, it came to him then. That was precisely what he didn't have the guts to admit, that he himself had roused himself to consciousness. There had to be the mysterious agent, for if Somebody got him into it, there was Somebody waiting to get him out. It was precisely because he couldn't make out where he'd gotten her, that terrifying old woman he'd dreamed of before, that he'd put her into the dream. *But she's fiction,* he told himself suddenly and violently *wherever she came from, pure fiction.*

Then all at once the intruder idea was back, not only the shock but the insight itself: *Obscurity: Burke's idea of the Sublime: the fallacy of precarious margin in Kant's idea of delight without interest.*

It seemed to burst full-blown in his head, not a fully developed idea but a certainty of intuition—an explosion of light, that final line of "Sunday Morning," an unexpected conversion of motifs in a Mozart quartet—bringing with it that sense of sudden release from the bounds of time and space that drove Anaximander to his theory of the infinite. He could have run naked in the streets crying "Eureka," and though perhaps it would have seemed to most people no different from the cry of an ordinary madman who'd found an unlocked door or, in a more mundane situation, a man who has found his credit card, it was not, for Chandler, an ordinary discovery but an insight into truth. The inner Eureka announced a philosophical advance, and if there had been among the passers-by, in that Syracuse where Chandler rejoiced, a man who had come to tell James Chandler that he'd just discovered Kant's mistake, his failure to see the disinterest in moral affirmation, that man would have understood Chandler's yelp of Eureka at once, and he would have burst from the crowd shouting, "So have I!"

It was agonizing that there was no one to tell. He thought, absurdly, of ringing for the nurse and then, the next instant, of asking for the doctor. But he merely lay in a kind of joyful anguish of suspense, waiting. It was not merely a wish to communicate his insight, share the joy of his discovery, though that was a very large part of it; it was also a desire—a positive hunger—for a chance to test it, work it out in detail, get it out where he could look at it as a man would look at a painting, search out its flaws.

And then, to Chandler's wonderment, the door opened and an angel of the Lord walked in—in the shape of his wife, Marie.

"Listen," he said excitedly.

Marie brightened. "Why, you're awake! And they've taken off the straps!"

He nodded. "Listen, let me tell you something. Did you ever come across Burke's *Enquiry?*" She looked uneasy, and he added, *"A Philosophical Enquiry into the Origin of our Ideas of the Sublime and Beautiful."*

"James," she pleaded, "I can see you're just dying to tell me another of those wild ideas, but you don't *know* what I've been *through."*

Chandler swallowed, then looked down at his covers. It was ironic, he thought, that it was Marie, not himself, that his ridiculous bleeding fit had frightened. But he saw, the next instant, that he'd misunderstood.

"I met a fool i' the forest," she said. "An old, old man. He's really strange. Mad, I think. A lawyer who writes for philosophy journals. He says he's published somewhere you have, in the same issue." She laughed and began to tell him all about it. Chandler smiled politely, helpless and miserable. She chattered on, gently, sweetly, her hand on his, but his find had gone off, or rather, his mind continued to hover over the casual sentence that had not yet exploded into sense. Suddenly he sat bolt upright.

"What did you say?" he exclaimed.

"I said he wanted to convert me, or at least that's what I *think*—"

He shook his head. "No, before. About philosophy journals."

"Oh. I said he writes for—"

But Chandler was already out of bed, hunting in the dresser and under his pillow for his glasses.

Her face was white. "You're not supposed to move! If you start to bleed—"

Chandler's mind raced. "Where did you see him?"

She caught his arm as he started out into the hall. "Please," she hissed, "stop." And then, absurdly seductive, smiling, her eyes wide and unblinking: "Let me get you a wheelchair."

He hesitated, though those words, too, took a moment to register in his mind. He nodded then, and she was gone from him, running down the hall, her outrage burning the walls on all sides like an aura.

But downstairs, where Marie had left him, they found no sign of John Horne. It was as if he'd been swallowed up in a puff of smoke.

8

SINCE writing, working the idea out on paper, was the only course open to him, Chandler wrote. He worked until three in the morning. The pencil grew slippery in his fingers, and whenever the heel of his hand touched the paper, the paper stuck; nevertheless, he was hardly aware of what effort the writing took. His mind raced, seemed to be burning up, and he was astonished at (as he put it to himself) how well the old machine still worked. But the strength of his mind was in part illusory. Again and again he would lose the thread of the argument, the machine would come to a standstill, and without knowing it, Chandler would slip into a kind of faint, to awaken four minutes later with the unfinished thought on his brain. When at last he laid the pencil and his odds and ends of paper down—Marie had been able to find only scraps: half of a prescription tablet, some mimeographed forms the backs of which were clean, a few sheets of stationery that the Indian girl happened to have—Marie came to him and moved them to the dresser top, where he could reach them if he needed to. She tucked him in for sleep gently, grimly, as she would a child who had displeased her. The flesh around her eyes was gray and puffy from lack of sleep.

Chandler slept until nearly ten the next morning. When he opened his eyes he saw Marie curled up sideways in her uncomfortable chair, reading. He thought at once of the writing he'd begun, but he did not turn to it at once. He felt calm now, well rested and even something like happy, despite his vague aches and the feeling of deadness in his back and buttocks from lying too long in one position. He closed his eyes again to lie in a kind of reverie.

After a time he found himself remembering perfectly distinctly the room where he had slept in his grandfather's house as a child. The late-morning sunlight was brilliant and friendly, and he remembered the pleasure he'd felt in his odd sense that there was no question whatever of anything's being anything else. Every object in the room was familiar and sure and wholly itself, and all the objects in the room were *in* the room, and nothing that was not there was there, though at night he was never so sure of that as he was in the morning. Even the glossy hardwood bedroom floor was distinct from the hallway floor: There was a low, rounded wooden thing below the door (which stood open, in his memory, looking into his grandmother's room), and on one side of the wooden divider lay the bedroom, on the other, the hall. On the floor but sharply separated from it was the dresser, which had drawers with wooden knobs that would come off, he knew by experiment, and above the drawers a long flat top like the top of a table, and it was all part of the dresser, though not all one thing; and on the dresser top, but not part of it, there was a clock and beside it, separate, a tray with brushes, combs, pins, and beyond that, boxes and bottles. Between the bedroom and the world outside there was glass, which sunlight could come through but not dust; and when he opened the window, the world was still outside, the room inside, and he himself, leaning on the windowsill smelling the air—flowers, apples, hay drying in windrows on the hill to the west—he himself was both outside and inside the separate, himself.

All this, those mornings, he had known in an instant: the manyness of things grown familiar and therefore one. It was because of that that the world was so large, and time, the span of a single morning, so vast. It was because of that, too that he felt such inexpressible joy: He felt intensely what later he would learn words to explain, the interpenetration of the universe and himself. For if he was distinct from all he saw, he was also the sum of it. He was even dimly conscious of the fact: Beyond the farthest hill or cloud, beyond the farthest star he saw through his window at night, stretched the shell of his own mind. When he closed his eyes it was all still there and, strange to say, it was as vast as ever—the garden, the orchard, the meadow, the hills, the sky. It was himself, then; all the rich profusion of it; and beyond the farthest hill there was more that was also still himself but not known, not safe. He had actually tried at times to remember what it was that was farther away, forgotten, but the memory would not come. He began to see that there was something else, perhaps within him, perhaps outside, something threatening, related to the mysterious intrusion he sensed around him in his room at night, when the law of clean distinctions broke down. And so one morning—a morning in his third year, perhaps—when his mother and grandmother were busy (But perhaps he had simply wandered off, unaware that they were to be avoided, unaware even that he meant to go), he'd gone not simply to the orchard fence at the end of the garden—he'd often played out as far as that—but past the fence to where the geese were and where he'd been once in his grandfather's cart, and he'd gone on farther, tree by tree, from shadow to light to shadow again through the long projection of his mind, and when he looked back, if it *was* back, the house was gone, and it was as if the world, once coherent, succinct with intelligence, had turned bestial and insane. He began to run, crying for his mother, and the sun was low and red, burning up the sky. The horses were coming, throwing their heads, crazy. He felt himself falling. The next instant the sky was dark and the tractor lights were shining on him where he lay on two crossed fenceposts and a tangle of barb-wire, the lights very white in the grass, making spidery shadows. His grandfather's dogs were barking and his father was shouting his name.

The horses were standing quiet now, over in the meadow on the other side of the fence, blowing steam through their noses and looking at the tractor.

His father held him in his arms, on the way back, and scolded him. His voice was small and thin in the enormity of the night, and even the roar of the tractor was small and thin. But the world was in order again. Even though he didn't yet know where he was, the center had reestablished itself: Space circled out from the tractor seat, the clean, white little lights on the gauges, the larger lights that were mounted on the fenders, the warmth of his father's body like a halo. They came to the road and then, far off, he saw the house, every window lighted, and that became the center now, his mother and grandmother waiting on the porch, his grandfather and one of the hired men waving lanterns from deep in the field across the road. From their different places they all floated in toward the house like chariots drifting through air—the image stood timeless in his mind, like one of the engravings in his grandfather's Bible—moving toward a high, resplendent, rock-walled island.

When he opened his eyes Marie was looking at him. "I slept late," he said.

She smiled, and after an instant: "You had a visitor. Mr. Horne. He'll be back, he said; and he probably will. He's the type."

"Where are the children?"

"They're at home," she said. "Viola Staley's there, helping out. It was Viola that brought you in."

"Yes, you told me. I remember now."

"Would you care for something to eat?"

"I'm starving, now that you mention it."

"The nurse said to call her when you woke up. The doctor didn't want you disturbed." She rang for the nurse, and before long Chandler's breakfast came, oatmeal that tasted warmed over, toast with tasteless jelly, coffee. *Your mother and Viola are getting along just beautifully,* Marie said. "It's funny. Yesterday morning you'd have thought Viola was Jezebel herself, as far as your mother was concerned."

A vague worry, or some question, perhaps, came into Chandler's mind, then escaped him. He was tired again. It was as if he had put in a long, long day in front of classes. He lay back and closed his eyes. There came to his mind—in precise detail, he would have said, though in fact to focus on any part was to blur it—an image of the orchard as it had looked that night in his childhood when he was lost. Something came to him about it, but it slipped between his fingers before he could catch it. And then there was another image, a sky full of screaming blackbirds, hundreds of thousands of them, and he stood looking up at them, terrified. But even as he quaked, part of his mind stepped back, calm, professorial, thinking, "It means something, something perfectly obvious but what is it?"

"What, James?" Marie said, leaning closer.

"Nothing," he said. He let his eyes remain shut and was dimly aware of her kiss. The image was gone, and he couldn't get it back. He could summon up in imagination an identical image, but he knew it was only a reconstruction, a museum arrangement of lifeless bones; the emotional shock was gone.

Then, deeply, he slept. He awakened to find Marie missing, the room full of shadows, the doctor and a redheaded nurse standing over him.

"Good afternoon," the doctor said formally.

Chandler nodded and drifted back into sleep.

9

WHILE Chandler was eating his supper, Marie seated on the side of his bed eating too—Miss Sundown had brought in a meal for her as well as one for Chandler—Viola Staley came in with Chandler's mother and the girls. Chandler's eyes filled with tears. He kissed his mother on the cheek, hugged each of the girls, and pressed Viola's hand as though she were an old, dear friend. His warmth toward Viola was a mistake, he soon discovered. (The discovery, like all discoveries now, was almost painful, or anyway exhausting, tolerable only because, like a drunk, he had lost involvement in his own discomfort: He sat across the room from himself, so to speak, wearily observing.) Green eyes wide, she spoke of having realized how much he must want to see his children (It was Marie's brief trip home last night, Chandler knew, that had arranged their coming), but she did not seem to guess that he would rather talk to them than to her. She stood close to the bed, embarrassingly solicitous, at first, and then irritatingly cheerful—very much like a church-school teacher he'd had long ago (a toothless old Baptist-brained bitch, he thought, and he thought the same instant how uncharacteristic of him that thought was, both the words and the childish escape to emotion: his sickness talking: and so a man was his blood condition: the platelets were all. Very well then, he thought. All right.)—showing the girls off, patronizingly, forcing them into the role of dolls, or good little dears, or Jesus' little angels. "Can you tell Daddy what we did today?" "Suzie, did you remember Daddy's present?" And to him: "They're such little *ladies,* Mr. Chandler"—a phrase she'd picked up from his mother, no doubt, and the phrase James Chandler hated more (at least just now) than any other he could think of. His mother stood at the end of the bed, beaming through her tears, her lips stretched, her hands folded at her waist like those of a singer counting measures of rest. All this he saw in the sharpest possible detail, and he felt his own heart and mind a vital part of it, and yet another part of his mind ran its own course, independent of forces outside, existing in the same world only as ghosts and people may occupy a single room, each oblivious of the other's time and place.

But if Viola was overwhelming with all her exaggerated, distorted emotions, the hint of inner disturbance that seemed to flow from all her body like waves of deep-blue light, Chandler had no time to be seriously bothered by it. He had not known until this moment how much he had missed his daughters, and now that they were here he felt he had to seize every moment, explode it into eternity, catch and hold fast every look, every gesture, every nuance in their voices. He seated Anne beside him on the bed and held on to Susan's hand, as she stood on his left, and Karen's, to his right. He looked at their faces, now one, now another, as he could not remember ever having looked at them before. Anne studied him curiously, the first few minutes, then turned to examining the head of the bed, forgetting all about him. It brought a sharp pang to his chest, a desire to cry out *"Look* at me, Annie!" but he was sensible at the same time, in that wilder realm where his second mind moved, of the rightness and naturalness of it; for how much worse it would have been, after all, if Annie knew that their time was running out. He too had lived outside time, once, or previous to time. How strange it was to see it in his child, and humbling.

Susan said brightly, brushing the soft, light hair from her eyes, "You know where we're going tomorrow, Daddy?"

"Where?" he said, smiling with unnatural eagerness, as Viola would, as though her presence had poisoned his reactions.

"We're going to Letchworth Park." She almost squealed it, her eyes blinding blue, her dimples splendid.

"How wonderful!" Marie said, and Chandler, catching the uneasiness in his wife's voice, was suddenly on guard.

"You'll be careful?" he said. An image of Letchworth took possession of his mind: endlessly pitted, ancient gray rock walls, narrow rock stairways winding down the gorge to the river, brown and turbulent water breaking to white, the falls roaring above, below, on every side, like steady thunder, a chaos of motion crying out to the chaos within: One knew that one could fall, that one had a choice.

"Of course we'll be careful," Susan laughed.

"We won't go near the edge, will we?" Viola said gaily. Then, to Chandler, in a voice different from the one she used on the girls, "Your mother and I will be watching them like hawks all the time, don't you worry. We thought they ought to have something very special to do just now, while you have to be away." She smiled. "I always loved Letchworth when I was a girl. My father used to take me there every time we'd visit my aunts." She spoke lightly, but there was intensity in all she said, as though she knew the room to be full of demons.

"It's a beautiful place," Chandler said, touching his chin.

Abruptly, Viola said, "Oh! We brought you some mail!" She opened her purse and brought out a thick bundle tied up in a rubber band. She slid it onto his dinner tray, and he nodded and left it there for Marie. "I was interested to see that you're a member of the NAACP," Viola said. "I'm glad, though of course I should have known from just looking at you. I wish *my* father had ever had any sense of social responsibility." Again he heard the irrational anger moving beneath the smooth surface of her voice.

Chandler said nothing. He lay with his head tipped, on his face the half-smile, half-wince that, even when his health was good, had always come when he was forced to make precise distinctions—when he was reading Plato, say, or when, as now, he was confronted, in conversation, with a sentence that seemed to say sixteen conflicting things at once. Of all the things she seemed to be saying —that she was enlightened and just, that she had a keen eye for character (she "should have known"), that she wanted him to think her an adult (she was capable of rejecting her father's opinions), that she was not absolutely sure of her own social responsibility, and so forth—the thing James Chandler's mind fixed upon was what seemed to be implied by her stressed word, *my* father. She was comparing herself to his children then, wasn't she—and finding them far better off? Could it mean that she wanted some sort of help, support, fatherhood, from him? The idea was unsettling, and he recoiled from it angrily. He was running out of time. He had come here to be with his mother and his family, to squeeze out the essence of the hours he had left; and as if that weren't enough to keep him busy, he'd stumbled now on his aesthetic theory, something at once significant and possible to bring to completion—he could get it all down, at least in outline (Ken Roos would be willing to polish it up) in three or four days. But perhaps his analysis of what she was saying was wrong, rooted simply in the inevitable paranoia of the dying. Yes, surely, he decided. He'd often been wrong, even at his best, about things like this.

With a part of his mind he heard her saying—almost hissing, he thought, her green eyes smoldering—"He was a Republican, you know, like my aunts. As far as any of them are concerned, the best thing to do with people who aren't exactly like you is machine-gun them, or sterilize them, maybe, just to be on the safe side with *God*." All her false cheer was gone now; the streak of irrational violence was out in the open. His mother saw it too, Chandler knew. Her eyes were fixed on Viola, alarmed, perhaps angry. One did not put down the Grand Old Party in the presence of Rose Chandler.

"I'm a Republican myself," Chandler said carefully, still with his half-smile, half-wince. He stood on a pair of powder-kegs, he knew, and only by the most careful choice of his words and tone could he keep them both from going off. The effort of caution was exhausting. He wished they would leave.

Marie snapped gaily—and the minute she opened her mouth he knew he'd been arming the wrong battlements— "Really, Viola, *I'd* say it's your father that's the freak. We Republicans have always been good to darkies."

Chandler snapped his eyes shut, helpless. He thought wildly of trying to explain what it was that she really meant, but her meaning was already all too clear. She meant pure anger and revulsion, and it had nothing whatever to do with Viola's words. It had to do with her sudden intuition of Viola's neurosis, and with Letchworth Park—for she too had looked down from the rim of the gorge. And it had to do, also, with something still more complicated: jealousy. For now he was certain—though he hadn't had time yet to think out why—that every detail of his analysis of Viola had been right. And Viola knew, he could see, that Marie had attacked her. Her face had gone white, and in an instant she would turn on Marie in rage.

"Listen!" he said. Everything stopped, all their emotions hanging weightless, and he knew, as surely as he could have known if it had actually happened, what it was that he had averted, at least for the moment. Twice in his life he'd seen breakdowns in class, explosions of mind into pure, howling passion, the transformation, within a matter of seconds, from what seemed mere sentimentality —the lie for effect—to madness, the violent defense of the lie in the soul. "Marie," he said, "why don't *you* take the children to Letchworth? We can't keep imposing on Viola.

And anyhow, you mustn't go on sitting here by my bedside, moping your life away. You ought to be seeing something for the children."

"Oh, do come, Mommy!" Susan exclaimed, running to her.

He glanced at Viola. Susan's "do come" made Marie an addition to the group already intending to go, and thus subtly, disastrously altered his plan. Viola met his eyes, understanding exactly what had happened, he was sure, but she did not leap in to seize the advantage.

Now Karen said, reserved, "Yes, do, Mother. I *would* like you to get to know Viola. We'll really have a wonderful time."

He flinched from the hint of affectation in Karen, and again he couldn't tell what to think. Her instinct was right, urging Marie to go with them on the trip; and he sensed, too, that she wasn't feigning her fondness for Viola, though perhaps it wasn't Viola herself but the fact that Viola was part child, part grown-up that attracted her. Just the same, it made him nervous, that tone of hers. Would she too someday not know—as Viola did not know—what emotions she really felt?

Marie hedged, confused and upset, and all of them begged her to change her mind. Their voices went hollow in Chandler's head, and his attention closed around Viola, now shouting fiercely that Marie simply must come along, if only for her own sake. At last, reluctantly but with clear relief, Marie gave in. Chandler too was relieved.

"It's settled then!" he said. The words rang false—theatrical, a line from a hundred television plays, but not because Chandler was fooling himself. He knew what it was that he was evading: the explosion all too likely to come tomorrow, when he was not there to play superego for Viola.

At last Viola—all joy now, eyes bright as daggers—decided it was time for them to leave. She and Marie began to get the children's coats back on. Chandler's mother said, struggling with her emotions, "I'm sorry you can't be with us, James. But I know you'll be home again just as soon as you can."

Out in the corner of his eye he saw Marie pause for an instant before going with her on buttoning of Susan's coat.

"I'll be home in a day or two, don't you worry," he said. His voice sounded cross, he realized.

His mother came around to him and kissed his cheek.

Marie said, "Tell Daddy bye-bye, Annie."

Anne said, "Go car. Ouseye."

Susan kissed him good-bye; then Karen came to him. When she'd kissed him on the cheek, she said, "I brought you something to read, Daddy. It's what you were reading before you came, so I thought—" From inside her sweater she pulled out his battered old copy of Aurelius.

"Why, Karen!" he said. A sudden emotion almost like fear leaped up in him. His two minds became one, and time seemed to freeze. He saw the room, for an instant, as a tableau, Marie holding Annie's hand, Viola with a smile of sudden and furious jealousy, his mother vague, half turned away, Susan holding the open door; but all this was at the edge of his vision. At the center was Karen, her head tilted, her eyes not meeting his directly, her lips forming a mysterious smile that made her seem not a child but a grown woman, or, no, some beautiful changeling, an elf-queen.

"Why how thoughtful!" Viola said, supremely false.

The words broke the spell, and Karen was merely a child again, standing with crossed legs and a sheepish, self-conscious, unpleasantly prim look. But Chandler said quickly, "Thank you, Karen. I love you."

She met his eyes.

"I want to kiss Daddy good-bye again," Susan cried, so blatantly jealous that, wearily, Chandler laughed.

"Good-bye, Susan honey," he said.

"Kiss," Anne demanded. "I wan kiss Daddy bye gin."

Marie smiled and lifted her up to him.

"You're a wonderful, wonderful father," Viola said huskily.

He met her eyes, point-blank and at close range for the first time, and a shock jarred his system. *She's evil,* his mother had said. But his mother was wrong. The girl was innocent, her whole soul twisted with her hunger for absolute goodness, and Chandler was afraid of her.

Merely to lighten the farewells, he said: "And you're the world's best baby-sitter."

She stared at him as if believing he'd cunningly insulted her, then laughed, bristling, exactly as she'd laughed in the hallway at her aunts'.

10

THE following day Chandler was, as it seemed to him, almost as strong as ever. He spent most of the morning writing, falling asleep sometimes in the middle of a thought, suffering brief, peculiarly unlocalized headaches, but progressing well, all things considered. In the afternoon, exhausted, he read Aurelius with a part of his mind and with another part confusedly turned over problems in the theory he was trying to elaborate. After supper he slept briefly, and then, with his doctor's permission, walked down to the library on the main floor. It was there that he met John Horne.

It was a room no larger than an ordinary hospital bedroom, lighted by one high, narrow window, which looked out on North Street, and fluorescent lamps on the two long tables that filled up most of the room. On the bookshelves there were, as far as Chandler could see, only mysteries and the novels of Lloyd C. Douglas and, on a shelf by themselves, the historical rambles of Arch Merrill. There was no catalogue or principle of order (though some of the books had been marked *F*, presumably for *Fiction*, in India ink, and others *M* for *Mystery* or *Mur-*

der) and there was no sign of a librarian, no doubt because sick people and their friends were considered, prima facie, honest. When Chandler entered, Horne was the only person he found in the room, though the hallway outside was crowded.

He stood at the far end of the far table, smoking, a book open in his hands but his eyes not on the book but on something outside the window. An obese man, with a fat, loose mouth drawn up in what seemed at first glance an obscure, sly smile. But that was perhaps the effect of plastic surgery. Most of the lower part of his face had been rebuilt after the removal of, perhaps, a tumor of some sort. (The ledges of his cheeks had irregular bulges that threw his eyes a trifle out of line.) The destruction of the lower parts of his cheeks, especially the left one, made his great bald dome seem even larger than it was. He was wearing, as he'd been when Marie had met him (according to her description), a heavy black coat. The black hat was on the table. When Horne turned, Chandler was an instant late in looking down and so caught the sudden confusion that came over him. The cigarette in his mouth jiggled violently, and he snatched at where his hat-brim would be if the hat were on his head, then remembered and caught it up from the table. He said nothing for a moment, and Chandler nodded distantly, not wishing to upset him further for fear it might mean explanations and struggles for which Chandler hadn't the energy. But the man said with forced delight, "Well, well! You're James Chandler, I believe." He came over to Chandler quickly, sliding his left hand along the polished tabletop, struggling with his right hand to stuff the book into his coatpocket as though the cover had a nude on it. "My name's John Horne," he said. "Let me give you my card."

"How do you do," Chandler said tentatively. "I believe my wife ran into you the other night." He smiled and glanced at the card the man held out, then reluctantly took it from him.

"Yes she did, she did." He mopped his forehead with his sleeve and smiled nervously. His teeth were yellow-gray.

The man's nervousness was contagious: Chandler began to feel as jittery as Horne appeared. He would have liked to sit down, but he could see no way to manage it. He had to think to keep from sickening at the smell of the man. He said, smiling, reading the card, " 'Attorney at Law.' It's a shame I don't need a good lawyer!"

"Perhaps you do," the man said intensely, trying to joke but managing to make the remark sound ominous. " 'Which of us knows his crimes?' to paraphrase Aurelius."

Chandler laughed, then said, struck by the curious coincidence, "You've been reading Aurelius lately, I take it?"

"Yes I have, yes. The incurable's friend."

Chandler laughed again, politely, touching the side of his face, not perfectly sure what Horne's remark might mean. "I've been looking at Aurelius too."

There was no response. Horne's cigarette had somehow gone out, and he took it as a major catastrophe. He stood fumbling with it for a moment, then turned to the nearest of the maple tables, put his book down, got his matches out, and hurriedly got the cigarette relighted.

"As a matter of fact, I came looking for you the other night, just after you'd talked to my wife," Chandler said then.

But Horne said: "I'm not a lawyer of the usual sort, Mr. Chandler. Spent most of my life as a librarian for a powerful and respected firm, Hawley, Hawley, and Poacher, of Buffalo. A specialist in research, in short." He sucked at the cigarette, then continued, looking at something just over Chandler's head, "I develop labyrinthine arguments: *Smith* vs. *Baker* and *Donoghue* vs. *Stevenson:* How much like a spark from a traveling locomotive which ignites a nearby haystack are the decomposed remains of a mouse in a bottle of Dr. Pepper's cola which causes psychological harm to the plaintiff? or a volley ball knocked out of the court which injures a blind old lady walking in the middle of the highway? or the slip of a stuttering accountant's tongue which results in pecuniary loss? Behold we are led into the most abstruse questions of metaphysics. *Nomina sunt consequentia rerum,* as we read in Justinian's

Codex." He leaned close, saying fiercely, "What is negligence? What is adultery? What is a 'cold' salami sandwich?" He laughed loudly, some great point scored. "And in all this, of course, I remain a free spirit. I never darken a courtroom door."

"Very impressive," Chandler said, leaning back from the man.

"Yes it is. Beyond the shadow of a doubt. Like all things of any importance at all, it's utterly and completely unreal. Immaterial, as we say in the trade. Shadows on Plato's wall. Reality, as we all know, has nothing whatever to do with philosophy or law—or science, for that matter. No man can reason about things, as Hobbes says, but only about the names of things, which is to say, words, air, the arbitrarily selective attention of a given culture at a given time and place. Which makes us completely ludicrous and drives us to art and religion. At bottom, the universe is sexual. Creative force, *élan vital*. I'm glad you're up and around, by the way."

"You've read Bergson?" Chandler broke in, missing Horne's last remark.

Horne lifted his hat from the table, reflected a moment, then replaced it. "I'm not very good at talking with people," he said, turning to Chandler again, his face a mask of agony. "I frightened your wife half to death, I'm afraid."

Chandler waved it away. "Oh, no—"

"I'm an old man. It's difficult to change one's ways. I don't know what came over me."

"Yes of course. Don't even think about it."

"The existentialists are right about this, at least: One has to be *engagé*."

"Yes, that's so, I imagine."

"You have a lovely wife, Mr. Chandler."

Chandler nodded, wincing, watching the man.

"And children, no doubt?"

"Yes, three. Girls."

"That's good. Fortunate. I have nobody, nothing. I think a great deal about it now, now that it's too late. I'm dying, Mr. Chandler. I mention it only as background.

It's strange what a trifle it is to die. A shortness of breath, a click, a moment of disquietude in the middle of a dream. . . . Are you religious, Mr. Chandler?"

Chandler looked at the floor. "I've never been able to decide." He laughed.

Horne seemed to consider it. At last he brought out, "No reason one should, to tell the truth, unless one's compulsive, of course; unless one's compulsive. Or in very great physical pain." He fell silent.

The silence between them grew, threatening to become unbreakable.

At last Chandler said somewhat doubtfully, seeing no other course open to him—it was clearly not consolation that John Horne wanted, or at any rate not consolation of the usual kind—"I wanted to talk to you about a theory of aesthetics, something I stumbled onto in a dream, or at any rate by means of a dream."

"Ah?" His nose moved, a little like a rabbit's nose, and his eyes bulged more than usual.

"What would you say art is, exactly?"

Horne turned his head away, looking for something, saw an ashtray at the end of the table, and hurried down to it. A nurse came in, looked over the shelf nearest the door, selected three books, and went out again, excusing herself with a nod and smile. Horne crushed out his cigarette clumsily and got out papers and a can of Prince Albert and began to roll another.

At last he said emphatically, as if only after doing hard battle with himself, "Atonement."

"Atonement?" Chandler echoed, almost in alarm.

"Art is the self-sacrifice of a man incapable of sacrificing himself in real life. I could easily have shape-shifted into an artist, Mr. Chandler. Does it ever occur to you that every man is required to be crucified?" He paused, flicking his tongue across his lower lip. "Perhaps I'm mistaken though. No doubt I am."

"I'm afraid I don't follow," Chandler said, squinting.

"A man must be born again, Mr. Chandler. I believe that. I'm a living demonstration of it. I sometimes think I've been born again, but those are moments of error, I'm afraid. I'm a man incapable of love. That is to say, a freak of Nature. Or worse yet, I'm a man who can love only what is gone already—my mother and father, for instance, whom I learned to love only after they were securely decomposed, and a cat I had once, a cat which, I must confess, I hated all his life, though I persuaded myself otherwise at the time. A miserable failure of a man, a botch. The Lord forgive me. But does anyone succeed, I wonder?"

He took, suddenly, the pose of an orator, one hand behind his back, and intoned, growing passionate as the poetry took possession of him—

> " 'Beyond the shadow of the ship,
> I watched the water-snakes:
> They moved in tracks of shining white,
> And when they reared, the elfish light
> Fell off in hoary flakes.
>
> Within the shadow of the ship
> I watched their rich atttire:
> Blue, glossy green, and velvet black,
> They coiled and swam; and every track
> Was a flash of golden fire.
>
> O happy living things! no tongue
> Their beauty might declare:
> A spring of love gushed from my heart,
> And I blessed them unaware:
> Sure my kind saint took pity on me,
> And I blessed them unaware!'

Do you know the meaning of those lines, Mr. Chandler? Do you see the horrible depth of the poet's vision?"

"Perhaps I don't," Chandler said uneasily. "Actually, my *own* theory—"

"There are indeed the damned and the saved—that's what Coleridge has to tell us. In a blind, unthinking moment an old man shoots an albatross—why? For no reason under heaven! There's the truth of it! He shoots the albatross because it's *there*, that's all. He sees it, and because of the sickness in his soul, hundreds of fathoms below consciousness, he kills it, symbolically crucifying Christ, out of sheer indifference, you understand, and on the astrological level of the poem, symbolically murdering his brother Abel. (It's under the sign of Cain, I could show you, that the albatross is shot.) But he's lucky, supremely lucky, you see, because at another time, with no more conscious volition than ever—*not* because of his atonement, no, out of utter absurdity—he saves himself by blessing them 'unaware.' You see? They're wrong, Coleridge is saying,—Locke and Hartley and Wordsworth and so forth: You don't just open your eyes to God's creation, passively receive impressions on the blank sheet of paper, and change your life. You don't even *actively* change your life. You happen to see or you happen *not* to by virtue of a health or sickness deeper than consciousness. He says it again and again, Coleridge, as only a man who knows himself bound for eternal damnation would need to. Have you ever looked closely at *Christabel?* Do you know what happens in that poem?" He paused for only an instant. Chandler frowned, waiting, and Horne continued, "Christabel makes that monster herself. *Unaware.* By Druidical magic. Can one really speak of *the remission of sin* in such cases?"

"It's an interesting theory," Chandler said, somewhat skeptical.

Horne nodded ferociously, hunting through his pockets. He found a piece of tissue and mopped his forehead. "Art is atonement," he said. "Good poets atone for the evil in their lives, evil poets atone for the evil in their very souls, which they cannot help but continue to affirm. By writing the poem, the poet hopes to exorcise his devil. God help him."

It was hard to know what to say. All the man said and did was frantic, violent, but it did not seem madness, exactly—though heaven only knew what a pychiatrist might think. To Chandler, at least, it seemed quite the opposite of madness, more like the terrible sanity that so frightened Bishop Berkeley. To look at him, one would have said that John Horne was a man who would never dare speak to anyone, a man who would shy from human contact as a bat shies from light. Like a man desperately timid, humiliated from the first, he kept his shoulders hunched; his glowing eyes were evasive; and his lips trembled almost constantly, like those of a man in mortal terror. And yet he forced out his confession not as if compelled, driven by an irresistible impulse, but like a man taking an almost impossible course because he had chosen to do so. It was less a confession that a sermon, judging from the tone; a hell-fire warning from a creature newly returned, if only for a moment, from the burning lake. Whether Chandler was right or wrong about why the man spoke, that is, right or wrong in his intuition that John Horne knew what he was saying and spoke for a reason—if only in the hope of discovering a reason— Chandler was prevented from turning the talk to something else (supposing that were possible) or interrupting the monologue so obviously discomforting to them both. Horne asked now, pacing back and forth between the two tables—over to the window, back to Chandler, over to the window, back again, reaching out to the large, dusky world-globe to give it a spin each time he started back— "What if it should be true? Think of it! Suppose men really do have no freedom at all. Or rather, suppose that only certain of us—the elect, let us say—can freely choose, while the rest, damned by predestination, corrupt in our very chemistry, have no choice? How *can* we be born again?" He stopped short, bug-eyed, waiting for an answer; but there was none.

"I might tell you," Horne said, "for the sake of dramatizing my state, that I'm a pederast, that a blind old man (a dear friend of the family) very early set the ugly pattern of my life; or I might say I'm a drinker, or an opium eater, or that without especially meaning to, I butcher little girls. But I will not stoop to melodrama. The case is much simpler. I despair, Mr. Chandler. There it is. I despair."

"Surely a great many people—" Chandler began.

"It's irrelevant what many people do." He was suddenly enraged, his eyes like a crazy toad's. "I'm an old man. No interest whatever in the pastures of the herd, some cheap and miserable consolation. I'll tell you a fact of experience: The question *'What is the meaning of life?'*

is a meaningless question to the simple, saintly plowman —which is to say, most of mankind. He looks at the life of the man beside him, and he sees the meaning of life at a glance: An end in itself. 'This man beside me is beautiful, and beauty justifies itself. As for my own life, if it's revolting to me, it's sweet as a rose to my good wife Madge.' Thus the fundamental law of Nature becomes the law for man, Mr. Chandler: Just as the components of an atom are components of anything at all only if you give them time to establish their rhythm— or just as (to put it more elegantly) the molecules within a rock are molecules within a rock only if you give them time to work out Zeno's paradox of the arrow in flight— so the meaning of man is defined by his relationships in time and space. In sort, as physicists tell us, *form is function.* And what is a man to do if he has no function— whether by virtue of his character or by virtue of his social condition?"

"Come now," Chandler said, his voice more tentative than he felt, *"talk is function."*

"Ha!" Horne cried. "But is *rhetoric?"* He stood motionless now, his head drawn back, smiling wildly. "Properly speaking, rhetoric is purposeless proliferation of once-utile figures. Do you deny that there is such a thing as love?"

Chandler squinted, trying to find the connection. After an instant he gave up the search and answered, "No, of course I don't deny it."

"You affirm that there is love?"

"Certainly. It's not debatable. To question whether one has experienced one's experience is misplaced argument."

"Excellent! Yes! And you mean *love,* not ego-gratification, the effect of what Coleridge calls delight in the agreeable?" He added quickly, jabbing his finger in Chandler's direction, "Because if so, you see, you're defining love as delight apart from any interest. And that's the idealist definition of the *beautiful*—and we're back where we started! A man incapable of love—incapable of aesthetic response—is a man congenitally damned. For such a man, providing he has the intellect to perceive his condition, life must be a continual but hopeless search for something he can find it in his heart to die for." He stood with clenched fists, his face dark red as if with rage.

Abruptly, mildly, Chandler said, "I refuse to believe that any such man exists."

"You refuse?" Horne echoed, furious, shaking like a leaf.

Chandler nodded, touching the side of his glasses.

Horne's eyes bulged with indignation. "Then I am annihilated." He laughed grimly.

"That's one possibility, yes," Chandler acknowledged.

"The other being, I suppose, that I'm a liar."

"Well, yes, perhaps. Or that you trick yourself—spirit cuckolded by brain." Chandler looked at him for a long time, squinting as if he saw John Horne not as a man but as a problem in formal logic. He said at last, as if tentatively, tilting his head, looking up at the top of the window,

> *O Rose, thou art sick; the invisible worm*
> *That flies in the night, on the howling storm. . . .*

Horne's eyes widened and he began to laugh raucously, like a creature deeply hurt. It was as if it were the poem that gave pain, and he laughed to drown it out. He stopped suddenly and nodded, beginning to weep. "Yes. Forgive me," he said. "God forgive me." He sobbed— a great, whooping noise—and Chandler winced.

After a moment Chandler asked suspiciously, "Do you really understand?"

"Oh I do! Yes, yes! I do!" He clutched his face in his hands.

"You insist on finalities," Chandler said, "—if not final salvation then final damnation, no mixture of judgments, no confusion of—"

"Say no more, I beg you!" Horne shouted, bending down, beating the table with his fist. "I understand!"

Chandler stood watching the incredible performance, wincing, unable to make out what he ought to do. At last, still uncertain, he withdrew, removing his glasses to polish them as he walked. At the door he startled three middle-aged ladies in bathrobes, who had obviously been listening with considerable interest and amusement. He took in their faces irritably, with a part of his mind: one was long and rectangular, with broken veins on the cheeks and nose; one was small and round and white; one was tipped back with obesity. They did not hide their leers from him; it was Horne they mocked from the heights of their virginal stupidity. Rage swept over him without warning. He turned back to the door of the library, his anger hammering in his chest. He shouted, "I wanted to *talk* to you, Horne." The great frog-face turned, gaping, bleary with self-pity, but Chandler turned away again and left him. His explosion left him shaken and frightened, and at the first chair he came to in the hallway he had to sit down.

11

WHETHER it was a memory or a dream, or the memory, perhaps, of a dream, he could not make out.

They were sitting on a high, green hill that fell away like a cliff toward the Pacific—Susan, Karen, Marie, himself, Wilma and Ken Roos. Marie was perhaps eight months pregnant with Anne. It was the time of some sort of vacation—semester break, probably—for the world was like a lowering animal, the grass and the stunted, windbattered trees gray-green, touched, on the seaward side, with a supernatural yellow, and the bare earth, where the sun hit it, was red as blood, and the sea and the sky were gray as lead in a mold. There were gulls, hundreds of thousands of them, caracoling over the water, below them, and screaming. When the lunch was finished, Susan and Karen danced away over the rim of the hill to look for treasures—pine cones, pretty rocks, some tough little winter blossom. Ken and Wilma and he fell into intense conversation about something or other; yes, now he had it: the show at the Legion of Honor. Ken was detached, amused, as always, sitting in the highest tower of his inexpugnable castle. "Introspective," he said. "The last gasp of Romanticism." He smiled, a smile that made one think of a minister at a baptism, or a dentist making x-rays. He was flatly wrong about the show, in Chandler's opinion. Wrong as he was about many things that demanded more than a reasonable response. (He remembered now, vaguely, huge obscene images by Rico LeBrun, corruption lifted to the full heroic—great manlike turtles, struggling upward against the weight of their own monumental deformity—in another room sculpture by Mallary, old clothes cast in bronze, in human poses but no figure inside—lifeless gestures of inextricable terror and joy. He, Chandler, had been wild with excitement, and Wilma Roos had said "Oh my God, my God!" and clutched her temples. Marie had simply smiled with pleasure, her hands resting in the pockets of her maternity smock; it was as if she had seen it all before and was perfectly at ease with it. She too was a grotesque, she knew—her face lean and dull with pregnancy, arms and legs thin, ankles large, her belly riding before her like the prow of a ship. And she too was a tangle of emotions: at once proud of herself and ashamed, joyful and full of dread. Chandler went over to her quickly, ashamed that for a time he had forgotten her vulnerability and had left her side. He hovered around her now like a sycophant without a function, as if eagerly hoping for the fall of a royal handkerchief. They were both aware of the ridiculous figure he cut beside her, and they reveled in their absurdity. But Ken Roos polished his glasses, Wilma's glove slipped through his arm, and with his head slightly cocked he considered the texture and composition of the rags cast in bronze.) Now out on the hillside, Wilma hugged herself, her head thrown forward—black hair neatly parted in the middle and brushed straight down, severe, eyes wide and full of nightmare, lips dry and slightly parted, as usual, as if pleading that Ken come kiss her again and hold her, reassure her. They were always kissing, as it seemed to Chandler. When you came out of a restaurant with them, they would drop back for a moment; when you went to the kitchen to fix them drinks she would cross to him at once; when you glanced into the rear-view mirror, saying, "There's Paoli's, the place we were telling you about," they would be clamped together. Chandler would feign extreme near-sightedness; Marie's reaction, usually, was to fan herself or clasp her hands and look heavenward for strength. Wilma's father was a psychologist. Wilma was saying, shuddering, "I couldn't *stand* many creations like that. It's all so *true*." Ken grinned and drew her hand to his lips, and Chandler labored over his pipe. Marie hand't said a word all afternoon—she seldom had much to say to the Rooses except when she felt like teasing them—but all at once she said, with enormous conviction: "This is much truer —whatever that may mean." All three of them looked at the same time, as if perfectly understanding her, at the miles of gray-green, dwarfish trees, the cliffs to the right, the ocean falling away to Japan, the wide storm of birds. What Chandler, at least, had seen that instant was Death, wheeling and howling, and two little girls in red coats running down the path toward them, laughing. Marie sat like the Buddha, her legs out like sticks, her red hands resting tranquilly on her enormous belly. Her face was full of light.

When Chandler awakened, sometime towards the middle of that night, there was someone standing at his window, beyond the uncomfortable chair where Marie slept. The back of his neck knew before his conscious mind made out who it was. The room was dark, but it was a starry night, and he could see the woman at the window very clearly. A slight woman with long white hair (her face was turned away from him), a gray shawl, a gray, old-fashioned dress that came to a little above her shoes. He knew at once that his mind must be playing some trick on him, that he was caught up in one of the favorite experiences of philosophers, the twilight impression of an animal sitting on the chair by one's desk, or the inkstain seen at dusk on one's table, which a moment from now will resolve itself into the form of one's sleeping cat. He himself had observed and recorded a hundred such experiences, had culled from the writing of others a hundred more, and had arranged them as well as possible into their proper classes, derived from Collingwood's *Philosophical Method:* false distinction, false disjunction, precarious margin. He knew that his eyes had made some mistake, that his mind had fallen—not by accident, of course—into a kind of rigidity, a refusal to shift to a new angle of vision, perhaps more accurate depth perception. He waited for the transformation, but it refused to come, and he remembered all at once a queer, essentially ridiculous experience that had frozen him to the bone one night in his undergraduate days. He'd been a counselor in the men's dorm, morals of freshmen and sophomores in the dorm. One that is, an upperclassman responsible for the manners and Friday night when he was studying down in the lobby, all alone in the dorm—or so he'd thought—he'd heard (or perhaps, just conceivably, had dreamed he'd heard) someone walking in the hallway upstairs, opening and closing the doors of the rooms one after another. He'd gone up, expecting to find some prankster, but there was no one. He'd looked carefully through all the rooms, but there was no mistake; there was nothing. He'd gone out to stand on the fire escape. There was no one in sight, and no way onto the roof. He'd stood thinking, rubbing his nose, and then, just to be on the safe side, he'd locked all the doors, including the john, with his master key. Then he'd gone downstairs again, dismissing the whole thing from his mind, and had settled down once more with his book. After a moment, as clearly as before, he heard— he was as sure of this as of anything on earth—footsteps in the hall upstairs, and one of the locked doors opened, then closed again. That was all. He had never managed to explain it, nor were there campus legends.

Coupled with the memory, the figure at the window filled his chest with panic. He closed his eyes, getting control of himself, and he reasoned calmly that when he opened his eyes again, if he opened them quickly and looked at once toward the window, his perception would get a fresh start, so to speak, and the figure he thought he saw standing there would snap into what it really was—a curtain, a tree outside, a shadow on the glass.

When he opened his eyes there was nothing. There was nothing, even, that could conceivably have suggested the apparition. And then, with a sudden flush of terror, he realized that the door of his room—firmly shut before, he was certain of it—was open. He turned his head quickly, and for just an instant he thought he saw her again, looking in at him with remote eyes and smiling; and then she was gone. Chandler got out of bed and crossed to the door to look out. The hallway was empty. He closed the door and snapped on the light. Marie continued to sleep.

He could not remember getting back into bed, but when he awakened the second time, he was lying as before, the room dark now. Marie was still asleep in the chair. He thought of waking her and even raised his hand, preparing to do it, but on second thought he decided to let her sleep. She'd get little enough rest, sitting up as she was, and today had been the day of the family trip to Letchworth. He knew without asking that something had happened, though nothing serious, finally. Otherwise she'd have talked about the outing. He wished he had a pencil—he'd somehow misplaced the one he'd been using earlier today. It was a habit with him, thinking on paper. He needed it as some men need their cigarettes, or as others need to pace. He closed his eyes.

It was all very well to say that all logic, all common sense must flatly deny the apparition's existence. But the senses were not easy to send packing. He wiped his forehead with the back of his hand, but his hand was as wet with perspiration as his forehead. He could describe her clothing in minute detail—the close-set buttons down the front, the wrinkles in her skirt, the faint discoloration on her sleeve—*mold?* he wondered in panic. She had smelled of newly turned earth, or old wet boards, the pungent scent of the fruit cellar in his grandmother's house, where he'd gone in the dark sometimes at night to steal a mason jar of canned peaches. There were rats there, and sometimes the pump would start up suddenly behind him, or a bat would explode into flight three inches from his groping hand.

He checked himself.

Very well, he had seemed to see the old woman clearly. No doubt he had imagined or perhaps dreamed her clearly. Which was to say—because the "unconscious" was a myth, a handy device for scientists, a latter-day phlogiston, a fancy description of ordinary selection and interpretation of experience, but more feeble than that in ordinary consciousness. . . . He paused, panicky again. He'd lost his place. Then it came back: Which was to say, then, that he himself had made her up. And the question, obviously, was Why? And the answer equally obvious: Because the mind could not take hold of the idea of dying. It was unthinkable, as unthinkable as the idea of total reality. And so his mind had constructed a symbol, so ambiguous as to be completely satisfying, a perfectly symmetrical paradox. Her return from the grave, a denial of the power of death; her seeming to come for him—or for Marie? Was that the dodge his mind had taken?—her seeming to come for someone, an acceptance of death's power. And so it was as simple as that. Again he wiped his forehead. His hand was dry and he knew that somewhere in the middle of a thought he had slept—perhaps for hours. He forced himself back to the problem. Understanding the monster he himself had created, he had now the power to destroy it. He was not mad, then, after all. Intelligence was still in control.

Marie's cigarettes lay on the dresser, her purse beside them. The matches would be in her purse. All this time in the hospital, even when he was working out on paper his outline of an aesthetic theory, he had not smoked; but now he needed to. Once again, quietly, he got out of bed. He had the cigarette lit and had carried the pack and matches over to the bed before he realized that there wasn't an ashtray. He went to look in the bathroom and realized when he got there that he needed to urinate. As he did, he began to feel faint and cold as ice all over. He leaned with both arms on the back of the toilet and compressed his lips. He leaned there for a long time after he'd finished; then, by an effort of will, he straightened up again and went back to his search. At first he couldn't remember what he'd been looking for, knew only that he was engaged in a desperate hunt for something. He needed to flick the ash from his cigarette and the thought of the ashtray returned. At last he removed the narrow top drawer of the dresser, slid it onto the bed, and crawled up after it. When he was under the covers again and propped half-sitting, half-lying on his pillows, he let himself relax completely. He hadn't felt so comfortable for months, he said to himself; but it was a lie, his nerves were ringing like telephone wire.

He lit a second cigarette from the first, crushed out the butt in the wooden drawer, and drew in deeply. *Had* he created her, really? Or had he drawn her there, perhaps,— or served as the passive means of her coming? The very fact that the idea was flatly ridiculous was a point in its favor, Chandler thought, his mind suddenly crafty as a witch in a tree. His own wish that she be imaginary and thus controllable established his powerful bias. It was admittedly true that, as Kant said— *Was it Kant?* He concentrated. *Kant.* All thought must begin with the assumption that the universe is available to us; that external reality is discoverable through reason and the senses; and admittedly it followed from that—as Chandler himself had argued in "Am I Now Dreaming?"—or somewhere— somewhere—that probability was sufficient to test the validity of . . . something. But suppose the assumption were false? What did it matter now that his psychological account was consistent and convincing? What he had to know was, Was it *true*? If not, a new question reared its head: What did her coming mean—if anything?

His mind shied away from it to a sharply recollected image of the old woman standing at the window. Was it possible that he actually had struggled with her on the roof of the porch? Was the rest true too, then? Had she come, somehow, to destroy his wife and children? He tried to remember clearly the dreams that had come to him at his mother's, but they were gone from his mind completely; he knew only that they had seemed convincing, at least while he slept. Why hadn't he written them down? Oh, foolish! Foolish! Suddenly, without the slightest warning, he began to weep, covering his face with his hands, sobbing in perfect silence.

Again Chandler caught himself. It was absurd, letting himself go this way. Once and for all, he would put it out of his mind.

He called out softly, "Marie!"

She was up at once and coming toward his bed, swimming against the darkness, not yet fully awake. "What is it?" she asked in a frightened voice, shaking her head, trying to drive out sleep. "What's wrong, James?"

"Listen, Marie. I want you to go home and stay with the children." Again he was crying.

"You what?"

"Stay in their room with them."

She studied his face, her lips pursed, her eyes a little widened with alarm. "James, you're being irrational," she said too quietly, as though she were only half sure of it. "I should be here with you. It's the middle of the night."

"Just go," he said. "Don't argue."

She drew back her hand, and he knew that she too was afraid. He wondered fleetingly what it was that had happened today at Letchworth. She said, "It's—crazy."

"I don't know," he said.

She looked at him a moment longer, her face white. Then, snatching her purse from the side of the bed, she left.

12

IN the morning when his wife returned, Chandler was ready to meet her. He had slept hardly at all, as far as he knew, since sending her away. He knew very well that, at least in theory, reason—especially *his* reason—might not be sufficient to deal with the lunatic questions raised by the old woman's coming; but reason was the only weapon he had: Even if it was the case that he was mad, the blood in his brain too thin for its proper function, perhaps, or white cells clotting some crucial passage, it was nevertheless a fact that logic, philosophical method, was the only road open to him. And so he'd considered carefully every possibility that would come to his mind, fighting all the while to hang onto strict objectivity—not to mention consciousness—examine every theory for the bias behind it, suspicious of every turn in his thought, more skeptical than he'd ever been before, even in his most painstaking investigations, for if thought was a game, now as always, the search for the center of a labyrinth that for all he knew might have no center, it was a game this time for higher stakes than usual: It was not a case this time—for Chandler, at least—of developing a thoroughly credible theory, but a question of decision where dispute remained after all the evidence was in.

He had seen (he squinted as he thought) or perhaps he had imagined he'd seen, an old woman standing at his window. He'd perceived, very soon after that, that she was either real or imaginary. And he saw that the grounds which most strongly supported the idea that she was unreal, namely, his characteristically human mode of apprehension, equally supported the hypothesis that she was real: For the world mankind has hacked out of chaos—all science, art, religion, and indeed civilization itself—depends for its existence on the basic limiting principles: that no effect can precede its cause, that effects must be physically related to causes, that cause and effect if separated in space must also be separated in time, and that mind cannot operate independent of brain. That the basic limiting principles should not be absolute is a proposition unthinkable for civilization (so Chandler reasoned), but unthinkable not because demonstrably untrue; unthinkable because useless and, moreover, threatening, tending toward the annihilation of all the work of the human spirit. He remembered vaguely, and with more emotion than he could comfortably explain, Bergson's remarks on telepathy, a thing analogous, Bergson suggested, to the phenomena of endosmosis. "If such endosmosis exists," Bergson had written (Chandler recalled only the general sense of the argument), "we can foresee that nature will have taken every precaution to neutralize its effect, and that certain mechanisms must be specially charged with the duty of throwing back into the unconscious the presentations so provoked, for they would be very embarrassing in everyday life. One or another of these presentations might yet, however, at times pass through as contraband, especially if the inhibiting mechanisms were functioning badly." C. J. Ducasse had gone even further, Chandler remembered with a jolt. (Once for some reason he'd missed Ducasse. He couldn't remember the reason now.) According to Ducasse, three of the basic limiting principles were no longer absolute even for modern physics, and he suggested a "physical" interpretation—the energy of sub-sub-atoms—of what Rhine had reverently handed over to God. It was true that Rhine's statistics for ESP were not overwhelming evidence that ESP really occurred. It might be the science of probability that was at fault. But it was true, too, that Mesmer's demonstrations of animal magnetism had quite often failed, and that the

Académie des Sciences had come out and had stood for a hundred years against him.

For hours, off and on, Chandler battled with the question in his mind, knowing all along that there could be no answer—no answer even if he had at hand the books he desperately wished he had—Bergson, Ducasse, Rhine, C. D. Broad, Soal and Bateman, even Joseph Glanvill or Increase Mather. Or there could be no answer, at least, until he was willing to make the leap into one assumption or the other. He was sweating so badly that his nightshirt was pasted to his skin, and when he noticed it, he laughed all at once, seeing with perfect clarity how comic he was—Professor Quixote with a vengeance!—but even that did not release him. The plain truth was that he simply couldn't shake the idea that she was real, the idea he hadn't quite admitted to himself when he'd found himself scratched up after his dream of the struggle on the porch, and hadn't admitted even when, on an irresistible impulse, he'd gone up into the Staley porch.

Suppose she *was* real, he thought (minutes later), for at least he might follow the two hypotheses out to their conclusions. If she was, and if her coming had any human meaning, it was only from the old woman herself, if from anything, that he could learn what that meaning was. It was a frightening step, but a logically necessary one: The next time she came, if she came again, he would seize her, if that was possible; try to talk to her. In his mind there rose an image of great, dark oak trees hung with moss, a circle of stones, a low flat platform of rock in the center, with runes chiseled into the platform's sides. He felt his fear draining out of him; it was as though he'd escaped the imprisoning vulnerability of flesh and had become the trees, the raised stones, the heaviness of the night. There he would wait. He slept.

But he couldn't, it came to him then. At once he was as wide awake as a child. There was no way of ruling out the possibility that he was mad. There could be no harm, except possibly to himself, in seizing her if she was entirely imaginary; but suppose she were a distortion of reality: Suppose she were Marie, for instance, or one of the nurses, turned monstrous by a trick of diseased consciousness. His physical condition gave *prima-facie* weight to the madness hypothesis. He had terrified Marie already. That was enough. The memory of the fear he'd communicated to her stood quite as vivid in his mind as the memory of the figure at the window.

He couldn't even tell her, he thought then—couldn't conceivably warn her about his possible madness so that she too could be on guard. For that course was based on the madness hypothesis, and inevitably it would be his madness that she feared, not the thing itself, if the thing were real. And if he were not mad, it seemed to him, exciting her fear that he might be would be pointless and brutal. There was nothing for him to do, then, but watch over the children himself, behave as though everything were normal, keep them all as secure and happy as he could, and watch: not the Druid seizing the secrets of the world by the throat but the Druid of a later age, the watcher of the forest. Again he slept, and again he awakened with a start, his mind once more turning on itself like poison sumac.

How could he know, accepting the madness hypothesis, that he wasn't potentially dangerous? Then he thought: *But under either hypothesis, one thing is certain: It's to me that she comes. If I were dead—*

So it was that Chandler came in feverish thought to the common wall, the fundamental paradox of consciousness, namely, that the very existence of a nonomnipotent, nonomniscient being is a potential threat to life. He saw with a shock what he had known abstractly for years, that the ultimate proof of love is premeditated self-destruction—the ultimate betrayal of love. And from that wall Chandler shrank back in confusion.

The night was suddenly quiet. He remembered standing with his father on the roof of the shop. He could look over the edge of the flat roof and down the gray, dingy wall of the building at small figures on the sidewalk below, or he could look to the left or right at the tops of trees, and seeing them from this new perspective was as frightening to him as looking down. He could see Mr. Cooper coming up through the skylight next door, that roof lower than this one, and beyond Mr. Cooper's roof other roofs, a clutter of things not meant to be seen—black vents, pigeon droppings, rough, discolored old chimneys —and far, far in the distance the spire of St. Joseph's Church. There was a heavy, supernatural smell in the air, and huge black clouds—great, tumbling, shifting mountains—were sliding towards them from the west. It was flood season; the Tonawanda was already far over its banks, and the Creek Road, south of Batavia, leading out to his grandfather's place, was under water for miles. In the sky—it was this that they'd come up to see—there were birds, hundreds of thousands of them: hawks, starlings, sparrows.

Clinging tightly to his father's hand, he had said, "What does it *mean?*"

His father had said, still looking up, his mind busy with other thoughts, perhaps, unaware that it was required of him that he speak with oracular certainty: "I don't know, Jimmy."

The words had struck terror into his heart.

He thought now: *And so when Marie comes back in the morning there's nothing I can say or do. Trust to the seven (seven? is that right?—the nine, perhaps) legions of angels*. There came into his mind a jingle that Marie had made up one night at a party:

> *The lizard is a timid thing*
> *That cannot dance, or fly, or sing;*
> *He hunts for lunch beneath the floor*
> *And longs to be a dinosaur.*

He half-smiled, half-winced, trying to think what had brought it to mind. He thought then briefly, for some reason, of Ken and Wilma Roos; and then he thought of walking on Market Street on New Year's morning, in the rain. He remembered Horne's asking him: *Are you religious, Mr. Chandler?* and he said in his mind, *Oh yes,*

quite religious. Also staunch Republican. And Mason.
Definitely believe in believing, at this time. Disbelief be-
ing, like belief (in my present opinion), a word-game.

He'd solved his problem, though—or solved it insofar as
it admitted of solution—and now he could sleep. He was
sure that this time he wouldn't be troubled by nightmares,
for he'd faced up at last to his dilemma; he'd thrown away
his cape and had opened his arms to the thing, prepared
to receive it in courtesy and peace, and surely the dilemma had no course, as a feeling creature, but to bow, ac-
knowledging its triumph, and retire like gentle Ferdinand
to the flowers at the edge of the ring. About this, however, Chandler was wrong. The moment he relaxed, his
nightmares were back, as threatening as ever, allowing
him only one consolation, the knowledge that they were
mere dreams. He could change them by turning onto his
side, but there was nothing he could do to check their in-
vasion.

. . .

When Chandler awakened in the morning, the world
was shiny from rain in the night. He got up and went
over to his window, opened it a little, and breathed in
deeply. There lay before and around and within him a
hundred different shades of green, a hundred different
birdsongs, a thousand-thousand distinct, familiar shapes.
One could understand, at moments like this, the great
Romantic flight to Nature—the concern his mother and
father had felt, and his mother felt still, if only from
habit, with temperature and wind direction, or the concern that had sent two hundred years of painters like
Aunt Emma scurrying to the trees.—Except, it came to
him, that Aunt Emma's paintings had nothing to do with
that. And then he knew all at once what it was in Aunt
Emma's paintings, crude as they were, that gave one that
sense of sudden release, unexpected joy, that one experienced in the presence of true works of art. And what was
more, Chandler saw then, his heart tripping rapidly and
lightly, with that one insight the whole aesthetic theory
fell into place. She painted the soul's sublime acceptance

of lawless, proliferating substance: things and their motions.

> A. A violent order is disorder; and
> B. A great disorder is an order. These
> two things are one. (Pages of illustrations.)

He obtained a pencil from Miss Sundown, and when Marie arrived he was chin-deep in papers. On the first page he'd written that morning, he had set down with an enfeebled flourish: *Time, Space, and Affirmation: Notes Toward an Aesthetic Theory.*

Marie said, after some preliminary fencing, "What was it that frightened you last night?"

"Nightmare," he said. "Terrible things, nightmares." He went on writing.

She studied him, dubious, apparently somewhat annoyed at his dismissing the thing so lightly.

"It's this bed," he said. "But I've figured out the cure. Today we go home. Anyway, I need my typewriter."

Her eyes widened, but he meant it. When his lunch came, Chandler was dressed and—despite an ominous touch of nausea—jubilant, sitting in his wheelchair ready to leave.

PART THREE

1

SHE had not stayed for his homecoming. She had meant to. She had been nearly as excited as the girls, in fact. But at the last moment she had changed her mind and fled. Her thought shied away from the reason, but each time she half-remembered what James Chandler would by now know—surely his wife would have spoken of it—a thing he would perhaps understand more clearly than Viola did herself, a feeling of shame and confusion came over her, so stifling she thought she might faint.

The day at Letchworth had been cold and dismal. The sky was bright blue, but there were huge clouds hurrying overhead, moving so fast that the earth under her feet seemed unsteady, and the air smelled more of winter than of spring. She had ridden to the park in the back seat of the car, with the children. The three girls had been happy and noisy, crying out in delight or pointing to every country windmill or wooded ridge or sagging, old-fashioned barn. She had never seen country more beautiful—the steep drop down the great, wooded hill into the peaceful, white little town of Wyoming, wooden bridges, long rows of gleaming milkcans in front of enormous red barns, beyond the barns the new-plowed valley, broken by panes of yellow-green spring wheat, in the center of the valley the silver brook, willow trees lining its banks like golden umbrellas. At first she had joined eagerly in the children's chatter. But from the front seat where Mr. Chandler's wife and mother sat there came no sound, and their silence began to weigh on her: Their sullenness was somehow her fault. She knew she had done nothing to make them cross, but her knowledge was no help to her. Little by little she grew angry and sullen herself.

Marie drove too fast, as if purposely to frighten and annoy her. She sat rigid—motionless except for her arm and the blowing wisps of hair at her neck and ears—watching the road as if in a trance. She swung wide on the corners, holding the speedometer at seventy, not slowing even when a tractor and wagon pulled out on the road a quarter-mile ahead of her, but for all that she moved the steering wheel with deadly efficiency. As they shot down the straight flat stretch approaching the town of Castile the car hit a pheasant. Viola's heart jerked, hearing the thud, feeling in her blood the otherwise imperceptible bump, but the car shot on as though Marie had not noticed.

When they got to the park it was virtually deserted. The car plunged down the steep and twisting tree-lined road along the gorge, and still neither of the women in the front seat spoke. The children's talk was irritable now. Susan wanted to know how much longer they had to ride, Anne insisted on climbing around in the crowded seat, and Karen snapped at them and, once, gave Susan a furtive pinch. Susan howled, and Viola said, "Susan! See how far down the river is!" Marie glanced over her shoulder angrily, and Viola would have sworn it was not at Susan she was angry but at *her*.

Somewhere in deep woods—a little beyond the huge, garrish yellow inn—the gorge yawning away to their right, to their left black trees and mounds of unmelted, dirty snow—Marie slowed down abruptly and turned onto what looked like no more than a paved path climbing sharply into the woods. At the end of the road there were old log cabins and a statue and, surrounding it all, what looked like a graveyard fence. It was cold here, and damp. Evergreens and maples and birches with chalk-white trunks scarred with black stood on all sides of the little clearing where the cabins were, and their branches, interlocking overhead, strained the sunlight and filled the sky with scratches.

"Where are we, Mother?" Karen said. But Mrs. Chandler only said, as if gaily, "Everybody out!"

There was not a bird or a squirrel in sight, not so much as a distant whistle, but as if from all sides came the unbroken roar of a waterfall, and riding that sound, lightly, like white froth riding churning water, the rustling of leaves and the ratlike squeak of branches. Karen slid out and took Anne from Viola's lap. When Viola and Susan were out too, she and the girls took hands as if to stand together against the darkness of the trees, the earth, the ancient, crumbling cabins.

"These are Indian cabins," Marie said. She reminded Viola of the nursery-school teacher she'd had a long time ago: a voice honeyed and dangerous.

"Are there Indians in them?" Susan asked.

Here even the softest voice stood out like a cut on smooth white skin, isolated and alien, and Viola shuddered. "The Indians are all dead," she said. Marie glanced at her.

"These are cabins where Indians used to live a long time ago," Marie said, her voice still sweeter, honey in an iron jar. She bent down, resting her hands on her knees, and looked with them toward the cabins. "A long time ago, before there were any white men here, the Indians used to live all over New York State. They had beautiful cities a little like medieval castles, with walls around them, and inside the cities there were houses and places like churches, and even stores. There were stores for baskets and stores for jewelry; and down the street a little there would be a store for dishes and things. They had their fields outside the city. Every night they would come in from the fields and be with their children, and then in the morning they would go out again to grow their corn and wheat and vegetables. They had doctors, too, and some of the things they used to do are still too hard for us to understand. The Senecas taught us how to cure malaria. You know what that is. They even had a kind of writing. There were very few Indian tribes that had that."

She loved the Indians, it came to Viola. She actually loved them. She thought: *I wonder if she ever saw one.*

"Is all that true?" Viola said.

Marie smiled, casual, and she spoke as if without a trace of indignation. "Why of course it is."

They looked through the wired-up windows of the cabins, but inside it was pitch dark and all they could see was the windows on the other side. Beyond the windows, dark leaves stirred rhythmically, back and forth, nodding, pausing for an instant, nodding again, gesturing without meaning, like Aunt Emma.

"Did someone live here?" Karen asked softly.

Marie said, "This was a longhouse. This was where they had their meetings and worshiped God."

"They believed in God, too?" Viola asked, wry.

"Of course," Marie said. And then: "Come see the statue of Mary Jemisen."

They stood near the iron fence around the statue. Old Mrs. Chandler read them what it said on the pedestal, or pretended to. She knew it by memory. They had come here often, then, Viola thought. Why was it so attractive to them? The place was morbid. Death lay over it like fog. Perhaps it was true, all Marie had said, that they had beautiful cities with fields all around them, a beautiful civilization with writing and medicine and religion. How horrible, then, these rotting log cabins, this harsh green figure of a white girl who'd been turned into an Indian— or no, worse, turned into dirty bronze, streaked and stained by a thousand rainstorms, bird droppings on her shoulders and on the dead bronze head of her papoose! The place repelled her and at the same time drew her toward it like a chasm. She bit her lip lightly, watching the children and carefully not listening to what Marie was saying; and yet she heard it all.

"The Senecas were farm people, not fighters. But when the white men took away their land they were very angry, and they struck back as angry people always do—much more fiercely than their enemies dreamed they would. They would come at night and burn up the houses of the people who settled on their land, and they would kill people and torture them in terrible ways."

"How?" Karen said.

"In terrible ways," Marie said. "And then one day they came to the Jemisens, and they killed them and took one child away as a captive—a yellow-haired girl named Mary. She grew up with them, and she learned to understand why they were so angry and why they behaved like wild animals, and she loved them."

"What happened to her?" Viola asked darkly.

Marie paused, thinking—turning over not the question itself but the tone of it, Viola guessed. She said: "She had two Indian sons. One of them murdered the other and ran away. She never saw him again."

"Horrible!" Viola whispered.

Marie seemed to think about it, undecided.

Now Annie was wandering back toward the longhouse. Viola wheeled and followed her, grateful to escape the blind gaze of the white Indian. But the longhouse was no better, empty and dead for a century, scarred by a thousand initials, telephone numbers, dirty words.

Anne said, looking up at her with what seemed only the faintest hope, "Ammie want yunch."

She patted the child's head, smiling grimly, thinking of the picnic tables down by the gorge where it was warm and there would be sunlight. "I'll see what I can do."

To her amazement she found that Marie was planning to spread the picnic lunch right here, in the grassy place between the log cabins.

"Why?" Viola said. "I mean, there are wonderful picnic grounds down by the gorge. I don't think you're *supposed* to have picnics up here."

Marie and old Mrs. Chandler exchanged glances and Viola flushed. She lashed out, "Well, what's *wrong* with the regular picnic grounds? There are railings, you know. And there are three of us—four of us counting Karen." Her heartbeat quickened. "Do I look like I'm going to push somebody over?"

Marie started. "Well for heaven's *sake*, Viola! I never said——"

"I'm sorry," Viola said. Her panic seemed to make the clearing grow brighter, every line sharper. She was amazed at herself.

"Maybe you're right," Marie said. "It's probably against the rules to eat up here." She looked at Viola, troubled. "I didn't mean to jump on you like that, Viola."

"It's all right. It was my fault."

Marie met her eyes a moment, then smiled, pretending to dismiss it. She turned to the others. "Everybody back in the car."

While the two Mrs. Chandlers spread a cloth over the shale table, Viola walked over to the railing and looked down. Three feet beyond the wooden rail at the edge of the path the earth dropped away, straight down for hundreds of feet to the boulder-littered floor of the gorge and the narrow ribbon of turbulent water, the Genesee. Across the gorge—the far side was lower than this side, and warm with sunlight—she saw miles of rolling hills, heavily wooded in places, in other places prairielike, all of it wild. There would be deer there, and foxes. Perhaps once it had been the farmland of a Seneca village. The thought of people who had been dead for a century coming out to work their fields filled her with restlessness. She looked away. Up the gorge to her right, far, far below her, was a double waterfall and, farther away, a railroad trestle, complex and delicate as a spider web stretched between the two cliffs. There were birds flying, down in the gorge. Swallows perhaps, for they moved very swiftly. Directly below her, broken on the boulders, lay the body of a deer. "Look!" she called back to the others.

"What is it?" Karen called. She dropped the silverware to the table and ran over. Viola put her arm around her protectively. The same instant, Marie's voice rang out: "Karen, come back here! Susan! Stay here!"

Karen moaned, Susan whining behind her, then turned back toward the table.

"It really is all right, Mrs. Chandler," Viola said. But she knew that for some reason it was not. She started back toward the table herself, slowly, frowning, trying to make out what it was that was escaping her. At the table, Marie was slicing the bread old Mrs. Chandler had made. Viola said, "I can take care of them, Mrs. Chandler."

The motion of Marie's knife stopped, then quickly

started up again. The slice dropped away to the table-cloth and lay still.

"It's better if we all look together," Marie said.

A trembling came over Viola's lips, and her whole body was charged, all at once, with meaningless anguish. Looking at Marie, she felt now—overwhelmingly—her separateness from her and all the family. A gulf yawned between them, wider and more terrible than the Letchworth gorge. The very fact of Marie's existence—not even her eyes, for she did not look up—had turned Viola into a stone, or some grotesque, bare tree, or a word carved into a log. She saw herself as Marie Chandler would be seeing her now in her mind, flat-lipped, stoop-shouldered, foreign. As if defensively, she stared at the stringy wisp of hair hanging down in front of Marie's ear, the bluish white of the wing of her nose. At the slot of her collarbone Marie's skin was red and wrinkled. She was old. Viola had never seen the woman so distinctly before. She was repelled, but it was not hatred she felt. She could no more hate the woman than hate a twig. When she turned her head to look at the others, she saw that they too were transformed to clarity. Every feature stood isolated, every pointless, familiar gesture—Karen's prissy lift of the chin, Susan's pout, Anne's intense concentration on taking a leaf apart—filled her with disgust. She said, "I wanted to show them something."

"Oh?" Marie said, polite.

"Come see," Viola said suddenly.

Marie cut off one more slice of bread, then put down the knife. "What is it?" she said.

"Come and see."

They walked side by side to the rail, the old woman looking after them. Marie rested her hands lightly on the wood and looked down.

"It's a dead deer," Viola said.

"How *awful!*" She remained bent forward, looking.

Leaning over beside her, Viola slipped her hand to the small of Marie's back. Her hand rang as it touched the cloth of the woman's jacket, and a dizziness came over her. It seemed to her that Marie shrank, or hardened, perhaps, at her touch, but Viola's own emotions were in such a turmoil she couldn't be sure. For an instant she believed she was actually falling, desperately clinging to Marie and drawing her with her toward the boulders like bits of sand far, far below. But the next instant she was leaning as before, safe.

"Poor thing," Viola said, withdrawing her hand. "How could such a thing happen—to a *deer?*"

Marie said nothing.

Viola said, laughing abruptly, "You're right, this *is* no place for children!"

All of them talked as they ate their lunch, and sometimes they would burst into laughter for almost no reason. They went to St. Helena after that, where a town had been once, now gone without leaving a trace. And then they stood behind Glen Iris Inn, overlooking the waterfall, and an old friend of Mrs. Chandler's told them of the Indian Joninedah—a strange story that filled Viola with feelings she could not tell whether or not she liked. The sensation of standing at the railing with Marie was still in her body—would perhaps be with her, at odd moments, as long as she lived.

And then they were standing in the garden behind Mrs. Chandler's house, the sky red as fire, whippoorwills singing in the grove beyond the garden, Marie Chandler facing her in the near dark. Marie was meeting her eyes directly, studying her, perhaps weighing whether or not to confront her with something. Viola felt like a child before a teacher. Marie said abruptly, "What were you thinking, Viola?"

"Thinking?"

She shrugged as though it were really too trifling to pursue. "When we were looking at the deer. What was in your mind?"

"Nothing. Why?"

She shrugged again, turning her face away a little but still watching her. "No reason," she said. "It's just—" After a moment: "I was afraid."

"It was a long way down, all right," Viola said with a little laugh.

Marie turned to face her squarely again, cross. "I was afraid of *you*, Viola."

Viola's heart caught. "What?" she said. And then loudly, violently: *"What?"* Then it was as if she'd been struck by lightning: She felt herself swelling like an adder, poison boiling in her blood. "You *monster!*" she hissed. *"You bitch!"* She was so angry she couldn't breathe. She howled, her whole body gone out of control, and she began to rock back and forth, sobbing, her hands clinging to her face.

"I'm sorry," Marie said, and without conviction: "I see I was wrong."

"She's sorry!" Viola brought out. "My God! My *God!*"

"You must remember what we're going through," she said. The words threw all the guilt on Viola: a bitter injustice—vicious! *vicious!*—but unanswerable. "Christ!" Viola whispered.

Marie said again, "I'm sorry." She turned with a jerk and marched back to the house.

But really, of course, it had been nothing more than a misunderstanding, Viola had realized later. The truth was, they'd both been upset. It was nothing more than that. She too must apologize; then everything would be the same as ever. Nevertheless, she had not wanted to be there when Mr. Chandler came home from the hospital, for fear he'd heard of it.

2

JOHN HORNE leaped to his feet in alarm, snatched his hat from the magazine table beside his chair, and rushed out into the hall. "Ah! Chandler!" he said. The wheelchair stopped at the head of the ramp leading down into the hospital drive, and both Chandler and his wife turned their heads. Chandler had on street clothes, a paper bag and a book in his lap. "You're leaving us?" Horne said. He smiled fiercely, and his hand jerked to his coat pocket for cigarette papers and tobacco.

Chandler nodded, remote. "So it seems."

"You shouldn't," Horne said. Then quickly, because he'd blurted it out, "There was a great deal I needed to talk to you about." He spilled tobacco on the floor. "We've hardly exchanged two words," he said. There were tears in his eyes and he had to compress his lips tightly to keep from breaking down altogether. He tried a laugh, goatish and terrible, but seeing Chandler's tired frown he let it pass. "*Exchanged* is hardly the word, I admit it. Ha. But you understand me." The cigarette slipped from his fingers and he bent down hurriedly to scoop it up, then on second thought bent again to brush the scattered bits of tobacco into a small neat pile beside the wall. "You *do* understand me," he said angrily, laughing. "You see through me completely! It's obvious to you (without my stupidly pointing it out) that an exchange—a mercantile term, alas—was what I hoped for. And you know the value of such things—the 'coin' as it were—unlike the common herd. Not the *friendship* in it (ugliest and most debased of words, as Nietzsche tells us) but the insight, the 'shock of understanding,' as someone has said, the fire of good minds in a single pursuit—" He shattered into laughter like hail. Chandler was not meeting his eyes, and Horne tried to hurry. Drops of sweat ran down his sides, inside the nightshirt. "There it is, alas—my character always rising in the way! Ego! Yes! Cruelest of tyrants! But so it goes. There are chatterers and listeners, eh? But of course that isn't the point I intended—" He wiped his forehead, shaking violently. He said, "Betrayed."

"I'm sorry," Chandler said.

He sucked at the cigarette, powerfully moved by the word *betrayed,* and he glanced at Chandler's wife to make sure she showed no signs of breaking in where she had no business. She was glaring at him, her lips parted, and the sight of her uncovered rodent's teeth was revolting. Let the woman think what she liked. Chandler understood what he was saying. Oh, one could see how strange it must sound to *her* kind, this talk.

He imagined himself bending down to Chandler's ear, hissing, "We're dying, Chandler, you and I. And we have the sublime good fortune to know it! This is no time for foolishness, sentimental waste! Our minds are at their keenest pitch. Think of it, sir!"

But there she stood, his idiot guardian, and so Chandler would say, "I'm sorry, Horne," and this time there would be brutal finality in it, as if Chandler had reached down and cut the rope, letting Horne drop free, abandoned to his endless fall.

Chandler's wife made a move to start down the ramp with the wheelchair.

He thought of exclaiming, "Stop!" running around in front of the chair; thought of saying, "I've been lying. I admit it! I need you, you don't need me. Nothing to do with the pitch of the mind, Mr. Chandler. Have mercy on me!" He imagined himself sobbing, unable to stop. Only Chandler's hand was visible, on the wheelchair arm, very still, riding away. His wife walked with great dignity behind him, like a new usher, staring straight ahead.

"You condemn me, then," Horne thought. It was like a howl, inside his head, though from without he seemed more or less calm, fat, stooped, frowning like a maculate old ram.

"Nonsense," Chandler's voice said.

Horne covered his face with his fists. A nurse put her hand on his shoulder—he knew their touch and scent without looking. "We'd better get back to our room."

But he'd spoken the truth. James Chandler would know that, at least. However Chandler spent his last few days, they would all survive, would remember him kindly; what he did for them made no difference. But John Horne would not survive. The last few days would have made all the difference in the world. And so Chandler had betrayed him, and Chandler knew it. The herd would say it was because James Chandler did not like him. That would excuse it, for the herd. But Chandler knew better! He was still weeping. His teeth hurt from his grinding them together, and his fists were clenched inside the pockets of his coat.

The elevator stood empty, and Horne stepped in. He pressed the button that would take him to his refuge in the basement. The doors hummed shut.

For it was not a question of liking, but one of sacrifice. His claim was clear and just, a need more desperate than the needs of the others, and Chandler had rejected it for nobody's sake but his own. He said aloud, angrily, pretending Chandler was standing beside him, "Concupiscence, Chandler! A grand old concept, and one more relevant to modern affairs than *some* people may believe!" Chandler caught the irony all right. ". . . The desire for the things of this world, rooted in Pride in the old sense, a greater concern with one's own private welfare than with the welfare of the whole. Lack of Charity. You, my friend, *you*, Mr. Chandler—"

The elevator stopped and Horne stepped out, biting his lips together. He stood wiping his eyes and looking around the dim brick hallway. Old operating tables lined the far wall. He turned right, watching carefully for intruders. He was alone. At the blue door near the end of the hallway he paused and bent forward to listen. He heard nothing. No light showed at the crack under the door. When he tried the knob, the door opened and Horne stepped in quickly, closing the door behind him, and stood in darkness.

"In a word, Mr. Chandler, you have no charity." The word *charity* had the same deep effect upon him as the word *betrayed*, and his weeping started again. When it was over for the moment, he felt in his pockets for his matches. He moved forward carefully—he could now make out dim shapes—until he came to the first of the long rows of shelves on which x-rays were stored. He reached to his left and found by touch one of the manila x-ray packets, tore a strip of paper from it, and held a match to the paper. The flame gave him light enough to get to the lightswitch halfway down the first aisle. He switched it on—it turned on only the four bulbs just beyond where he stood—and settled the position of the switch four aisles over, then turned the first one off. He hurried to the further switch, groped for it, and switched that one on. He stood motionless and wide eyed, listening like a fat old spy. He knew exactly where his own packet was and went to it at once. He carried his packet to the far end of the aisle and, breathing heavily, squatted down close to the wall.

"I will tell you the truth, Mr. Chandler," he whispered. (Mice skittered across the floor somewhere behind him, but Horne was used to that.) He raised an index finger and shook it, preparing to speak, but he frowned and let his hand drop. He could think of nothing to say that would fit the gesture. "Look," he said then, seriously. He drew out the first of the photographs and held it to the light. They leaned their heads together soberly, studying the x-ray, though neither of them knew what it might mean. Horne pointed out the shadowy places the doctor had pointed out to him.

"It looks a little like a photograph of the moon," Chandler said.

"Yes it does," Horne said very thoughtfully, touching his chin and moving his elbow cautiously toward Chandler. "I'd noticed that myself. The inside of the moon or the outside?"

Chandler bent closer, squinting.

3

ROSE CHANDLER sits at her dining-room table, resting a moment before plunging into the million and one things she has to do. James will be home this afternoon. Outside her slightly opened window it is a warm day, yellow and green, full of voices and movement and pleasant smells. She hears the children laughing with Viola in the yard. St. Joseph's Drum and Bugle Corps is playing, some six or seven blocks away, probably in the yard of the church, and the thought of their red shirts and white suspenders comes into her mind.

(There were twenty-three drum and bugle corps gathered at Woodward Field, and George had brought the movie camera he'd made from instructions in one of the *Popular Mechanics* he had in the den—and in the spare bedroom, the attic, the bathroom, the cellar. It was a bright, hot day, so bright they had to squint a little in all that color—the dazzle of the grass and sky, the white of the bleachers, the reds, blues, yellows, oranges, greens of flags and bunting and the uniforms the corpsmen wore, the gold and silver of bugles and batons. The rattle of their drums came from everywhere at once, like a noise of machine guns, and the music the bugles made had a silver buzz in it that ran like an electric current along the bleachers. Jimmy wanted to go home, but George was excited. "Be still," he said, and Jimmy began to cry. He put his thick-lensed child's glasses beside him on the bleacher and covered his eyes with the heels of his hands, and George said, "You lose those glasses, young man, and your troubles will have begun." "His troubles have already begun," she snapped, and she put the glasses in her purse. Jimmy was still crying. The marching went on for hours, the unearthly racket of the blazing corps going back and forth like enormous wind-up toys, stepping through intricate, confusing maneuvers that made her head ache. But that night, at home in their cramped little living room, George had shown the movies he'd made, and in the silence and darkness, watching them jerk slowly across the screen, Jimmy had laughed with delight and had clapped his hands. *I don't regret it,* she thought. *Praise God, there's nothing I regret.* There were things she would change, but nothing she regretted.)

I was going to get the piano tuned, she thinks. *I had it on my list.*

It had belonged to her Uncle John, or, rather, to Uncle John's wife Kate. A small, red-headed Welshwoman who would sit very prim on the long, glossy bench, her wrists raised high above the keys, her eyes as blue as the water of a Catskill Mountains lake. They had no children. She would play, and Uncle John would sit with his hands clasped on his enormous belly, white hair growing out of his nostrils and ears, and he would rock slowly with his eyes closed, thinking about Black River, perhaps, or about the waterfall near his father's house back in Wales. Sometimes all the uncles would be there—Uncle Charley, Uncle James, Uncle Ed, the two Uncle Hughs, Uncle Griff— their wives beside them—and they would all sit there old-fashioned and formal, with their eyes closed or staring into space, like people posing for one of those black and white engravings one never sees anymore. Sometimes they would sing. After the music the women would go into the kitchen again and the men would go out on the porch to watch the last of the red fade out of the sky, Uncle John's mill going blacker and blacker against the night, yellow lights going on in window after window the length of Remsen— Jack, they called it—and in farmhouses up on the hills beyond, and one would hear the men's voices from one place, the women's from another, talking quietly in Welsh, laughing sometimes, like the music of the little falls across the road, below the blacksmith's. When she died he'd closed off that part of the house, or at any rate had never used it any more: had hired a woman to keep it dusted and cleaned—the great soft carpet, the huge old chairs, the lamps, the pictures in their oak-leafed frames, the table where once Uncle John and Aunt Kate had played dominoes, the piano. When James was four he'd gone in there to play it, and they'd all been surprised at how sweet it still sounded after all these years, though James was not really playing music, merely random notes, clusters that were only occasionally and accidentally chords (his owlish face in a half-smile, half-wince of careful attention, prepared to laugh at any moment over some ingenious remark from inside the piano). Two weeks later, when they were back in Batavia, a truck had come, and there the piano was, and on the music rack a note, unsigned, as though it were not from Uncle John at all but a gift handed down through a gap in time from Aunt Kate. But now they too were dead and gone: Uncle John, Uncle Charley, Uncle James, Uncle Ed, the two Uncle Hughs, Uncle Griff, and all their wives. And the mill was gone, and the blacksmith shop and the big old frame houses and the cobblestone streets; even the waterfall was gone. Nothing left but the yellow pictures in the album, a yellow tablet or two upstairs in the desk, which said at the top *John E. Jones, Quality Feeds.* And the piano.

No, they were here; it slipped my mind. They were here last Saturday.

Two blind men, one of them old, one young. She'd opened the door thinking "Who on earth can that be?" and the two blind men, or man and boy, had taken off their caps and the older one had said, "I'm Mr. Williams and this is my helper Irving." They looked like brothers. Not father and son because blind men never seemed fathers or sons: Strange, pale-skinned creatures who had come from the bottom of some wooded lake or appeared like mushrooms one morning in a grove: Their shoulders sagging, their faces infinitely weary, brightening for an instant when they spoke, then sliding away once more to a deadman's repose. She saw them often, young blind boys hurrying up Bank Street in pairs, spreading out through all the city, from Roosevelt Place to Harvester Avenue, selling the brooms they'd made at the Blind School, walking faster than other people walked, talking more loudly than other people did, laughing huskily, like Negroes. Once when she was first married, when a blind friend of her father-in-law's was there at the home place for a visit, there had been a thunderstorm and the lights had gone out. They could hardly find their way from one room to another, but the blind man had gone at once to the pantry where the candles were, and had set them up in their pewter holders and had lighted them with a look of unspeakable indifference, like an alien god intervening to resolve some idiotic dilemma of his creatures; and she had been alarmed.

The older man said, "Could you let us see the piano?" She realized only then that they were piano tuners—though the long, black, coffinlike toolbox ought to have told her at once. No doubt Marie had called them.

"Yes, right this way," she said, turning back to the living room.

They followed her as though they could see her, and the older man said, putting his hand on the corner of the piano as if casually, "It's a beautiful old instrument," and then, playing two or three notes, "I see it hasn't been used much lately."

"It's been in the family for years," she said.

(George had stood in the doorway smoking his pipe, his back round and his head thrown forward, and sometimes as Jimmy played some particular passage or chord George would nod. "Doing well," he would say later, with exactly the same expression he had when he commented on his own progress with his perpetual-motion machine or when he mentioned the nest building of the swallows in the garage. Jimmy wasn't even taking lessons yet—his hands were still too small, Betsy Staley said)—but he played the piano incessantly. He would play any note or clump of notes his fingers happened to fall on, and sometimes it was enough to drive you wild; but as the weeks passed it came to sound more and more like music, order imposed on the earlier chaos. "Good," George would say excitedly sometimes. George had taken lessons once himself, but all he'd ever known was gone from him now, and his fingers were wide-ended and clumsy on the keys. She, for her part, would merely listen, and the chords would bring pictures to her mind. She would remember the Black River, smooth as glass, every seaweed leaf distinct as a leaf in a painting, down in the water. (It was late afternoon. The sky was peach color, and the trees across from Uncle John's cabin were dark green, almost black.) Or she would remember the drowned man she had seen as a child—how one day he had quietly risen like some new kind of plant from the sludge at the bottom, and how the sight of him had overwhelmed and, in a queer way, thrilled her. His coming had had the force of a long day's berry picking or the sight of a mountain torrent or the sensation one had looking down from the rail of a steamer on Lake Erie: She could not shut it out of her mind even when she slept; it was as if the walls between herself and what lay outside had fallen. Or she would remember the bobcat she'd seen when she was ten, out by Uncle Si's milkhouse, or the weasel Ez Hammond had trapped. Or George's experiments in taxidermy. When Jimmy was two and a half, George had stuffed a bear, out in the workshop at his father's place, and Jimmy had watched with wide, superstitious eyes. "Bear will hutt Daddy," Jimmy had said, though they'd both told him the bear was dead—(and they knew he knew what it meant). And they saw, or rather George pointed out, that in the dim light, in the unfamiliar room, the innate dangerousness of a bear had, for Jimmy, nothing to do with its being alive: Its threat was not conditional but absolute; its meaning had nothing to do with cause and effect. (So George had explained, and she had understood none of it but nevertheless had understood.) And for a split second she too had seen the bear in a new way, or rather in an old, old way, her eyes innocent again. It was hard to believe how happy they'd been in those days, when they were young and Jimmy was a baby. Had James any idea? Did he even remember it? It was a shame they weren't more talkative, she and James. Always it had been George who did the talking. She remembered kneeling by Jimmy's bed with her hand on his hot, dry forehead; or singing beside him in church when he was nearly a grown man, the leader of the Westminster Fellowship, director of a dance band of his own, and the first Eagle Scout Troop 7 had had in years. He would scoff at those things now, no doubt, or he would change the subject in embarassment. But she had the Eagle Scout badge in her dresser drawer, and nothing on earth would be sufficient to buy it from her: not an object, a life. But no doubt all that would mean nothing to James. He'd been young then, and other things were fresher now in his mind. Only she had really lived those years, drinking deep of the present, not tasting and hurrying on, and mindful of the past not because it was the past but because it came to fulfillment in the present and gave the present its soul. Not that she had lived for others. She'd seen the world in a way she would not have seen it otherwise, and others were a part of the world, and ultimately it was the world itself that was changed by her having lived. The piano was a different object from what it would have been if James had not played it, and, before James, Aunt Kate. In the same way, the living room was smaller than it would have been if George had not set up his projector here when company came. Had James ever noticed that? she wondered. Was it the kind of thing people wrote philosophy about? Perhaps it was, she thought with a sudden flicker of excitement. In James's typewriter she had once found a sheet of paper with just one word on it, a title: *Memory*. What would he have said? She would never know, even if he had finished it (as perhaps he had), for she had tried, sometimes, to read his writing. It filled her with a terrible longing, what seemed to her a deep sense of the lack in her life: She experienced things but she could not understand. How much more fully they lived, those who understood what her son had to say! Someday perhaps everybody *would* understand—it would come down through the schools— She must not go on like this.)

The blind man played octaves, his head tilted to listen, his expression weary and lifeless. Then he straightened up and took off his coat and laid it neatly over the chair he could not know was beside him and said: "We can't bring it up to four-forty, you know. These old pianos——"

"I don't know about these things," she said. "My son James—he's here from California——"

"These old pianos go down and down and down." he smiled, his glass eyes focused on the center of her forehead. "You check it, you know, you try to pull them back, and maybe they'll hold for a day or two, even a week, but there's nothing you can really do, nothing permanent. You nail them to pitch, try to make them what they used to be, but one of these days you sit down to play and they blow up like dynamite under your fingers. It's a terrible thing, the way these old pianos go. And you can't replace them, that's the truth. These new pianos, I don't care what kind of a brand name they've got, they're not built the way the old ones were. People don't know about woodgrain any more. These new pianos just don't have the *energy*."

She'd sighed. "I've always loved good piano playing. My son's a piano player. James Chandler. Perhaps you've heard of him?"

"Don't think so. You ever hear of him, Irving?"

The boy shook his head.

"No," the man said with finality, "we've never heard of him."

4

SHE thinks, sitting at the dining-room table: *I've still got George's old desk to clean out.*

It was Marie that had gotten the cabinet-maker, too. A man named Jensen. He'd stood looking at it with his hands on his hips, a great, greasy fat man with his shirt hanging out and his broken shoelaces tied in shaggy knots halfway up the tongue. The three girls stood beside him, a little behind him, watching with exaggerated interest. He smelled as if he hadn't had a bath in years. He was chewing gum, moving his gray-bearded jaw very slowly, squinting behind his steel-rimmed glasses, and he reminded her a little of a Chinaman. "Mmmm," he'd said, noncommittal. She'd said, as though it might help him, "It used to belong to my husband." He'd nodded, saying "Mmmm" again, still offering no opinion. At last he'd said, "Have to get them old books out of there." Marie had gone down the hall and up the attic stairs for boxes, and when she'd come back the two of them, she and Marie, had begun to unload the desk. Handling the books that hadn't been touched since the day he'd died, Rose Chandler's mind had been troubled by memories sharper than any that had come to her for years. She remembered the way he would sit reading in the shop when there weren't any customers and hadn't been for a long time. She would be nervous, herself, when business was bad. "People don't want this old stuff," she would say, waving angrily at the roomful of stirring, tinkling gadgets. "We don't *carry* enough, George. I don't mean those things you make aren't clever, but people just don't *want* things like that. Not these days. They want something useful. Birthday cards, for instance, or pens, or picture cards, or books." He would say nothing, just go on sitting by the window with his long legs stretched out in front of him, his sharp elbow resting on the wooden chair arm, his fingertips supporting the side of his head, that infernal pipe in his mouth. Or if he did say anything it would be only, "Something'll turn up." And, to her disgust, something always did. Some farmer would come in and would ask him what a man ought to do to cure a horse of spavins, or to make him quit nipping or crowding in the stall, and George would do the job for him for twenty-five dollars; or someone would hire him to find them the place to sink a well, and George would do it, taking great pleasure in making it seem more mysterious than it was; or the church would hire him to put on a sleight-of-hand show, for George had invented a number of things for the magic trade and had traveled all through Western New York, in his younger days, doing "scientific demonstrations," as he called them. For years after he'd died she'd left his chair by the window and beside it the little table with three of four of his books; but finally she'd had to make more room—when the boom in paperbacks began—and his place by the window had gone. It was a wrench to her, seeing it go. She'd been right all along, though; she would say that. The store had made money, with her in charge. And it was still making money—though she was out of the business now —selling the same sorts of things she'd stocked. Except that there were a good many things she would never have had on the premises. She would drop by and visit now and then, to relive old times: to see herself standing at the counter again, little James straightening out the shelves or sweeping or talking to the parrot George had kept. Or at any rate she *had* dropped in from time to time. The last time she'd gone back they'd just finished remodeling. Everything was white now—it made her think of a creamery—and there was ugly ceramic flower-pots and tall, slick-paper greeting cards that were sup-posed to be funny, and all the books were novels she'd never heard of, with tiresome, irritating titles. (She had carried, in her day, the novels of Grace Livingston Hill —titles like *A Patch of Blue*—or the poetry of Grace Noel Crowell, or occasionally serious history books.) Some-thing had happened to books since her day. She never spoke about it, of course; she didn't feel confident of her opinions. But she couldn't help but notice. They were all pale and full of uninteresting things, and there seemed to be so many more of them, hundreds of new ones every week, and all of them dull and full of Serious Prob-lems and Troubled People and ugliness and places she'd never heard of.

She thought of the way George would rub his finger on the side of his nose and close his eyes for a moment when something in his reading seemed doubtful to him, or hard to understand.

After Marie had packed and labeled the last of the boxes and had carried all of them up to the attic, Rose Chandler had gone up with a pencil and paper and had carefully unpacked them again and had made a list of what was there. It was always a good idea to know just exactly what one had. Some of the books might be valu-able someday, old as they were. She had always hoped James might want them. Well, perhaps now Karen might. She was very much like him, in some ways.

Rose Chandler gets up and takes her piles of lists from the little top left drawer of the buffet, then returns to her chair. Viola Staley comes into the room, looks at the lists from a distance, curious, then smiles and goes on.

1. *The Book of Magical Art, Hindu Magic, and Indian Occultism,* by Dr. R. Cohn
2. *The Master Key,* by Dr. Chas. Parish
3. *MacFadden's Encyclopedia of Physical Culture* (set), by Bernarr MacFadden
4. *Ideal Suggestion through Mental Photography,* by Forrest Orr
5. *Reading Character from the Face: Or, The Key that Unlocks the Secret Nature of Man through his Face,* by Dr. A Wildavsky, D.D.
6. *Fasting for Health,* by Bernarr MacFadden
7. *Eating for Health and Strength,* by Prof. Carl Dennis, Ph.D.
8. *The Truth About Tobacco,* by Bernarr MacFadden
9. *Youatt on The Structure, and the Diseases of the Horse, with their Remedies* (brought down to 1849 by R. Rainbow, M.R.C.V.S.)
10. *Modern Starting, Lighting and Ignition Systems,* by Wayne Petersen, M.E.
11. *Automobile Repairing Made Easy,* by G. F. Patterson, M.E.
12. *The Model T Ford Car: Its Construction, Operation and Repair,* by Robert Griffin, M.E.
13. *The Law of Psychic Phenomena, a Working Hypothesis,* by S. Burns, M.D., Ph.D., LL.D.
14. *A Scientific Demonstration of the Future Life,* by Edward L. Epstein, Ph.D., LL.D.
15. *The Law of Mental Medicine,* by Thomson Jay Hudson, Ph.D., LL.D.
16. *The Mysteries of Astrology and the Wonders of Magic: Including A History of the Rise and Progress of Astrology and the Various Branches of Necromancy, etc.,* by Dr. N. Snortum
17. *The Poetical Works of Thomas Moore,* ed. D. and C. Finkel
18. *Oscar R. Gleason's Practical Treatise on the Breaking and Taming of Wild and Vicious Horses*
19. *Diseases of the Dog and How to Feed,* by Prof. E.M. Glenn, V.S.
20. *Dr. Irene Solomon's Treatise on the Horse*

21. *Prof. O. R. Gleason's Horse Book*
22. *Selections from Homer's Iliad,* by Rev. M. Harris
23. *Diseases of the Horse, and their Cure,* by Harold Armstrong, M.D.
24. *Hunting, Trapping, and Fishing,* by ???
25. *Capturing and Training the Elephant,* by Prof. P. Nordhus
26. *A Treatise on the Horse and his Diseases,* by Dr. R. Partlow, S.J.
27. *Historic Sites of New York State,* by Hilligas
28. *Dr. Wm. Somerville & Sons' Veterinary Medicines*
29. *The Horse's Friend,* by Prof. C. Zimansky
30. *Thaddeus of Warsaw,* by Jane Porter
31. *The Poetical Works of Sir Walter Scott* (complete)
32. *Favorite Methodist Hymns,* ed. J. Thurston
33. *Shakespeare's Complete Works*
34. *Physics,* by W. H. Gass
35. *Mesmerism for the Salesman,* Prof. Lennis C. Dunlap
36. *The Complete Writings of Alexander Pope*
37. *Forbes' Cyclopaedia of Mechanics*
38. *Mathematical Tables* (pamphlet), W. Dickey
    7 notebooks

The cabinet-maker said—this was two days later— "Well, lady, good as new, put-near. Can't get cherry like that no more, and them little pieces of glass, they nobody makes it. I made these here hinges myself."

5

SHE had expected that James would want to go out to the country with her. They'd always gone out there at least once or twice when he'd visited in the past, and when she'd mentioned it this time, he'd seemed interested. But in the end she'd gone alone. It was the day after they'd taken him to the hospital, and why she had gone she could not say. Perhaps she had thought it would be restful and comforting to talk to Dave, the man who lived there now, for there was no denying she'd somehow found it restful in the past. And so, with Viola Staley there to take care of the girls, she had started up her old black Chevy and had set out, driving slowly, as always, bending nearsightedly over the steering-wheel, keeping to the exact middle of the street, her gloved hands gripping the sides of the steering-wheel stiffly: up Bank to Main and down Main to Harvester Avenue and over to Ellicott Street and back to Jackson, circling the stretch where the sewer lines were all torn up, then out past Max Pies' and Jefferson Junior High to the Creek Road. The flats along the Tonawanda were flooded—the WBTA transmitter rose out of what might have been miles of choppy, brownish water—but the flood was not as bad this year as she'd sometimes seen it. She drove past the new little matchbox houses springing up around Walt Cook's farm, past the bend where Judge Cone's girl tipped over that time, past Coverts' and Humes' and the Polish peoples'—Charley Walls' place in her day—and up along the DL&W railroad tracks to what had once been the village of Brookville. When she came to the place she pulled off the road into the spongy, spring-yellow weeds and sat looking for a long time at where the house had been. There wasn't a sign any more that it had ever stood there. Woodbine and purple nightshade covered the stone foundation, and what had once been a lawn shaded by English walnut trees had turned into a disorderly grove, the walnuts' old bare skeletons rising over volunteer locusts and maples and elderberry thicket that almost hid the black remains of the barn. She started up the car again and turned down the two-rut lane that led off the road to the right, rising toward the cinder-block house where the present owner lived. He met her at the turnaround by what had once been the wellhouse, with a branch saw hung over his shoulders. "Hod-do," he said, his hands inside his overalls' bib, his bare shoulders sweaty. He'd been sawing limbs from a tree he'd cut down beside the house. His eyes were always a little too wide, his eyebrows too high, as though he meant to seem more interested than he felt. He smiled. He was a hermitish sort of man, unmarried at fifty, but he liked to see company now and then. He said heartily, "You're a little off your road, ain't you, Mrs. Chandler?"

"Well, yes," she said with a polite, awkward laugh. "How's everything with you, David?"

"Oh, can't complain," he said. "Yourself?"

"I still get around, thank you."

He made no move to open her door or invite her in, merely stared, wide-eyed and smiling, as he might at a fox cub he'd found beneath a burdock or a lunchbox beside the tracks.

She said, "I see you're keeping busy." The old orchard was gone completely, and he'd cleared the maples from the side hill and put in Scotch pine.

He nodded. "You care to see something?" He turned before she could answer and walked over to the corncrib. He came back in a moment with what she thought at first was a kitten.

"Why, a baby woodchuck!" she said.

"Yep. Ole groundhog. Cute little feller, ain't he?"

"Where did you find him?"

"Up in the bean lot. Old Juniper got his maw." He spread the woodchuck's paw on his glove, smiling proudly, showing the claws. "Don't weigh but a pound and six ounces," he said. "Eats whatever a rabbit'll eat. Face just like a squirrel with the eyes of a pig."

"Why, so it is," she said, struck by it. When she reached toward it a little, the woodchuck hissed, and she drew her hand back sharply. They both laughed.

He put the woodchuck away in the corncrib and came back to stand by her window again, smiling as before, his hands in his bib. "You ought to see the pond this time of year."

"No thank you," she said. "I'm too old for traipsing over hill and dale."

He leaned on the fender and turned to look off at the hill beyond which the pond lay, and after a minute he said, "You'd never believe how much living goes on, a little old place like that. Little early yet, but you go out there two weeks from now and that place will be teeming. Down under the red maples and alders there's ferns and mosses and a thousand different kinds of herbs, and then in the shallows there's cattails and water hay and pond lilies—little plants that grow out of the mud, plants that grow out of sunken logs, plants that ain't rooted at all but just hang onto rocks. And then there's algae, what people call scum,—they're little floating plants. And animals, you couldn't name them all: May flies, water beetles, dragonflies, mosquitoes, water boatmen, back skimmers, diving beetles, snails, redworms, water spiders, whirligig beetles: one time I found a great big bug that would carry his eggs on his back. And let's see—" He stretched out his fingers and began to count on them—"we got spotted newts and sunfish and frogs and snapping turtles and eels. You couldn't count 'em all. And I haven't even mentioned the birds. Must be sixty different kinds out there. All living off one plain ordinary pond, no different than any other pond in Genesee County."

She said, "It must be very nice to live close to Nature the way you do. You ought to write a book about it. You'd make a lot of money."

"No thank you, ma'am," he said. "What good would money be to me? Just buys you things that clutter up your house and keep you awake all night worrying. And raises your taxes. I got taxes already that I ain't got around to paying yet."

"Well, it's a shame to let all that experience go to waste."

He shook his head slyly. "Everything in this world was made to go to waste, ma'am. May flies eat algae, and dragonflies eat May flies, and sunfish eat dragonflies, and people eat sunfish, and polar bears eat people. That's only thing I've learnt in fifty years. Things was wasting before the first human beings came down from the tree-tops, and there'll still be things wasting when all this world's turned to cinders and ice. Only real difference between people and trees is trees don't fret about it. People ought to be more like trees, Mrs. Chandler. That's my philosophy."

She scowled, studying him critically. All at once his smile seemed stupid to her. "People aren't supposed to be trees, Mr. Plumber," she said. She felt shakes coming on. She started the car up angrily, nodded, and bounced out to the road before he could think of an answer. On the way home she had to stop and cry.

She has written:

> *Things for Marie and the children:*
> *Tea service*
> *Silver*
> *Cut-glass goblets, etc.*
> *Books*
> *Piano*
> *George's desk*
> *The good bed*
> *Japanese dishes*
> *Ceramic statues Marge made*
> *George's Copper kettles*
> *Tools in the workshop*
> *Bibles*
> *Good chairs*
> *Tablecloths*
> *Pots and pans, appliances*
> *Inlaid tray*
> *Uncle Griff's pistol*
> *Photo albums*
> *American Heritage books*
> *George's movie camera*
> *Trunk of clothes in attic*
> *Good flag*
> *Carving set*
> *Tea cart*
> *Lawn furniture*
> *George's paints and colored pencils*
> *Printing press in garage (if fixable)*
> *Silver bird cage*
> *Seth Thomas*

Quilts
Eiderdown pillow
Old churn
George's bust of Cicero
Aunt Kate's artificial roses

She gets up, puts her lists away, goes to the window, and stands looking out. There is no one in the yard now; she can hear the children on the front porch. The Negro woman who works for the Donaldsons next door is hanging out the wash.

She has a million and one things to do. On the way down to the Bendix she stops, leaning on her cane, and looks in through the open door of George's old workshop. His pride and joy stands, as always, in the middle of the wide old piano table. It consists of three wheels made of nickel suspended in a rosewood frame and connected by belts which are now as stiff as dried-out cardboard. On the side of the largest of the wheels there hangs a small, glass, bottlelike thing, sealed off at both ends and so discolored that one can no longer make out the mercury inside. In its day the machine would run for forty minutes, and to his dying hour George Chandler had believed that with a little more work he might solve forever the problem of perpetual motion. Now the wheels are frozen on their axles. The sunlight falling in a dusty shaft from the little rectangular window above strikes fire as it hits the pitted nickel. Not as prettily as it once did, of course. Nevertheless, a beautiful machine, a handsome achievement.

She goes into the room, mysteriously impelled, or drawn, and she touches the central wheel, gently at first, trying to turn it. It will not budge. She pulls harder, and, almost without a sound, the polished wooden axle snaps. The wheel clatters to the table, the mercury-chamber bursts.

6

ACCORDING to Kant (Chandler wrote) Beauty is that which calls up a response of "delight without interest." A picture of a grapefruit, Kant would say, must have *interest* for a starving man, or for the owner of a grapefruit grove: for them it is not *beautiful* but *agreeable*. In the same way, a representation of Christ emerging from the Tomb must have interest for a minister or for a lady dying of leprosy: for them it reflects *what ought to be,* in other words, it is a *good* which has practical consequences. To experience the true aesthetic response, the onlooker must be indifferent to whether the thing represented exists, has ever existed, or may exist in the future.

Now as Croce and Collingwood saw, if Kant were right it would be of no aesthetic importance that Mann's exploration of Venice grows out of a close and literal scrutiny of place. But in fact Mann's reader draws pleasure (whether or not he likes Venice or believes Venice "good") from the observation that Mann's symbolic apprehension has its basis in the *actual*. Clearly, there is a kind of interest which is *impersonal,* and which goes by the name of *scientific curiosity*. And to the extent that reality offers both food for intellect and food for intuition, the aesthetic response to art grounded on *realism* must be termed not "delight *without* interest" but "delight *beyond* interest."

The same holds in the moral sphere. We have only to consider the relative impact of Homer's *Iliad* and, for instance, Humbert Wolfe's little poem on the gray squirrel to see that Kant's sharp separation of the aesthetic and the moral is *a mistake*. We know from experience that (as Wittgenstein thinks) aesthetics has something to do with ethics. Our problem is to determine the connection.

Art, like Nature (as human bias perceives it) *contains affirmations which transcend procticality*. If a mountain suggests to me, as it did to Wordsworth, dignity and highmindedness, my response to the mountain may or may not have consequences in my behavior. In either case, what I affirm (or what I imagine to be implied by the mountain) I in fact affirm for all mankind, for all time and space, as *an absolute* (human) *good*. Responding to aesthetic stimuli I say, in effect, "This belongs in my civilization," or, *in another case*, "This belongs between my civilization and chaos."

I am suggesting that affirmations can be of two kinds, in Kierkegaard's sense *ethical* or *moral*. These kinds correspond precisely, though Burke did not notice it, to the two kinds of aesthetic experience elaborated by Edmund Burke, *viz.*, the experience of *the Beautiful* and the experience of *the Sublime*. What Burke identifies with *the Beautiful* (the small, the curvilinear, the smooth, the pleasant) we may associate with *ethical* (*i.e., social*) *affirmation;* that is to say, with affirmations of what is to be sought, what will "do," what must be tolerated (the harmlessly ugly or ludicrous), and what will not do in a given culture. All that belongs in Burke's realm of *the Sublime* (the large, the angular, the terrifying, etc.) we may identify with *moral affirmation;* that is to say, with human *defiance of chaos*, or the human assertion of *the godlike magnificence of human mind and heart*. Thor's annual circuit around Midgaard, hurling his hammer against trolls and monsters of the night—his back to the order his existence maintains, his face towards darkness—is Sublime, *all the more sublime for the fact that every year Thor grows weaker, the circle of order smaller*. In such terms, the voyage of the *Pequod* is Sublime; the teas of Jane Austen are Beautiful. That the two exist *on a continuum* is evidenced by the existence of Henry James or, better,

Chaucer. Needless to say, designating a work Sublime is not the same as asserting its high *artistic* merit. Melville's *Pierre* is sublime but unsuccessful: we understand what moral emotions we are expected to feel, but our thought is distracted by the writing.

Whereas Kant's theory of delight without interest asserts that utility corrupts the response, a theory of delight beyond interest asserts man's potential for selflessness. When Iphigenia—in Euripides' *Iphigenia at Aulis*—declares that she will die joyfully for Greece, we share her emotion and, though Greece fell long ago, experience *interest:* We hope that we too would die for country, or for mankind; but hope and, indeed, assert that *there are always human beings capable of such goodness.* What we mean when we say that Art *imitates* Nature, then—or at all events what we ought to mean—is this: Whereas in Nature human consciousness discovers and enlarges itself by learning to categorize and choose between brute sensations (or the emotional charge in brute sensations) and later to choose between passions, in Art a gifted consciousness simplifies, extends, or reorders categorization and choice for the rest of us, speeding up the painfully slow process of evolution toward what, hopefully, we *are.*

The aesthetic impulse may thus be understood to be *moral,* and Nature, or life, is indeed, as Pope said, the *end* or purpose of Art. By this we mean that the highest state a man can achieve is one of *aesthetic wholeness.* As Collingwood saw in *Speculum Mentis* (but forgot when he came to write his *Principles*), the end of aesthetic evolution, *wholeness,* is analogous to the end of religious evolution, *saintliness,* that state in which one is capable of embracing all experience as holy and some experience as *more* holy; and it is analogous too to the end of intellectual evolution, *scientific knowledge.* But *aesthetic wholeness* is nobler than *saintliness* just as *saintliness* is nobler than *scientific knowledge.* The concern of knowledge is with *form and function* abstracted from the sensual richness of *substance;* one grows *saintly* by rejecting both *form* and *substance* from their supposed *es-*

sence, in other words, *by evading the question.* (Whether one chooses to speak of shoes as *God* or as *a faint odor of turpentine,* one is not in fact talking about *shoes.*) Aesthetic wholeness affirms with total selflessness the universal human interest in what is—as Wallace Stevens says, "the finale of seem." The good life, then, *towards which Art points the way.*

It seemed to Chandler that no one might more easily have achieved it than he—that good life of which he wrote so feelingly—if only he had understood in time. He could now understand the state perfectly, could construct a clear and complete conception of its emotional quality. Indeed, he had achieved it; but the achievement was poisoned. His sense of being in two places was constant now, a thing that should have been all to the good. From the ceiling he watched himself laboring slowly, tortuously, struggling against idiotic bafflement, rereading a single sentence sometimes twenty times, straining to remember what he had meant when he began, and he felt, looking down at himself, compassion and faint amusement like that of a parent at sight of his child's struggle with the colored balls on her crib. Like God he could affirm without personal involvement the beauty of the struggle, the beauty of a good mind, seen here in ruins, the beauty of the larger life process in which this man's individual success or failure did not matter as much as the success of his kind, which must depend upon work like his, or like any man's. From his place near the ceiling he watched the man's wife bring food to him, kiss the top of his head, and tiptoe away to avoid interrupting his work. In that too, in the universality of human love, however twisted in its manifestations, he could feel the beauty.

But he was sick. His mouth was sour, as if from gulping tar from an unrested pipe, and his stomach floated with nausea. His head ached dully, and no matter what he put on, he could not get warm. It was as bad when he lay down as when he sat at his desk, and he could not see that the pills the doctor had sent made very much difference. All this did not rob him of his sense of the beautiful—the softness and warmth of his wife's hand, the sheer music in his children's voices—and neither did his sickness rob him of his sense of the value of beauty. His misery was a separate sensation, not infecting the others but intolerable in itself. With a single motion of his mind he wanted to listen to his children's calls and wanted to sink into unconsciousness; in the same instant he might have moaned with pleasure at the soothing warmth of his wife's hand pressed against his forehead and howled against the infuriatingly endless turmoil in his body.

And there was mental torment as well. He went through periods of terror, a groundless quaking of the heart that came over him without warning or apparent cause and made him want to howl. A clot of white cells somewhere, perhaps. He would believe the old woman to be somewhere in the room with him, or standing downstairs in the middle of the night, listening. Or he would see her, even hear her speak, murmuring words that didn't quite make sense but hovered teasingly on the edge of sense. While the terror was on him he couldn't think and when it was gone, he was afraid to think back to it. He began to long ardently for death.

More than "in the world but not of the world" (he wrote). More than Platonic. The wisdom of old people when, as sometimes happens, old people chance to become wise. To whom the death of a child is tragic but tolerable, as it is not to us. In whom no trace of self-pity remains. Who are not overly grieved by tragedy in life, and not because they have no commitment, no interest in the central figure of the tragedy, but because, having loved repeatedly, having survived by the skin of their teeth many times, just as those who love them will, despite their own wish, they can give of themselves unstintingly, fully prepared to pay back all they have spent. To see life's beauty whole implies at once the ardent desire to look and the necessity of backing off.

"You betray me," Horne had said.

He got up unsteadily from the typewriter and went over to the closed door. He leaned on the doorknob, listening. The television was on downstairs, and it reminded him that Anne and Susan had their innumerable dolls and stuffed animals assembled on the floor around the screen to watch. "It's the funniest thing you ever saw," Marie had said. "I'll see if I can get them to leave it until you come down."

"Do, yes!" he'd said, and he had laughed, imagining it.

Now he stood musing on whether or not he should go down. His legs were shaky when he stood too long. He shuffled over to the bed and sat down, still undecided, leaning his sharp elbows into his legs. He felt a faintness coming on and leaned back on the pillow. After a moment it passed.

7

VIOLA STALEY returned to her aunts profoundly changed, as it seemed to her. It seemed to her months ago that she'd heard those screams in the street and had rushed out into open air and sunlight, a world drastically and, she was soon to feel, beautifully changed. She had fallen in love. She'd been with the Chandlers for only four days, but every minute of that time, as it seemed to her, she'd been strangely alive, awake. There was very little required of her at her aunts' house—no more than had been required of her when she'd lived with her moth-

er in Effingham—and yet it had been at the Chandlers',
where it was important to be listening every minute for a
child's cry—listening even while she slept—and where re-
sponsibilities kept her running from dawn to dark, that
she had felt, for the first time in her life, really free,
really happy. Sometimes alone in the kitchen or up in
young Mrs. Chandler's closet, choosing the dress she
would wear today (Marie Chandler had insisted that she
make herself at home with her clothes), she would find
to her surprise that she was singing. And sometimes,
looking in the mirror, she would find that, strange to say
(for Viola was in her own opinion hopelessly plain), she
was beautiful.

It was not that those four days had been pure joy,
a comfortable feeling of being loved and needed, or the
pleasure of being in command, or, least of all, a sense
of being caught up in real life instead of some sickly
make-believe, though at first she had thought that all
that accounted for her feeling. (There, where Marie
Chandler had novels and even books of poetry and where
Mr. Chandler had a whole library of philosophy books,
it had hardly crossed Viola's mind that she might stop
whatever she was doing, if she liked, and read. Yet at
her aunts' she had read incessantly.) She *was* loved and
needed at Chandlers', that was true, but the three girls
had loved her no more and needed her no more, really—
though in a different, somewhat more pleasant way—than
the three old women she lived with; and if she was in
command at the Chandlers', it was a delicate, difficult
command, one that had to be constantly modified to take
account of old Mrs. Chandler's wishes—for it was she,
at least technically, who ran the house—and modified to
take account, too, of the wishes of the children, for she
had no more power over them than they freely gave
her. It had at first seemed to her an entirely new situation.
At her aunts', her position was clearer—or so she would
have said. Aunt Betsy was the master, and Viola's only
task was somehow to guess Aunt Betsy's will and execute
it as well as she might. The only danger was that she
might guess wrong or do clumsily what was required of

her, that is, do it in some way that Aunt Betsy herself would not have done it; for when she made a mistake, all three of them became the masters, by a sudden change in the rules, and Viola became the stepchild alone in the cinders. Yet Viola's first sense of the thing had passed; the two situations were the same, really—except for the mysterious fact that she'd fallen in love, quite literally, with the Chandler family. The two situations were even the same in specific ways. Aunt Betsy and Karen, respectively, were the rulers of the two establishments, at least in the sense that they were the ones who laid out plans when plans were needed or functioned as final judges. Aunt Maud and Susan were the especially demonstrative ones, the representatives of love to whom one turned for reassurance or a moment's rest from the complication of things. And Aunt Emma and Anne were, in their exactly opposite ways, the mysterious ones, the centers of turbulence, the holy ghosts of excitement or uneasiness or trouble. And not only that: Except for that one enormous difference, the fact of her transmuted heart, the two situations were the same with respect to Viola's place in them. It was something that had dawned on her on the second afternoon at the Chandlers', while she was watching the children play.

It was the queerest game she'd seen in all her life, she was sure. Anne and Susan would stand by the fence, and Karen would roll an imaginary pair of dice, and then she would give one of them permission to take a certain number of steps, first Anne, then Susan, in turn. The child who first reached the other end of the yard was the winner, and the determining factor, evidently, was Karen's whim. It seemed to be clearly understood that only Karen knew the rules and that Karen's permissions or penalities for cheating—the penalties were often severe—were, at least theoretically, beyond dispute. Anne would cry sometimes when she lost, but it never seemed to occur to her to blame Karen rather than bad luck. Karen, on the other hand, would sympathize with what one would have sworn was perfect sincerity, and she would hope that Anne might be luckier next time. And indeed, Anne would win the next time, or at least would come within a hair's breadth, which proved, supposedly, that the game was on the level.

And of course it *was* on the level, Viola had realized all at once.

It was not that Karen alone knew the rules or that Karen's whim controlled the game. *No* one knew the rules, and each had as much control as any other. What determined the number of steps that Susan or Anne might take was Karen's calculation of how much Susan or Anne would put up with: How far, with the magical help of the imaginary dice, could one push Anne or Susan without triggering sufficient outrage to make them quit? On the other hand, if Karen called out "Four steps," Susan might quickly ask, "Six, did you say?" forcing Karen to another quick calculation: If she said, "No, four," would Susan decide to call her a liar, insisting that she had said six (believing it, of course, at least while she was saying it, exactly as she believed by choice in the imaginary dice)? Sometimes, in righteous indignation, Karen would say, "No, I said *four,* and you heard me *perfectly well.*" At other times she'd say, "Well, all right six," and at others, firmly, "Six." Now and then Susan and Anne would cheat, darting forward a few steps when Karen supposedly wasn't looking. If she caught them it meant still another calculation: She could send them back to the starting line, she could ignore it completely, or she could accuse them of cheating, but tentatively, so that they might go back or remain, depending on their mood.

Viola had bent forward over the rickety window table cluttered with plants, and she had watched for a long time. It made her skin crawl. The incredible seriousness of the thing! The silence like death when Karen studied the imaginary dice! It all had some powerful but indefinite meaning for her, but she could not find words for what it was that she felt. It was somehow more than itself—so it seemed to Viola—like familiar rooms seen in an unfamiliar cast of sunlight, or like old pictures in Aunt Betsy's album. The game seemed to tell her something, but something she couldn't make out. She heard

Mrs. Chandler come into the room behind her, and she said, "Come here, look at this"—pointing. Mrs. Chandler had come over to stand beside her, but of course she saw nothing—only the blurry forms of the children, apparently—for she said: "Poor dears." That was all. (Anne abruptly ended the game. She found something in the grass, and she sat down to examine it.) Viola had nodded absently, then had turned away and had gone on with her furniture polishing: the piano, the flower tables, the bookshelves, the wood on the arms of the couch. She thought (as if momentarily confusing the family and the furniture) *How beautiful they are. I couldn't love them more if the children were my own.* She thought of James Chandler standing over Aunt Maud with his hand on her stomach. He had a startled look, as though he were wondering how he'd gotten into this. Viola laughed, all at once, remembering that look. Strange, she thought then. She'd lost completely her sense that he was dying. She knew, now as surely as before, that he was; but she had lost belief in what she knew. (The smell of his pipe would catch her unaware in a musty corner or on the attic stairs, or one of the girls would mention him very casually, and the tone of the man would change the surrounding world for an instant.) His family no longer believed in his dying either. The older Mrs. Chandler told long, pointless stories, as she might have at any other time, about old Mr. Donaldson, next door, who had arthritic knees but who nevertheless worked from morning to night every day in his garden. These were some of his tomatoes. He'd brought so many Mrs. Chandler had had to can them. Or she would tell of some woman who had bought a navy-blue coat, and come to find out, it wasn't navy blue at all, but *black*.

When Viola was dusting the dining-room table the thought had come, as if out of the sky, *That was my life they were playing.* Maybe everybody's life, she'd throught a moment later, without the faintest idea what it was, exactly, that she meant. The half-formed idea had shocked her, and she'd vowed never to think about it again.

But as luck would have it, she hadn't been given a chance to forget. Marie had come home that night, briefly, to look in on the children, and Old Mrs. Chandler had fixed tea for her and they'd sat at the table, talking. Marie Chandler told of some unpleasant old man she'd met, and old Mrs. Chandler, who knew him, had defended him. Marie said wearily, in no mood to argue—or rather, perhaps, in the perfect mood to argue and therefore careful to keep out of a fight—waving her hand hopelessly, as if to shoo away a huge bird that she knew would probably refuse to leave: "It wasn't really him that annoyed me. Life in general. 'All the world's a stage, and all the men and women merely players.' " The line, which she delivered with scorn, as though the line itself disgusted her, was startling to Viola, close as it was in some obscure way to what she herself had been thinking this afternoon. She said, "Who said that, Mrs. Chandler?" "Bartlett," young Mrs. Chandler said. Viola, had laughed, though she didn't think it was funny, and she'd said, "What does it mean?" Marie had turned to look at her briefly, unspeakably tired but hiding at least most of her irritation, and she'd said, "Nothing. It's merely a transition." Viola had laughed again politely, perhaps rather bitterly this time, and had withdrawn. The line continued to nag her. And then when she was putting the children to bed, something else had happened, and it seemed to throw all the rest into a new light, though again the exact connection would not come to her but stood in the dark of her mind like the undiscovered exit from a sealed room.

She had read Susan and Anne their bedtime books and had tucked them in for sleep—Marie had long since gone back to the hospital—and Viola was just getting up to leave the children's room when Karen said, "Viola?"

Karen had been quiet until now. Viola had almost forgotten she was there. "What is it, Karen?"

"Would you read something to me, please?"

Viola looked at her. She seemed, just that moment, small and frightened and lonely, lying like a prim, white doll in her bed. Viola that instant saw herself as a child and remembered vividly how she'd felt just after her father's death. She touched Karen's hand. "Of course I will," she said. Then, brightly: "What shall we read?"

Solemnly, a little timidly, as though she knew very well how odd it was, Karen drew a thick, black book from under the covers. Viola stared. She knew at once that this was no storybook for little girls. She almost laughed, but something told her that Karen had not chosen the book to impress her. She really did want it read aloud; and Viola knew by instinct that to mock the wish would be monstrous. She looked at the cover. At the top, *Immanuel Kant,* and below, *Critique of Pure Reason.*

"Are you sure, Karen?" Viola brought out.

She nodded, holding her covers tight to her chin.

Viola leaned toward the lamp—the younger children were asleep already—and began to read.

> *The idea of Transcendental Philosophy.*
> *Experience is, beyond all doubt, the first product to which our understanding gives rise, in working up the raw material of sensible impressions. Experience is therefore our first instruction, and in its progress is so inexhaustible in new information, that in the interconnected lives of all future generations there will never be any lack of new knowledge that can be thus ingathered. Nevertheless, it is by no means the sole field to which our understanding is confined. Experience tells us, indeed, what is, but not that it must necessarily be so, and not otherwise. It therefore gives us no true universality; and reason, which is so insistent upon this kind of knowledge, is therefore more stimulated by it than satisfied. Such universal modes of knowledge, which at the same time possess the character of inner necessity, must in themselves, independently of experience, be clear and certain. They are therefore entitled knowledge a priori; whereas, on the other hand, that which is borrowed solely from experience is, as we say, known only a posteriori, or empirically.*

Viola glanced at Karen and was startled to see the oddly grown-up look of suffering on her face.

"Could you explain that a little, Viola?" Karen asked softly.

It was as if the words had frightened her—as if, with her life depending on it, Karen had stepped up confidently to answer a riddle but had found now, hearing it, that the question was in ancient Hebrew, and the mind that had constructed it not human. Not, of course, that Viola Staley leaped to Collingwood's image of the sphinx. She leaped to no image whatever, having no need of one. She saw Karen's face and understood it without translation, the face itself pure language. She reread the paragraph to herself, word by word, carefully; but though she might have been able to make its meaning out at some other time, just now the sentences were too complex, the words, the concepts too unfamiliar. At last she said with a little laugh. "I can't make head nor tails of it, to tell the truth."

There were tears on Karen's cheeks, and Viola reached out ot her quickly. "What's wrong, Karen?"

"Nothing," Karen said, sobbing now.

Viola knew very well what was wrong, though she could not have put what she knew into words. She squeezed Karen's hand. "You'll be able to read it when you're older, honey."

The child turned her face away, and, helpless before Karen's helplessness, Viola bent down and kissed her cheek. "We'll try it again in the morning when we're fresh," she said brightly. Even as she spoke them the words sounded stupid and hollow.

Karen gave her no answer.

Viola got up at last and turned off the light; but she did not leave the room at once. She stood for perhaps three minutes in the doorway, her head bowed, lost in reverie, and when she left, she moved away quietly, as she might have moved from a temple where, at least for an instant, she had found herself persuaded.

She dreamed that night of a kind of playground, a place all alone among oak trees. It was a moonlit night and the playground was of smooth gray sand that seemed very old and beautiful. The only play equipment was an elaborate construction of monkey bars, black against the brightly moonlit sky. A radiant, naked boy with white hair crossed the sand toward the bars. As he walked, something happened to him. His knees began to knock together and his bony arms flung out. His eyes protruded, entirely white, and he bit his tongue from the effort of propelling himself. As he reached the monkey bars his feet began to sink in the sand. She watched him sink down, and when only his owlish face remained, she screamed. Instantly someone caught her hand and she awakened. "I'm sorry," she said. "I had a nightmare." "It's all right," the voice said softly. "Everything's going to be all right." Then she knew that her comforter was also a dream. And at last, really awake now, she knew something else. She was in love—and in no Platonic way, either—with James Chandler. Joy came over her like a warm wind, and sitting in the envelope of her joy, she was shocked. Nothing could be more ridiculous or more terrible; she saw it as clearly as any objective observer could have seen it. But knowing the complete absurdity of her emotion was no help. *No,* Viola thought, furious at the shameless and disdainful trick that had been played on her, seeing herself with perfect clarity as grotesque, comic, a ragged lady clown in a broken bicycle routine. She wanted to smash things, snatch down vengeance from the moon, O Lord, or drag it from the depths of the sea! She wrung her hands, weeping now, and her mind leapt wildly in its fury, but she did not think about what she was going to do. *I love him,* she thought. *I love him. Dear God, I love him!*

Everything was going to be all right. It *would* be all right.

Compared to the Chandlers', her aunts' house seemed dark and heavy and dead. The moment she came into the entryway, the dry heat leaped up around her like sharply recollected anger. As though she had been away for years, she saw the high old mirror on the wall, the wallpaper, the furniture, with brand new eyes. Everything was just as it had always been, standing in its accustomed place, timeless, immutable, deadly; and as the door swung shut behind her she felt, for a fraction of a second, trapped. But this was what she must learn to live with, she knew. This was real; the other, luminous illusion. Aunt Betsy was giving a lesson, and she went right on as usual; but Aunt Maud came as far as the dining-room door.

"Viola, dear. How are they?" She took Viola's hand.

"They're fine, Aunt Maud. Mr. Chandler's come home now."

The old woman smiled vaguely, leaning forward, and Viola said it again, more loudly, smiling this time, little as she felt like smiling, for that much at least Aunt Maud would get.

"Let me fix you some honey-bread and Ovaltine," Aunt Maud said.

"No, please," Viola said quickly, touching her aunt's arm. She wasn't ready yet to go into the kitchen. She had never known until this moment exactly how much she loathed that enormous, sterile old place. She would stay right here by the dining-room window, the only sun-lit place in the house, unless one counted Aunt Betsy's music room.

"How's Aunt Emma?" Viola said as if with great concern.

"Just fine, thank you," Aunt Maud said vaguely.

Viola was painfully aware of the music now, though once she'd gotten fairly used to it, before her trip to the Chandlers'. How had they stood all that banging, year after year, hour after hour? But they hadn't, of course. She wanted to laugh, furious, as the thought came. Aunt Maud had cleverly gone deaf, and Aunt Emma, cleverer still, had gone out of her mind.

"Poor dear, you're pale as a ghost," Aunt Maud said. "You've been taking your vitamins, I hope?"

"I'm fine, Aunt Maud," she said. Then, because she had spoken crossly, she said: "I'll run in and see how Aunt Emma's doing." Before Aunt Maud could misunderstand again, Viola slipped past her and crossed to

Aunt Emma's room. At the door she hesitated a moment. Aunt Maud was looking after her with a sweet, annoying smile. Viola turned the knob and went in.

Aunt Emma sat, as always, in the elegant old cane chair beside her bed, dressed in her finest, smiling pleasantly, waiting. Except for the scent of age, not quite negated by sachet and the dry smell of the yellowed lace curtains on the window, one would have thought no one had lived in the room for years. Aunt Emma's neatly folded towels, her converted china oil-lamp, her porcelain pitcher and washbasin, stood on the marble-topped commode like a carefully arranged display at the Holland Land Office Museum. On the dresser lay her combs and brushes, antique bottles, milk-glass boxes, her little white clock, the 1916 photograph of "Emma's Young Man." No one any longer remembered his name. One might have known, it occurred to Viola, that Aunt Emma would be the one who would fall in love, and with someone not from Batavia at that. In the black Japanese box she kept in her dresser drawer—Viola had seen it once or twice, long ago—there was a gold ring (a wedding ring, Viola would have sworn), a bundle of letters, and a diary.

"Hello, Aunt Emma," she said.

Aunt Emma lifted her head slowly and looked at her. With detachment, as though she stood outside herself, watching herself perform in some beautiful, stilted, old-fashioned play, Viola saw herself walking slowly, erect as a princess, to stand directly in front of Aunt Emma's chair. She stood for a long moment, meeting the mild, blank gaze of the gentle old woman, and it seemed to her that she saw herself and Karen Chandler and all mankind in Aunt Emma's waiting. The moment was holy, a strange reawakening of childhood, and Viola kneeled and pressed the side of her face to Aunt Emma's knees. She *is* good, Viola thought, remembering Aunt Emma's fixed idea. The sunlight on the bed beside her was lovely, and there were subtle shadows from the pattern in the lace curtains. After what seemed a long, long time, the old woman's hand came to Viola's head, gently, tentatively, like the hand of a child. *I love you,* Viola thought.

She was aware, the same instant, of the boniness of the old woman's knees, the shabbiness of her dress, the smell of decay. The moment was over, and she could not bring it back.

The following day (May 6th) she mentioned to Aunt Betsy, when they were eating their lunch—or dinner, as the aunts called the noon meal—that she'd gone to Letchworth Park with the Chandlers. Aunt Betsy was all nerves today. Tonight was the night of the recital, and though she'd been giving recitals for years, she had never learned to take them as a matter of course. They were (or so Aunt Betsy believed) an important social event in Batavia. All the best people's children came to Aunt Betsy for piano lessons; she was known to be the best teacher this side of Rochester, and, indeed, many of her students had gone on to Eastman and had later made names for themselves in "the world of music," as Aunt Betsy called it. (It brought to Viola Staley's mind a perversely literal image of great, unsubstantial cathedrals made out of solid bass-clef chords, staccato, middle-register crowds, glissando rain, and enormous yellow sun in the key of C♯ major.)

"Letchworth," Aunt Betsy said as if nothing on earth could be more dreary. "How nice for the children."

"What was that, dear?" Aunt Maud said.

But Aunt Betsy went on, "Father and William Pryor Letchworth were very good friends, did you know that? They served together on the State Board of Charities, I think it was."

"Oh?" Viola said politely. She toyed with the little gray sugar bowl, and she felt the beginning of that drowning sensation that came so often here with her aunts—or no, had come so often all her life, but expecially here with her aunts. There had been something she'd wanted to say. Now it was gone.

"Mr. Letchworth was a great reformer," Aunt Betsy said. "He did an enormous amount for the insane and for epileptics and underprivileged children. It was Mr. Letchworth who started the State School at Industry and Craig Colony at Sonyea." She sighed. "Father knew most of the important people of the time, you know." She reached for the honey and began to fix herself another sandwich. "He knew the Richmonds, too—the Richmond Library people, you remember. In fact he helped with the planning of the Library. And he knew Mr. Wiard, of the Wiard Plow Works—that's gone now, of course. You're probably familiar with Wiard Street?—I was just a girl then. We still lived in that big old house on East Main. But I remember the wonderful parties. (Mother never knew that I'd crept out of bed and slipped down to listen at the pantry door.) And I remember the music evenings. It was a wonderful time to be alive. Maud—" She raised her voice abruptly, imperious. For some reason Aunt Maud could always make out what Aunt Betsy was saying, even when she spoke in her normal voice. "Maud, do you remember the Armistice Parade? We went with Clara Williams, and Emma was in tears for weeks, poor thing, because of that young man."

"I remember, yes," Aunt Maud said, smiling wildly.

They talked on, but Viola's mind went to other things. She stood again by the rock wall in front of Glen Iris Inn, Anne's hand in her left hand, Viola's right hand on Susan's shoulder, and the man that old Mrs. Chandler knew was saying, looking down at the falls, "Thunder Water, the Indians called it. You ever heard the story of Mona-sha-sha?" He tipped his head toward the falls, indicating that there was some connection, and Marie shook her head, interested. (It was to her that he talked exclusively. Viola could understand it, of course: She was pretty, with that blond hair blowing, and those lumpy, Englishy clothes, And her sharp tongue made her seem clever. Just the same, it was annoying that the man should be so easily swept off his feet.) Viola had said, "Do tell us!" Her tone had perhaps been ugly, but the man had seemed not to notice. He looked at the water for a while. It was very dark and as smooth as glass, then suddenly white, hurtling away, deafening; and towering above the falls, on the far side, stood gray rock wall, and, above that, trees, and, higher yet, blue sky. When he had the story straight in his head he nodded, chewed his cheek a moment, then began. "Something like two hundred years ago, maybe more, there was an Indian hunter named Joninedah, a young brave with a beautiful wife named Mona-sha-sha, and one child. He brought his wife to the banks of the Genesee when the hunting was good, but then when she'd been there a while the hunting changed, and Joninedah thought she'd wrecked his luck. He came home one might and wouldn't smile, and he told her she'd brought him evil. As soon as Joninedah was asleep, Mona-sha-sha strapped her papoose on her back and went out. She found the canoe up half a mile above the falls, and she slipped into the stream with it and laid down the paddle on the floor and let the canoe float downstream. When Joninedah work up and saw that his wife was gone, he ran outside. There in the moonlight he saw a doe and a fawn, and they were white. He went to look where he'd left his canoe, but it wasn't there, as Joninedah'd known all along it wouldn't be. So Joninedah got out his knife and gave himself up to the gods."

"It's a beautiful story," Marie had said, looking at the water. Karen's lips were a thin, tight line, and involuntarily, guessing that the child was thinking of her father (and yet Karen could talk quite matter-of-factly about his dying, at certain times), Viola had covered her face with her hands.

Later, looking up at Table Rock, or beyond, perhaps, at the slowly moving patchwork of light and dark on the trees—the shadows of clouds—Karen had said, "There *is* no God, is there, Viola?"

"Hush," Viola had whispered fiercely, thinking of the man she would joyfully give her life to save, and of the hunter Joninedah. *"Nobody knows."*

8

MAY 6th. 6:30 P.M.

A vague unrest came over her as Aunt Betsy and Aunt Maud dressed for the recital, a gnawing, indefinite hunger not unlike that, perhaps, which animals feel when the days grow longer, the increased light transforming their blood, transforming even their colors and their voices. It was as though the aunts were dressing for a ball to which Viola had not been invited, an affair she had not been thought worthy to attend. She helped them with their corsets, listened to their nervous, pointless talk, put the finishing touches on their hair.

"Surely that's good enough, Viola," Aunt Betsy said, turning.

"Yes, you look marvelous now," Viola said with an eagerness that did not fit and caused Aunt Betsy to frown. Perhaps, with that knack she had, Aunt Betsy guessed the fantasy in Viola's mind, Viola herself dressed to the nines, prepared for a royal ball.

She said: "Perhaps we're wrong, not taking you and Aunt Emma along. We're making you into a homebody."

"Nonsense." Viola laughed, clean and sharp as glass.

Still Aunt Betsy was frowning, studying her. But then she remembered that she hadn't phoned Strohs' to make sure the flowers would be there, and Viola was free. Viola did not enter Aunt Betsy's mind again, apparently, until the time came for leaving. She pressed Viola's hand then and said, "I'm sorry, dear."

"Don't be silly, Aunt Bets," Viola said, and she observed with mingled dread and delight Aunt Betsy's grim smile. "Aunt Bets" was Aunt Betsy's least favorite form of address. Viola held the door for them, and Aunt Maud went feebly out onto the porch, her arms and neck blue-white as yeast in the black lace formal; Aunt Betsy, in her slightly too small turquoise gown, maneuvered her great bulk after her.

"Drive carefully," Viola called as they went cautiously down the steps.

Aunt Betsy waved her glove. "Don't wait up."

She closed the door and leaned on it and waited until she heard the car start. Then, heart pounding, Viola ran back to her room and changed to the suit that had belonged to her mother, a suit as black and spare as the habit of a nun, brushed her hair and pinned it up, slipped on her real Mexican silver charm bracelet, and put on her make-up. She was amazed at herself and a little frightened, it was as if she'd been planning it all day. It was 7:15. She thought of the game she'd watched the Chandler children play, and it seemed to her (but wordlessly, more meaningful than words) a proof that what she was doing was right, inevitable, outside choice. Her alarm grew in proportion to her joy, and she began to hurry as if in fear of being late for an appointment.

When she glanced in at Aunt Emma, the old woman was sitting exactly as she always sat, motionless in her chair beside the bed. With the key an inch from the lock, Viola hesitated, and then, changing her mind, she slipped the key back into its place on the nail by Aunt Emma's door. Now it was 7:30.

The Chandler house was completely still, completely dark, the high, narrow gable a sharp black shadow against the sky. Her heart caught in her throat, and she thought, *What if he's dead?* But she knew, the next instant, that it wasn't that. The house was not completely dark after all: There was a light on in the kitchen and another in the room where she'd slept while she was here, the bedroom-den, as old Mrs. Chandler called it. She could hear the rapid clicking of a typewriter. She ran up onto the steps, not making a sound, listened for a long time her heart hammering in her chest, then knocked.

It was the old woman who answered the door.

"Hello," Viola said gaily. "Is everyone out?"

Mrs. Chandler blinked. "They went to the recital," she said holding the door, not yet inviting Viola in.

"Oh," Viola said. "Did Mr. Chandler go too?"

"No, he's here," the old woman said, "—he and the two youngest. But they're asleep, the girls." She stepped back a little, opening the door wider. "Come in. James is upstairs typing something."

"I just wanted to give him my best," she said lightly. Panic flared up in her, but the old woman was nodding, welcoming her more heartily now.

"How's poor Maud?" Mrs. Chandler asked.

"Oh, fine, just fine," Viola said. She draped her coat over the arm of the couch and patted her hair. "I won't stay but a minute."

"James will be pleased to see you," Mrs. Chandler said. Then, doubtfully: "Let me call him." She opened the door at the foot of the stairs leading up from the living room and called in a way that might once have been musical, "James? Company's here."

Viola heard the typewriter stop and, after a moment, his footsteps slowly crossing to the head of the stairs. He called, "Who is it?"

"It's Viola."

She felt a tingle of pleasure at hearing herself called simply *Viola,* like a friend.

There was a silence. Was he scowling? Was she interrupting something important? It had not been especially *Mr.* Chandler that she'd wanted to see, really. Any of them would do. She'd merely wanted to come back to life for a little, breathe freely again. It was nothing more than that. It was only natural.

"Send her up," he said.

Viola blushed and wished desperately that she hadn't come. It was insane, leaving Aunt Emma like that, not even locked up! Three minutes to eight. She didn't dare think about it.

"He says to come right on up," Mrs. Chandler said. "He's not supposed to go up and down stairs. It could be very dangerous for him."

Viola nodded, smiled, delighted, and crossed to the stairway door. Mr. Chandler was standing there when she looked up. He was leaning on the railing with his left hand, leaning on the wall with his right, as though he were not strong enough to support his weight without help. He'd grown cadaverous. His thick glasses hung low on his nose, and he was frowning like a man who has just looked up from his book. But when he saw her he smiled, his whole, owlish little face lighting up, and she started up the steps.

He led her to the bedroom-den, propped the door open with a green-felt-covered brick, and, feebly, like an old, old man, pulled a chair over from under the window for her, then drew his own around from the desk where he'd been doing his typing and placed it directly opposite hers in a way that seemed to her queerly formal, a little unnerving. His skin was very white, splotched with red.

"This *is* a surprise," he said, his voice somehow guarded, as it seemed to her, the voice of a man very carefully minding his manners, an actor in a play. "I thought you'd be over at the recital."

She laughed and took her seat. "I would have been but—" She smiled. "Aunt Maud did so well taking care of Aunt Emma while I was over here that they decided to take her along to the recital. It meant I could be free if I wanted, and you know how it is. A girl can't spend every minute of her life with old people, even her own family." Instantly she was ashamed.

He smiled, or, rather, partly smiled, looking at her a little too closely. Then he said, as if conscious of helping her out, "We're grateful for the way you pitched in here last week, Viola. I don't know what we'd have done without you."

"Oh, it's nothing," she said, pleased. But even as her pleasure bloomed, she thought in alarm, *What's got into me, running here like this? What have I come for?*

She wanted to talk to him, yes, that was it, really *say* something—heaven knew what—but it was impossible; she should have known. He talked like someone in a book. *This is a surprise. The way you pitched in here. I don't know what we would have done.* She realized that she was bouncing her foot slightly, and she made herself stop.

To put her at ease, as it seemed to her, the man turned toward the huge shamble of a desk and pointed to a stack of neatly typed papers. He was working on the general outline of an essay on art, he said. He'd been at it for three solid days, both at the hospital and here, and with luck he might finish it by tomorrow night. He was eager to be through, partly to see how the devil it came out but mainly to give himself time to be with his family. It was criminal, he said with a laugh, to be spending all his time on a paper, at this particular-juncture. But the theory *was* an interesting one, he added then with a faraway look; it accounted for a good deal more than he'd dreamed when first it had come to him. He seemed on the point of launching into a complicated explanation; but then he checked himself, smiling, looking at the floor, and fell silent.

"What can I do for you, Viola?" he asked then, remote, professorial.

His wrists and hands were so thin she couldn't stand to look at them. She wondered if his life had been happy. Did he love his wife? Was there anything, ever, that two people so terribly different could find to talk about? She was younger than he was. Had he married her late, in a desperate snatch at happiness?—Or had he met her, perhaps when she was hardly more than a child, and had he fallen in love with her innocence, not guessing that, unlike himself, she would very soon grow jaded? Perhaps it was that, perhaps it was something else. In any case, Viola could see very clearly how terribly he suffered. Why else would a man spend the last days of his life fleeing from reality, hiding in his room? And yet how good he was, how really incredibly good!—forgetting his own troubles completely, putting behind him death itself—asking: *What can I do for you, Viola?* How beautiful!

There was nothing to say. How stupid it was, her coming here. She was sick with fright, suddenly—so nauseous she had to close her eyes. Her face burned, and she could feel Chandler's eyes on her, puzzled and far away, kind. She thought of the book that Karen had wanted to understand, and in the same rush of emotion she heard again the screams in the street and saw his look of distaste but also compassion when she'd laughed in the entryway that morning. Nothing seemed real or solid to her now; it was as though the world really had all at once turned into music, but terrible music, dissonance. She felt his hand on her arm, as gentle as Aunt Emma's hand and as sharp as fire, and she heard him saying, "Is something wrong, Viola?" She opened her eyes, and on a wild impulse, shame consuming her even as she did it, she caught his face in her hands and kissed him. "I love you," she whispered, terrified, pressing the side of her head to his cheek. She could not look at him until he answered, but waited in anguish for the heart on the altar to be taken or rejected. He was motionless, his hand still on her arm, and the moment stretched on. Then, casually, not even with pity but as if it were all completely natural and everyday, Chandler patted her hair and drew back from her.

"Let's go get some coffee," he said.

"Is that what I need, you think?" she asked fiercely, her heart utterly and finally broken. She laughed.

"It's what everybody needs," he said. His hand came under her arm to help her up.

She rose after an instant, feeling suddenly contrite and confused. "I'm sorry to trouble you this way, Mr. Chandler. I really am. I must be crazy or something."

He smiled a little absently, glancing over at the clock on his dresser as though he knew to the minute how much longer he had to live. The clock wasn't running. "Its good to be troubled. Leads to a condition a man named John Wisdom calls 'philosophical wonder'—a dread disease. For which he has excellent therapy, in case he should ever unearth some man who'd seriously consider being cured."

"Pardon?" she said.

"Nothing." He smiled and blushed very faintly, patting her arm. "Talking to myself."

She went down the steps ahead of him, giving him her shoulder for support. His mother appeared in the doorway below, looking up at them in horror, and Viola remembered that he wasn't supposed to go up and down stairs. But Chandler had made up his mind to it; there was nothing she could do.

"I'm sorry," Viola said when they reached the old woman, "when Mr. Chandler suggested—"

But the old woman is looking at her now in a way she has never done before, as though she is seeing her clearly for the first time. And Viola thinks, thunderstruck, caught up again for an instant in her terrible and splendid love of the dramatic: *Why, it's true! I come here to kill him!* She feels a sudden weightlessness a kind of vaulting joy. *And Aunt Emma?* she thinks. Clearly, as though right here in the room, she hears Aunt Emma's doorlatch click, and she hears the door swing open. She lets her gaze go blank, concentrating on the strange sensation, standing momentarily outside time, and for the first time in her life she knows what is wrong with her.

Then, abruptly, in real enough anguish but a voice not her own—if any voice was ever her own—Viola says, "Mr. Chandler, I have to go. I was lying when I told you that they took Aunt Emma with them. She's alone."

He turns, looking at her.

"I've got to get back," she says. She glances at the clock. Nine. She bites her lip, fighting back tears, and catches up her coat from the arm of the couch. She seems to herself like someone in a movie—Elizabeth Taylor in that scene from Raintree County.

"I see," he says. "Yes, go then." He touches his chin, looking past her, not judging. *Beautiful,* she thinks, and she loves him more than ever. She catches his hand.

"Thank you," she says. "God bless you, Mr. Chandler."

For a long moment he holds her hand as if torn between saying something and keeping still. At last, awkwardly, he kisses her fingers. "Goodnight, Viola."

On the sidewalk, under the clean white lights, she runs with all her heart, her coat flying out dramatically behind her. But she is of course too late. The front door at her aunts' stands open. The interior falls away from the door like a grave.

9

QUARTER to eight.

Emma Staley sits perfectly still, smiling her pleasant, ladylike smile, as though she has not seen her door swing shut or heard her niece's footsteps retreating to the front of the house. When the front door closes, she stands up, as if she's been listening for it, and crosses to her door and turns the knob and walks out into the living room. She looks pleasantly about the room, as if finding it all in exquisite taste and wonderfully livable as well, then takes a step toward the dining room. She pauses again, her eye caught, apparently, by the small silver bell on the desk. She picks it up with her thumb and first finger, and it clinks. She smiles, sly, and decides to keep it. She walks through the dining room to the little parlor outside the music room, then on into the entryway. She opens the front door and stands a moment as if in pleasant, crafty thought, her head tilted like that of a wise old gentlewoman thinking back. She walks out onto the porch, the bell closed in her gloved hand now, and in perfect silence she goes very slowly and carefully down the steps. She stands in the dark of the shrubbery for a long time, smiling like a fox, and then darts out onto the walk. She turns right and walks as far as Main Street, where she waits for the light, then crosses to the bridge and goes over it and walks on toward the edge of town. The street is wide, and there is traffic, but no one seems to see her. She passes like a small, prim shadow under the limbs of the maples along the street, in front of porches where people sit talking or reading their papers, past vacant lots, the railroad tracks, the city-limits sign. At the entrance to Law Street, with the city behind her, she frees the bell and lets it jingle softly as she walks. She moves past willows and scrub-oak trees and unlighted houses, to her left the whisper of the Tona-wanda Creek, ahead of her the music of crickets and frogs in the long, wide flatland where cattails grow thick and lush except in the little patches where the quicksand is, silver places under the moon. (She does not seem to hear the frogs and crickets.) She comes abreast of the open flats. There are wisps of fog, white in the moonlight, and far ahead the silhouettes of farmhouses, and on the hills, locusts and maple trees and pines. When car lights approach, she walks down into the marsh and stands, unobtrusive as an old gray fencepost, watching until they have passed. Some farmer's dog barks, far away. Otherwise, silence; the faint tinkle of her bell.

10

HE stood leaning on the porch banister, the cold night air tearing at the lining of his throat and releasing a fierce pain at the base of his skull. His nausea was worse, as if he had swallowed duckpond water. His throat, wholly independent of his will, hung uncertain whether to close on the foulness in his stomach or open to release it. Even as he leaned now on his arms, his legs shook with weakness. If he closed his eyes he would fall, but he kept them stiffly open, clinging by vision to place and time, clinging to the gray-white of the sidewalk under the streetlamps diminishing away like stars, and holding by a strenuous exertion of memory his knowledge of time if not his sense of it: Viola's running was an undistributed event, isolated in an intense present, but at least he could know that a moment ago, however fused that moment-ago might feel with the eternally present instant of his mind, she had been running in the aura of this streetlamp in front of him, not that one where now she ran. There were gnats in the air around his head, briefly turning into streaks of dull light, completely indistinguishable to him from dim, falling planets, except that, without evidence, he believed them to be gnats. If they brushed against his face or settled on the surface of his eyes, he could not feel it. What he felt was the rumbling movement of the world in its wobbly, top-heavy course around the sun. A lift and fall like a ferris wheel, a sickening outward rake like that of an ancient carrousel turning off center. Well might the oceans shift uneasily and rocks stir, deep in the earth, and mountains crack. He remembered from somewhere,

> *When stars from heaven begin to fall*
> *And mountains are on mountains hurl'd,*
> *We'll stand unmoved amidst it all*
> *And smile to see a burning world!*

He did not think he would smile. *You too wanted to talk, Viola said, and now you betray me!"*

Good-bye, Viola, I said. Goodbye.

And then for some reason—the release of a miniscule amount of some chemical in the forepart of his brain, independent of his will, or the break-up of some microscopic congestion—his mind cleared. He turned, frowning, toward where his mother stood framed by the door, her two hands pressed over her heart, the stiff, bent fingers extended. He said: "She left the old woman alone."

"The Lord only knows what's happened there," his mother said. "How could she do it?" Her face was death-white, not from emotion, it seemed to Chandler, but as if a light had quietly gone out.

"She wasn't thinking," he said. "That's all it was."

For a long time there was no sound behind him, no sound in all the city except for the heavy rumble of his blood.

His mother said calmly, as if from years away, "She's so young. It's such a little thing. And yet—"

He stopped listening, a new shock running through his system. All this time it had been there right in front of him—if it had been a snake it would have bit him—and he'd missed it! It was not the beauty of the world one must affirm but *the world,* the buzzing blooming confusion itself. He had slipped from celebrating what was to the celebration of empty celebration. *To keep a drowsy emperor awake.* Again the nausea welled up in him. If he should have to vomit he would rip himself open, and the whole thing would be over. He closed his eyes, but that was worse, and he opened them quickly and fixed them on the cracks in the warped porch flooring. He thought: *One must make life art.*

"Mother, I have to go help," he said, consciously dramatic.

She stared. Her hands were pressed more firmly to her heart, the elbows down straight from the effort. "You can't James," she said. It was final.

He struggled to think, and after a moment brought out, "Then you must drive me there."

"The children are asleep. I can't leave them alone."

"Only for a minute." He leaned away from the railing and crossed to her, reaching out for the doorframe as he moved. "You *must.*" He thought: *For Art's sake. As the play requires. We shall set our face to Jerusalem.*

"I'll phone Marie," she said. "Marie would be glad—"

But he shook his head angrily. "No."

She met his eyes, her lips parted, blackness in her

throat. She made as if to shake her head, refusing him, but half way through the movement her look clouded, not from a change in will but from confusion. She said nothing, grieving, knowing as clearly as he'd have known in himself what was happening—the mind weakening under the weight of time, weariness, old ideas, the tyranny of substance. At last, in despair, she said, "All right." She went to the living room for her purse.

The lights were all on at the Staley house. The sight filled him with dread, and at first he only sat looking up from the car, making no move to get out. At last he strained at the door handle until the latch fell, then pushed with his knee and shoulder to pry it open. On the sidewalk he leaned on the car door a moment and waited for his nausea to settle and the pain in his head to subside. Inside the car, when he looked back, his mother's dress was lost in darkness; her hands clutching the steering wheel were white, her face eyeless, ghostly.

"Tell Marie I'm here," he said. "And tell them all—" He paused. He had nothing to tell them. He blew her a kiss, his hand moving clumsily, comic.

He closed the door and waited while she got the car in gear, then turned out into the center of the street. She drove very slowly, squarely down the middle, her headlights on high-beam, lighting the trunks and lower branches of the trees from here to North Street. Every line of the bark stood out clearly, a labyrinth of ingenious connections. He watched the lighted trunks go out, one by one, as she passed them. Then he turned toward the porch.

It took him what might have been quarter of an hour, for all he knew, merely to mount the wooden steps. He watched himself with mingled horror and amusement from above as he stood clinging with both hands to the porch railing, sucking in the smells of the night, struggling like some grotesque vaudeville clown to lift his foot from the first step to the second. He couldn't do it; it was as if he'd been made for another planet, where the pull of gravity was infinitely lighter and where old, flaking steps sat with less intransigence against him. When he tried to lift his knee with his hand, the nausea washing through his belly and chest made his sense of balance fall away; he had to snatch at the railing quickly to keep himself from reeling. A whimpering began to come out of his mouth, and he no longer remembered how to stop it. He got down on hands and knees. He held himself still a moment, adjusting to the new churning of his nausea, and when he knew he would not pass out, he began to climb. At the top he felt as if had had come a great distance, and he no more dared look down at the street than he would at the moment have dared to look down from a railroad trestle. He thought of getting to his feet again, but the front door stood part way open; he didn't need to. He crawled into the entryway, thick with scents of overshoes and cloying roses. The rug smelled of, perhaps, cat urine.

The music-room door stood open, and there was a light on. The legs of the grand pianos towered above him like Cretan columns, the nearer pedal-box hanging to within an inch of the carpet, the pedals and the cover-plate bronze, the box itself like a plain but elegant coffin. He rested his head on the carpet a moment and closed his eyes, but again only sight could preserve him from tumbling weightlessness. The dining room, kitchen, and parlor were empty too. A sound came then. It seemed to come from all sides, a great rush of noise like an avalanche, but the part of himself that hovered in godlike detachment above him knew that there had been no more than a whisper, the sound, it might be, of a curtain turning over once in a draft. He crawled toward the open doorway. With a part of his mind, some half-dead nerve, he realized that on the blotched white of the back of his hand there was a brighter, more distinct blotch, and now another— blood. He ran the back of his index finger under his nose and it came away wet. He thought nothing, concentrating all his attention on keeping the room from spinning.

The girl sat perfectly motionless on the side of Aunt Emma's bed, staring straight ahead. Aunt Emma was not in the room. From above he saw himself crawling toward her smiling horribly, lifting his hand very feebly as if to say "Hi!" He wiped the blood from his chin with his sleeve. She was barefoot but still had her coat around her, the sleeves hanging empty. She refused to see him. He thought of Karen, who was beautiful, yes, and a class of vague faces squinting at him as he wrote on the board. Marie saying something he had no time to listen to now, though he loved her, yes, a vague mumble in the back of his mind, the chalk bright white and beautiful on the green of the board, the bare legs of the child on the bed shining. But she would not turn, and the sickness charging his throat would not let him speak. A scent of powder and old feet and sachet welled out of the rug, and the coverture on the bed smelled of cleaning. The girl's perfume filled the room and he thought hungrily, sickly, of her kiss. He remembered that there was something he must remember and strained to catch it until it came. Aunt Emma was gone. *I'm sorry,* he thought. And then his mouth went sour and he knew that in a moment his terror would be back. The room grew brighter, almost blinding, as though the old woman were emerging from every atom of the place at once. He lunged forward and caught the girl's bare foot and clung to it, and the room grew brighter still. He struggled against it violently, pressed tight to the rug, and then, as if by his will, he made everything dim. He saw her foot, his bloody hand closed tightly around it—an image out of some grim, high-class Western—and he remembered he had had to talk to her. Now it was dark, and he thought he was saying—shaking his head and smiling apologetically—"No harm. It's done us no harm."

11

THE end of the third floor hallway. 9 P.M.

John Horne says:

"Were all my elaborate theories wrong? Is love indeed what Proust thought, a magical battle of consciousness against consciousness, the lover's attempt to possess and thus annihilate the beloved, but at the same time, paradoxically and thus hopelessly, to *not* possess, to perpetuate, since only in the beloved can one find oneself, that very self which, through the possibility of betrayal, one's beloved must place in jeopardy? It's a view I've often denounced in the past. Transcending oneself, I have often held, one creates a shadowy other self, that luminescent Possible that one flies toward with all one's might. And love (I said) is the discovery in another creature of transcendence aimed in roughly the same direction. It is not (I said) the lover's purpose to fix his beloved like a bleeding butterfly on a mounting board—if butterflies do, as I think, bleed. Love is mutual flight (I said), transcendence-transcended, to use Sartre's terms, in the sense that two-winged creatures, whether they be angels or leather-winged bats, can know, can realize their flight in a way neither one could know it alone. So that the concept lover-beloved was wrong from the start: It's lover and lover in a double search, twin stars each of whose relative motion depends for its significance as motion on the other's. Not that the lover-beloved concept is inevitably wrong, you understand. One sees it sometimes, especially among those who are brilliant and sensitive but insecure.

A cancer of the finest kind of soul. But at its wisest, love is not simply the recognition of flight aimed in a similar direction but a recognition of the universality of flight itself: Thus saints (I am personally acquainted with a saint) can love everything that lives, from worms squirming upwards through the petals of a rose to the questing of the universe as a whole, exploding infinitely outward to find God. Transcendence-transcended, for a saint, is the astonishing act, inconceivable to an ordinary man, or at any rate inconceivable to me, except in theory, of affirming at once, and without contradiction, the Many and the One. It's the mystical recognition that one's own flight to higher ground is both itself and the indivisible flight of life toward life. And it is, after all, but a short step from the statement 'St. Francis knew the unthinking transcendence of birds' to the statement 'Birds loved St. Francis.' For at some point motion, the root of all, say, negative prehensions, transforms itself into thought, and a man is Nature!"

The blind old woman in the corner says nothing, merely hugs herself, whimpering a little, clutching the collar of her bathrobe, her face white as ashes.

"I speak for your good, you understand," John Horne explains. He lights another cigarette, then hurries on. "If my words confuse you, don't trouble about it. Words are merely our outward apparel. You and I understand these things, Miss Thomas. We understood them in grade-school, when I called you 'Grandma.' You remember that? You called me 'Grandpa.' We understood each other perfectly.

"But isn't it in fact the case, after all, that the one sure law of the universe is the law of blind force? In history, for instance. What was the rise of America but the growth of a plant where nothing happened to be there to kill it?— Absurd little colonies absurdly revolting when the oppressor happened to be up to his neck in European troubles. Or the case of Hitler—an incompetent, a lunatic, a fear-ridden weakling without a hope in the world, who came at precisely the proper moment, when all the mindless forces in Europe were right and who therefore shot up like air through a vacuum-tube: A convenient tool of the high command, at the start at least, a convenient symbol, a convenient hater—a convenient, wholly pointless explosion, like life itself, Alma Venus! Have you ever read him? An unbelievably stupid man! For instance: *Every animal mates only with a representative of the same species. In the exceptional cases of breeding with another species the offspring are sterile or else through lack of vitality succumb to disease or other dangers. Thus bastard forms are eliminated and uniformity is maintained in each species. Therefore it is silly not to recognize that any mixing of Aryans with lower human races is disastrous. In Central and South America there has been more race mixture than in North America, which accounts for their inferior culture.* I quote verbatim. A tissue of perfectly astounding bad logic and misinformation. The man's never heard of the gene pool! And yet people listened, apparently. Blind forces. No other possible explanation. Or take Marx. A philosopher laughed out of Europe, who could get a hearing nowhere but in a barbaric country, among peasants who had no conception of logic, no knowledge whatever of the philosophical tradition. There's your answer to that ringing question in *Aurelius: Hippocrates after curing many diseases himself fell sick and died. The Chaldaei foretold the deaths of many, and then fate caught them too. Alexander, and Pompeius, and Caius Caesar, after so often completely destroying whole cities, and in battle cutting to pieces many ten thousands of cavalry and infantry, themselves too at last departed from life. Heraclitus, after so many speculations on the conflagration of the universe, was filled with water internally and died smeared over with mud. And lice destroyed Democritus; and other lice killed Socrates. What means all this?* Nothing! Absolutely nothing! A game of blind forces. Epictetus with all the noble conclusions scratched off.

> *His son is dead.*
> *What has happened?*
> *His son is dead.*
> *Nothing more?*

> Nothing.
> His ship is lost.
> What has happened?
> His ship is lost.
> He has been haled to prison.
> What has happened?
> He has been haled to prison.
> Nothing more?
> Nothing.

An idiotic interruption of darkness, a sickness of matter. And what is the proper activity of man? The study of astrology, a life devoted to pursuit of the art of calligraphy. One simply goes on. One gets distance, detaches oneself from one's thoughts by speaking them aloud, freezing them into the wooden formations of the tongue and teeth, formalizing them out of all content. 'We shall grieve not,' as the poet says. I forget which poet. One makes up something to do, and one does it."

He pauses, looking at his cigarette, then corrects himself, "One makes up something to do and, insofar as one is able, one does it."

He begins to pace back and forth in front of her.

"But what does it mean, "One makes up something to do'? How can one make even this trivial sort of leap of faith when one has discovered that the center of the universe is a dark place, the 'coal pocket,' as astonomers say —if I've got the right term? How can one celebrate Alma Venus once one has seen that time and space are a bucket of worms?"

He stops in his tracks and stares at the floor, sucks at his cigarette, then bursts out: "How can I ask that the universe take me seriously? I can't do it myself! Here I stand, a fat grotesque who is dying, or so my doctor has decreed. What do I do? I play the creature in his death throes. Because I can't realize it, of course. I look at the world—" He paused, then turned and waved at the window for dramatic emphasis. "I look at the world and I brood on it, but nothing I see or brood on is there, only some unimaginable distortion, the reality behind the mask. I say that the sky is black tonight, but it has no interest in being the black I see. I say that the grass is grayish black, but the truth is merely that to a creature of precisely my size and shape, grass is grass and trees are trees and the laws of thermodynamics are true. So much for human consciousness. An ingenious and delicate instrument designed by monstrous reaches of time for the sole purpose of knowing that all it knows is wrong and, anyway, irrelevant. What then am I to conclude but this: that the only reasonable course for man is to hurry to his grave or, if he's willing to be made a joke of, to hurry to those who share his condition, keep them entertained with talk, implore them to entertain him in turn, distract him to dreams and elaborate rules—to shadows. Are you a religious person, Miss Thomas?—If I may ask?"

She says nothing. She moves her shaking hand toward him, seems to consider, then draws it back.

He says, "Love, then—the brotherhood of man—comes down to that, it seems: mutual flight to illusion. In the beginning was the void.

"They had an interesting theory in the Middle Ages, Miss Thomas. Perhaps you're familiar with it. The idea of a god who was infinite Wisdom, Goodness, and Power —Father, Son, Holy Ghost, you know—though I'm not sure I've got the three parts properly lined up; it may have been the Son who stood for Power. The brilliance of the concept, in any case, lay in this: that Wisdom, Goodness, and Power are precisely what human beings don't have. For anything to have meaning at all, we must posit a God who has what we lack and who for some mad reason wants to give it to us. It's a beautiful vision, and its progress is a beautiful thing to trace. From Moses to Job, for instance—Moses bending to the will of the Lord, Job grabbing the old man by the ear. Job says, 'God is a tyrant,' and when Job's friend tells him he's got to be wrong, he's got to have committed a sin of some kind to be punished the way he's being punished, God steps in and takes Job's side: 'You say the thing that is not so.' From that point it's all predictable: God stretched out broken on the rood; the remission of sin. It's a beautiful vision, and I've even believed it from time to time. One must, in a way. But it makes us even more ridiculous, don't you think? Better to know you're ridiculous and establish definite limits to the laughter. Isn't that so?"

He turns suddenly and draws closer to the old woman. "Perhaps I'm mistaken, Miss Thomas. Perhaps you can point out some error in my reasoning." Abruptly, frantically, he snatches her hand. "I must be wrong. You *know* it, don't you? My good woman, *I can see it in your eyes!*"

"John," she says in horror. Her gray face shakes. "Shame on you," she says. "*Shame* on you, John!"

12

ELIZABETH STALEY's annual recital was always a splendid event, in its way. All the important people would be there or, if they weren't, would have sent their excuses, and everyone would be dressed in his finest. Everyone who was anyone had taken lessons, at one time or another, from one of the Staley sisters, and though now Maud Staley had no vocal students, which meant that the traditional vocal part of the recital had been dropped, and though now Emma Staley had no student painters, which meant that the walls would not be hung with floral still-lifes or country bridges, everyone in Batavia who had reason to look back with pleasure or nostalgia at his or her cultural awakening at the Staley house was sure to be in attendance.

The Y.W.C.A. auditorium, as the little room was called, was lighted by tall white candles on seven-branched candelabra. The old damask sofas were pushed back to line the walls, with spaces left between them for the candelabra and the elevated bouquet stands borrowed from the Methodist Church. Metal folding chairs filled most of the room. The bouquets were of red roses and white carnations, tonight as always, because of the symbolic meaning of the flowers—though nobody including Elizabeth Staley herself remembered precisely what the symbolic meaning was. Maud and one of the older girls met the guests at the door, while Elizabeth saw to last-minute details in the kitchen. (There were always little sandwiches afterward, and tea, coffee, and punch.) The children who were to play in the recital sat, arranged by order of entrance, in the little dining room just off the auditorium, the boys in dark-blue suits and bow ties, the girls in party dresses or formals. They whispered in great excitement, every girl jealous of some other girl's dress, or suffering a vast, undisclosable passion (for the boy with red hair), or running over, one last time, in terror and hopeless confusion —fingers racing up and down an invisible piano—her recital piece. The younger boys poked one another in the ribs, or pulled the curls or the ribbon ends of the girls beside them; the older boys sat with their heads down, their hands on their knees, one neatly polished shoe on top of the other, sunk in gloom or talking loudly, with sudden bursts of maniacal laughter, about basketball, or baseball, or the girl with the daisies in her hair.

The entryway and the auditorium hummed with talk and the shuffling of feet, the rustle of mimeographed programs, the occasional click of one of the metal folding-chairs bumping another. The grandfather's clock—the chimes carefully left unwound—said quarter to eight. Two of Elizabeth Staley's older boys bowed politely to each cluster of guests coming in and led them, if they would be led, to seats, and a tall, thin girl in a white dress with a wide pink sash checked over the flower arrangements on the two gleaming Baldwins at the front of the room. She moved the benches, each a fraction of an inch, then stood back, her lips pursed solemnly, considering her work. At last, with a look of extreme satisfaction, she left the room. Elizabeth Staley appeared in the doorway, nodded and smiled briefly in the general direction of her guests, studied the room critically, then vanished. The crowd grew.

Arriving relatively late, Marie and Karen Chandler were shown to seats very close to the front. They sat, strikingly similar in appearance, erect and still, hands folded in their laps, their faces composed, modest, apparently prepared to smile politely if necessary but lost at the moment in thoughts of their own, or, perhaps, eavesdropping on some conversation nearby. Someone said, to Marie's left —nodding to her as well-bred ladies nod to newcomers who have inadvertently seated themselves in a family pew —"Isn't everything lovely?" "Lovely," Marie said, smiling and imitating the nod precisely. The woman said, "I've always loved Elizabeth's recitals," and Marie replied— unable to resist it, lover that she was of the absurd—"So have I." The lady smiled again, too sweetly, obviously baffled, and turned away.

At last, at a quarter after eight, Aunt Betsy appeared in front of the two pianos and the talk died down. When everything was quiet, Aunt Betsy began her welcome and introduction. Marie's mind—though she smiled or tittered with the others at all the exactly proper points— wandered off to tomorrow morning's shopping. (Life, as James Chandler would say with a laugh, goes on.) James ate virtually nothing, these days; she had to find something he really, deeply liked—something he'd never eaten before, perhaps; something delicate and at the same time, substantial. Marie scowled, but inwardly, not a muscle of her face stirring. She toyed with the idea of lamb, then rejected it. Karen leaned toward her, smiling and whispering, and Marie nodded with a brief twinkle, though she hadn't heard. Then Aunt Betsy was bowing and turning away—two or three people clapped, then saw their error —and was sweeping off, her pearls and her blue-white hair gleaming in the candlelight. A boy came out quickly, sat down at the nearest piano, and began at once to play. The piece was over in perhaps five seconds, and the boy was gone. A blond little girl came in as the audience clapped for the boy, played something only twelve measures long (if Marie was not mistaken), all in thirds, then curtsied twice, delighted with herself, showing her enormous dimples, and danced out. Marie glanced down at her program. No doubt the pieces would get longer very soon. The thing might go on for hours. *Well, that's three now,* she thought. She clapped.

"I wish Daddy were here," Karen whispered. There was a tear on her cheek.

Marie nodded, panicky for an instant, but with no change whatever in her expression. She raised one finger to her lips.

She could not have said what it was that made her remember. Something in the music, perhaps. She'd been six or seven. She'd gotten up very early one morning and had gone outside before she'd had breakfast—something she was never allowed to do. She'd gone to the sand pit at the edge of the woods on her father's farm, where the red and white wild roses were in bloom, and there she'd seen a shiny-faced, curly-headed boy of perhaps four or five. She'd talked to him for a little while, but the boy was grouchy and superior, and at last she'd decided he was hopeless, and she'd left him. She'd slipped back into the house, and she'd been lying in bed as though she had been there all the time when her mother came to wake her for breakfast. Later that day the troopers had come, looking for a little boy who was lost. Marie's father and older brother had gone off with the troopers and three or four other farmers of the section, and they'd looked all night and all the next day. They never found him. Marie had been horribly tortured by guilt. She'd known very well that she ought to tell them where she'd seen the boy that morning, but she'd been afraid, and, moreover, no one had asked her. She had no way of knowing, she'd told herself, that the boy was the right one. It was not that she had reached any definite decision not to tell— indeed, if anyone had asked her point-blank what she knew, she'd have told at once—but she had put it off and put it off until all at once she knew that it was too late. And so she had never said a word, never once in all her life, not even to James. It was a strange thing to carry around. She wondered if she herself could stand the sight of someone who had done it, someone else. Her fingernails bit into her palm, though her face remained tranquil, composed. *I'm sorry,* she thought, *but it's too late.* The fat, blond boy at the piano got up, and she clapped with the others.

She thought of the house in San Francisco—the white walls, the paintings their friends had done, the four big fireplaces, the plates and matchboxes and Indian baskets they'd found at Cost-plus, the thick, bitter-green carpet Gordon had gotten for them with his discount at the Emporium. The cat would be out of his mind by now, the vet calling him "My fine young man," dogs yelping in the next room, mere cat food in his dish. It had been good, their life there. She mustn't think about it. *But poor Hobbes,* she thought. (The cat.)

She thought of James building infinitely elaborate sandcastles with Susan on the beach, and tears filled her eyes and spilled over onto her cheeks. She wiped them away but more came and she let them come, merely biting her lips together, thinking violently. *What of it? Who cares?* She remembered Wilma and Ken, sitting on the couch, holding hands and talking learnedly about "form" in Schönberg. James was fond of them, though; and heaven knew she ought to be grateful that they were interested in such things, otherwise *she* would have had to talk learnedly about form in Schönberg! When they'd finally gotten rid of Wilma and Ken (Wilma had given way to weeping, toward the end, and stood hugging James, crying on his tie, Ken in the background, helpless as usual, James standing erect and dignified and dreadfully embarrassed, patting her shoulder as if absentmindedly while Marie stalked off in rage to the kitchen), James had lain down beside Marie on the bed and had unbuttoned her blouse and unhooked her brassiere, and moving his hands over her breasts in that unbelievably gentle way he had (his hair and mouth reeking of pipe tobacco), he'd said, "Wench, you and I don't realize how much we suffer. Wilma told me. Everybody suffers. Fact."

"It doesn't seem fair," she said, "that some people should suffer a lot, and others—"

He said:

> *That strange flower, the sun,*
> *It's just what you say,*
> *Have it your way . . .*

"Oh, I know, I know. But suppose a person can't *choose* the way he sees things? Or suppose there are some people who can choose, but others—"

"Hush," he said. "It's not meant to be fair. It's meant to be thoroughly perplexing, to drive you to Art and Scientific Progress and God."

"Do you think so?" she'd said, seriously considering it.

He'd said, "Damn it, Marie, you're supposed to turn off your brain when people seduce you."

Karen too was bending her head, crying, her shoulders hunched. In about two minutes they'd both of them be crying aloud. She mustn't allow it. She caught her daughter's hand and held it tightly, and Karen returned the grip.

Hours later, as Marie thought (it was nine o'clock) Aunt Betsy appeared before the pianos again and announced that, since this was, she was sorry to say, the last of her annual recitals, she would like to play them a little something herself. There was a moan, the queerly joyful sigh of people conscious of themselves as present at a moment of significance, the sad and splendid conclusion of an age. Then a tempest of applause. Aunt Betsy smiled and seated herself at the farther piano. Absolute silence. The silence lasted for nearly a minute, and then, with unbelievable power, there came four notes, a long pause, four more. Then there exploded a terrible holocaust of chords and runs, each note precise, overpowering, irremissible—not music but a monstrous retribution of sound, the mindless roar of things in motion, on the meddlesome mind of man. Karen said, "Mother, Miss

Staley's *deaf!*" "Be still," she said. The people sat listening, perfectly silent, as if deeply impressed, staring at their knees. And whether or not they knew what it was they were witnessing, no stranger could have said.

ABOUT THE AUTHOR

John Gardner was born in Batavia, New York, in 1933. He grew up on a farm, attended local schools, and received his B.A. from Washington University at St. Louis in 1954. Since 1958, after taking the M.A. and Ph.D. degrees at the State University of Iowa, he has been a teacher of English literature, most recently at San Francisco State College. He has published various articles on modern and medieval literature in the academic journals and is the coauthor, with Lewis Dunlap, of two textbooks, *The Forms of Fiction* (1961) and *Poetry: Form and Substance* (1965). He has also translated *The Complete Works of the Gawain-Poet* (1965). His short stories and poems have appeared in *The Southern Review, The Quarterly Review of Literature, The Northwest Review* and other little magazines. Mr. Gardner is married and has two children. This is his first novel.